*St. John's Baptism*

# St. John's Baptism

A DETECTIVE NOVEL

by William Babula

*An Irma Heldman Book*
Lyle Stuart Inc.          Citadel Press

Published by Lyle Stuart Inc.
120 Enterprise Avenue, Secaucus, N.J. 07094
In Canada: Musson Book Company
A division of General Publishing Co. Limited
Don Mills, Ontario

Manufactured in the United States of America


Library of Congress Cataloging-in-Publication Data

Babula, William.
    St. John's baptism : a detective novel / by William Babula.
        p.    cm.
    "An Irma Heldman book."
    ISBN 0-8184-0461-2 : $14.95
    I. Title. II. Title: Saint John's baptism.
PS 3552.A252S7 1988
813".54--dc 19                                          88-3037
                                                           CIP

5  4  3  2

For IRMA HELDMAN,
editor extraordinary

# 1

"So how are things, Rick?" I asked as I stepped into the air conditioned inner sanctum of San Francisco's foremost drug and sleaze attorney.

Rick Silverman didn't answer.

I looked at Silverman's shimmering aircraft carrier of a desk; he was supposed to be behind it, shaking his silver chain bracelet and swinging his silver chain necklace at me in his usual frantic way.

But he wasn't there. Rick Silverman was lying face down on the floor, looking like a collapsed pushup.

A small pool of blood was just beginning to thicken next to Silverman on the dark gray crushed pile carpeting. The blood matched the burgundy accent pieces in the room. A nice touch that was obviously lost on him. I kneeled down and felt for a pulse but there was none.

"Shit."

The second Monday in August had been another record hot day in the city, but now the evening fog was finally rubbing up against Silverman's third story office window with the great bay view, putting the room into shadow. I got up and turned on the light.

Under the fluorescents, Silverman's law office glittered like the sterling silver department of Tiffany's. Everything in the room was silver, silver-plated, or at least chrome: the clock, the pen and pencil desk set, a ruler, a letter opener with a Navajo sign on the handle, the In and Out baskets, the stapler, the telephone, the floor to ceiling bookcases, and even the wastebasket. And of course the huge desk and the high-backed executive chair behind it. I was mildly surprised that the papers in the In basket were white.

The office was always a shock to my senses but I had never had the opportunity to examine it so closely before. It had always just been a shimmering quicksilver impression. There was only one personal touch, a photograph of an adolescent boy in a silver frame. What else?

I looked down at Silverman's body. What I had left of common sense was telling me to get the hell out of there.

"Got to run, Rick," I said as I backed out through the silver-plated door into the dark uncarpeted hallway. I checked my watch. It was after seven. The office was deserted.

The suite Rick Silverman had shared with his partner Sam Fan ran north-south through the building, parallel to Montgomery street below. It was set up for maximum security, which was a good idea considering some of Silverman's clients. If you came in with an appointment through the double door entrance you stepped immediately into the waiting room. Like a doctor's office, it had uncomfortable chairs and old magazines. This area was sealed off from the rest of the suite by a massive wooden door that could only be opened by an electric switch inside the main office. The receptionist, sitting behind a steel partition and a sliding bullet-proof glass window, was separated and protected from the waiting clients. Her name was Victoria. She was a beautiful woman with blue-black hair and porcelain-white skin. I had once asked for a date but was turned down cold.

Once the second door was opened you were led into the central foyer where there were two facing desks and an open central area. Clients for Silverman made a right turn by the desk on the right; clients for Sam Fan made a left turn around the other desk. During working hours the two desks were used by a pair of very pretty twin blond legal secretaries.

Off to the left there was a series of doors that led to an office for a clerk, a storage room, a workroom, a bathroom, and Sam Fan's office. Down the hallway to the right were the doors to a clerk's office, a private washroom, and Silverman's office.

I had come in through the outside entrance to the building, right up three flights of stairs from the outdoor parking lot, just as Silverman's message had instructed. I entered through a fire door that was supposed to be locked but which Silverman had left open for me. It was at the south end of the suite, only a few feet from Silverman's office. It let him conduct business through a back door leading directly out to the street.

Almost involuntarily I backed down the hallway until I bumped into one of the two desks in the central foyer. As I turned I hit my elbow against the side of an IBM PC.

"Damn." I rubbed my elbow to relieve the tingling.

I checked the door to the inner offices and found it locked. So security was tight on one side of the office. But on the other side Silverman, doing his own business, had unlocked a fire door for someone he wasn't expecting.

I was about to release the lock on the inner door when I stopped and reconsidered my situation. Silverman had called about a delivery he wanted me to make and it was possible Fan or one of the secretaries would have known about it. My name might even be in an appointment book, making me a suspect for the police. I had also come to collect for investigative work done for Silverman in my capacity as a Board licensed private investigator in the state of California. Disappearing now could hurt my chances of collecting what I was owed for some work I didn't like very much—which was usually the kind of work Silverman had for me and my two partners in the Jeremiah St. John Detective Agency.

Reluctantly, I started back towards Silverman's private office. Before I went in again I took a deep breath and looked at my distorted image reflected in his hammered silver door. The effect was like a fun house mirror. My six-foot-one, one hundred seventy-five pound frame had collapsed into a squat shapeless body. My straight brown hair, which I had been growing out over my ears, looked like a wig, and my blue eyes darkened strangely in the silver, almost as if tarnished. My face had gone ancient and craggy and my once-broken nose had a new split across the bridge. My skin became protoplasm slowly dripping down a terraced series of ledges. I was thirty-one and looked a hundred. I wondered if that was how Rick Silverman saw himself every workday morning.

Inside, the corpse was still there. I had a crazy, wishful notion it might have disappeared.

With one arm behind his neck, I slowly raised Silverman's body just enough to see his arms and chest. And the surprised look in his eyes. It looked like he had taken two bullets but only one had done real damage. The front of his suit vest was soaked with blood. A bullet had hit him in the heart. There also was a red target-like circle staining the material of his blue oxford shirt on the right arm just below the shoulder. Another bullet had caught him there.

From the position of Silverman's body he was coming around the desk to confront his killer when he took the fatal hit. I lowered the body carefully.

On the wall behind his desk there was an oil painting of his most prized possession: a Rolls-Royce Silver Cloud. It was a marvel of detail down to the license plate that read SLVRMN. Vowels are superfluous in the new vanity language. The artist was Diego Hammond. I had thought Hammond's exclusive specialty was portraits of women, preferably nude. Boudoir painter or not, he was one of the most expensive artists in the city and one of the best according to the local critics. Alive, Silverman had the kind of style money could buy.

Apart from the nearly photographic rendering of the car in oil and the Hammond name, two things struck me. The first was the odd angle at which the picture hung, as if the rear of the car were thrusting out three-dimensionally into the room. I knew it wasn't Hammond's skill creating that illusion. I took out my handkerchief, touched the frame with it, and saw that it was mounted on hinges

12

which allowed it to swing free to the left. The second was a bullet lodged in the canvas at the left rear tire.

I pushed the picture away from the wall as far as it would go. Behind it was a fairly large safe, its door ajar. Using the handkerchief I opened the safe the rest of the way. Its hinges were well-oiled.

The safe was empty. Not even a few silver bars. I closed the door to about where it had been before and swung back the picture of the Rolls against it. Its angle was now less severe and obvious.

Rick Silverman had become a great drug lawyer in a relatively short time. Now all he had were a couple of slugs and an empty safe. All I had was the bill for the money Silverman owed me. Maybe there was an envelope with my name on it waiting for me in his desk. Maybe. I checked the desk drawers. Nothing.

I would have to try to collect from Silverman's partner, Sam Fan. Unfortunately Sam Fan was notorious for not paying—or at least not paying on time and never the full amount owed. And this would be a bill for work done for a dead man. Of course Rick Silverman wasn't the kind of guy to drop a check in the mail just because a bill was due. But if you caught him at the right time— when drug charges against an obviously guilty client had been dismissed on a technicality, for example—and he felt up, he'd pay with no problem. Always cash, always in small denominations, always unmarked and usually with a bonus. And the IRS didn't have to know a thing.

In a straight line across from the wall safe the spine of a book with the title *Civil Code Annotated of the State of California 46000 to 77999* had been badly damaged. I examined the book without pulling it from the shelf. Another bullet, but considering the direction, one that had been fired by Silverman, which meant that he had had a gun. Only it wasn't anywhere obvious. Maybe the killer had taken it for a souvenir. With three bullets fired at Silverman from somewhere by the door and at least one fired back from behind the desk it must have been like the O.K. Corral in here. I wondered who opened up first.

To the left of the desk was a wooden door that led to a closet. I opened it and found mostly empty space with a few high shelves.

On one of the shelves there were traces of a white substance that was probably cocaine. I shut the closet door.

I got down on my knees and looked under the desk and saw a large green trash bag shoved up against the solid front. I pulled the bag out. At its top the plastic had been pulled together and wrapped with a wire and paper twist-tie. I undid the wire and let the bag fall open.

"Jesus!"

The killer had missed it all.

The bag was full of cash. U.S. currency. Very old and very dirty, which probably made it very genuine. Some of it was wrapped in bands and some of it was just loose. There were mostly small denominations but enough fifties and hundreds to bring the count up to half a million dollars. A rough and modest estimate.

It was drug money of course. This was how the dealers operated: cash and carry and disposable trash bags.

My momentary impulse was to throw the green bag of untraceable money over my shoulder and disappear somewhere in the South Pacific.

Instead I counted out the fifteen hundred Silverman owed me.

"Bonus?"

I counted out a thousand dollar bonus.

"Generous, Rick."

I divided the money into two neat stacks on the desk and put them into the inside pockets of my sports jacket.

Maybe I should have taken all the money. There are times when I still daydream about it.

What I did was sit down on the edge of the desk and use the silver phone to call the police.

"I want to report a murder."

"In progress?" a female voice asked.

"Actually it's over."

"Then could you hold?"

"I don't see why not."

I held. When she came back on I gave my name and location and settled in to wait.

Silverman's message had mentioned "A Delivery." That trash

bag of drug money wasn't the kind of package you turned over to Federal Express or your local Post Office. But knowing some of Silverman's clients as I did, I thought it could go by Air Colombia.

I stared at the body of San Francisco's former top drug lawyer and wondered if he would be buried in a silver-plated coffin. I couldn't imagine that he'd be comfortable going six feet under in anything else. Except maybe his Silver Cloud.

# 2

Considering the nonchalance of the police operator, Homicide, in the person of Detective Oscar Chang, arrived sooner than I expected.

"He was a scumbag, St. John," the detective, dressed smartly in a dark suit that looked like it had just been pressed, announced as he stared at me with irises black as camera eyes. Under his dark, precisely parted, stiff hair the skin of his face was so smooth and taut it looked like planed and polished amber.

We were in the central foyer to let the Crime Scene Unit lab people get at Silverman's office. The body had already been taken away in a silent ambulance for the morgue and the autopsy. I was sitting in one of the secretary chairs, feeling uncomfortable because it had no arms to rest my elbows on. Chang at about five-eight was hovering over me, looking taller than he actually was. He was so close I could smell his expensive aftershave.

"So you're a P.I.," Chang said.

I nodded.

"You carry a gun?"

"I've got a license," I said.

"Let me see it."

"Here." I pulled out my wallet and let it fall open.

Chang shook his head in annoyance. "Not your permit. Your gun."

I reached into the shoulder holster under my left arm, careful not to expose the bulge of money in my pocket, and produced my Smith and Wesson .38.

"This piece isn't any better than standard police issue," Chang muttered as he sniffed at the end of the cold barrel. "It hasn't been fired recently. In fact, it looks like it's never been fired."

"It's new," I explained as he handed the gun back to me. As I holstered it carefully, I said, "And I'm not in the business of shooting people."

"Just working for scumbag drug lawyers."

"I didn't know the man personally."

"You play with fire . . ." He stopped and smiled, revealing perfect white teeth.

"Or matches . . ." I tried.

"You touch a tar baby . . ." he said.

"Evil companions . . ." I offered.

"By his friends . . ." Chang said and smiled again, looking like he had won whatever competition we were in. He was accustomed to having the last word and I let him.

Then he got down to business. "Did you touch anything in the room?"

"I know better than that."

"Sure." He paused. "We're not going to lift your prints?"

"No. Didn't touch a thing. Except for the light switch and the silver telephone. To call the police."

"You could have smeared some prints."

"Next time I'll use a pay phone," I said.

Chang pursed his lips.

"My prints are on the doorknob," I added. "I had to open the door."

18

Chang looked me over as though memorizing me. Finally, he asked the obvious question. "What were you doing here?"

"I had a message that Silverman wanted to see me."

"From Silverman himself?"

"I assume so. One of my partners took the call."

"What did he want?" Chang asked as he began to pace back and forth.

I thought about saying that it was a privileged communication. I also considered telling Chang that it was something about a delivery but I decided against both options.

"I don't know," I said instead. "When I got here he was dead."

"What did it have to do with the money in the trash bag?"

"I don't know."

"You don't know?"

"I didn't know anything about the money," I insisted.

He wasn't buying that. "Where were you taking it?"

"I wasn't."

"That money was going somewhere."

"Not with me. Not that I know of." At least not all of it. For all I really knew Silverman wanted me to deliver a singing telegram for him.

"So you just came by when he called?"

"Silverman owed me money. If he had another job for me I was going to collect first. Good business practice."

"Money talks," Chang said.

"You make this stuff up as you go along?"

"St. John, you are a wise-ass."

"Just making conversation."

"It's a lost art. Try to keep it that way."

The CSU lab team down the hall sounded like they were trashing the office.

"If there was no one here but a dead man, how did you get in?"

I told him about the unlocked fire door.

"Is that usual?"

"That's how Silverman told me to do it."

"Did you kill him?" Chang asked, making it sound like an afterthought.

"He owed me money."

19

"Did you kill him?" It was no longer an afterthought.

"How would I collect from a dead man?"

"You'd think of something."

"My gun hasn't been fired."

"This one hasn't."

"Would I have left the money?"

"Somebody did. Why not you?"

"Come on Chang. I didn't kill him."

Chang finally sat down, leaned back, and locked his hands behind his neck.

"So you claim. But claims mean nothing." He paused. "You know who said that?"

I thought it over. "No."

"My grandfather. He was a cook in a gold mining camp." Chang laughed.

I didn't laugh. I felt too damned tired.

"How long have you been a P.I.?"

"Long enough. Can I go now?"

"Don't leave the city."

"Christ, I've got a business to run here."

"St. John, have you ever been involved in a murder before?"

"No," I admitted.

"Have you ever seen a murder victim before?"

"Not in the P.I. business. Now, can I leave?"

Two lab guys rolled a wagon of police equipment out of Silverman's office. It rattled down the hallway. Chang waited for the noise to subside. "I'll ask you again. Why did Silverman want to see you?"

"I'll answer again. I don't know."

"Sure." Chang stood up and pointed a finger at me. "He was a scumbag, St. John. The city's a better place without him. Maybe we can keep a little cocaine off the street. And maybe we can keep some of the drug vermin behind bars instead of out on technicalities."

I knew how Detective Chang felt; I had felt the identical way often enough in the past. A year before I opened the detective agency I was a deputy district attorney in one of the Bay Area's most crime-ridden counties. It's the kind of job you expect to last less than five years in, according to all the statistical studies. I had gone into the D.A.'s Office right after law school, idealistically thinking that I would beat the odds, bring a modicum of justice to the county, and last as a prosecutor. I was wrong. I didn't even come close to five years.

What I saw in the D.A.'s Office was nearly everybody hustling to get out, looking for soft positions on special task forces, moving into less pressurized U.S. Attorneys' Offices, into well-paying criminal defense, or into private law firms that dealt with everything from divorce to personal injuries. To any job where the pay was several times better and the case load wasn't back-breaking and demoralizing. I left too. But not for the same reasons.

What happened to me was that I ended up on the wrong prosecution team. Not Team 2, which dealt with the usual run of felonies, or the prestigous Team 1, which handled homicides and death penalty cases, but on something like Team 50. Where I played alone in the minor leagues. I had made some wrong moves in the office.

Since we were all putting in seven-day weeks as we dealt with an unending series of cases, there was little time for socializing outside of the office. So internal socialization became the accepted practice. Affirmative Action and feminism had brought a substantial number of female Deputy D.A.'s into the office so the sexual opportunities were there. Five of these office romances ended up in marriage during the first year. Mine got me into love and into bed with Sarah, who turned out to be the wrong female prosecutor. She was also the woman of choice of my superior, a very well kept secret. From me. The result was a career disaster.

In any D.A.'s Office there is always pressure from the police to proceed with prosecutions that are hopelessly deficient legally, and potentially embarrassing to the prosecutor. Our district attorney tended to give in to this pressure and pass those cases down to Sarah's lover who knew exactly what to do with them. Down to Team 50 while Sarah herself was promoted to Team 1 and the big leagues.

Disillusioned, I left to spend a year in a San Francisco personal

21

injury law firm, dealing with the vagaries of whiplash and the intricacies of accident reconstruction. It was a year too much. But at least I met a few private investigators, got interested in the business, and made enough money to start my agency and buy a black classic Thunderbird coupe. I thought it was the kind of car a P.I. would drive in the city. I read too much detective fiction.

I hadn't lost my interest in criminals and justice, I just didn't want to be trapped in an unrelenting system again. I thought I could be more effective as an independent operator, outside the law enforcement bureaucracy. So I opened the agency.

I'm not sure what I expected, but so far in three years I had spent a lot of time investigating airline, train, and auto crash victims for insurance companies trying not to pay off, prospective jurors for attorneys trying to select the most favorable panel for their clients, political candidates for their opponents, and adulterers for other adulterers.

This was the kind of work that paid the bills and let us show a profit.

On the other hand, I did some rewarding detective work on an Indian reservation in Mendocino County and I did get ten grand back for an old woman on a pension who got caught in a variation of the "Jamaican Switch" scam. I also managed to find a reasonable number of missing, runaway, and even kidnapped children. There was an exciting, in retrospect, rescue of several teenagers from a religious cult in the South Bay. Some of this work was more emotionally satisfying than financially rewarding but all the books have to balance for me.

With Sarah and my experience in the D.A.'s Office behind me, I was glad to be out of prosecution and out of personal liability and on my own, with a functioning detective agency, working for my private and somewhat idiosyncratic version of justice.

So I looked at Chang with some understanding, but all I could say was, "Can I leave?"

"Go ahead."

I got up and started for the inner door, which had been wedged open by the police. The detective signaled to the uniformed cop on duty that it was okay to let me by.

"St. John," Chang called as I paused by the yellow plastic strips that read CRIME SCENE DO NOT CROSS, "that was a lot of money to resist."

"I know," I said as I went past the barrier and into the outside corridor. What I didn't know was how many people were not going to let me forget about it.

# 3

The next morning I sat at my desk staring at the two-column Tuesday *Chronicle* headline: PROMINENT DRUG ATTORNEY SLAIN.

A red light blinked on a panel by my telephone, which meant the front door had opened.

"That you, Mickey?" I called.

"Yes," she answered from the narrow hallway outside of our row of three separate offices.

"You're late."

"Only twenty minutes, Jeremiah," Mickey said as she swung into the doorway of my office, the third one back from the entrance to the old Stick-Eastlake-style converted Victorian that served as office for the agency and living quarters for me. She threw her Banana Republic straw hat onto the coat rack in the corner of my office.

"Cow's eye," she said and went back into the front room that doubled as her office and the reception area for her morning ritual of makeup repair. A redundant ritual if ever there was one.

Mickey was Michelle Farabaugh, my receptionist, secretary, assistant, hi-tech equipment expert, and actually, second partner. Like my other partner Chief Moses, a Seminole Indian who occupied the middle office, she was chronically late. Since they more than made up for it, and not just in hours, it was more of an inside family joke than a genuine irritant.

When Mickey reappeared I just looked at her as I did every morning, admiring her five-foot-eight frame, her long dancer's legs, and her splendid breasts rising and falling beneath the silky material of her blouse. She tilted her head at me and her shoulder-length honey blond hair shifted to cover one green eye.

"It's your turn to make the coffee," I said.

She walked up to my desk. "Can't you plug in a damn Mr. Coffee machine?"

"I made it yesterday."

"You were already downstairs." She spun around and went off to the modern bathroom, which had been built off the hallway under the staircase that led up to my second-floor rooms. I heard her running water for the coffee maker, which was in the Chief's office between us. This was one of the games we played.

The house was a convenient if expensive arrangement. My apartment upstairs had two bedrooms—one turned into a personal gym—a bath, a kitchen, a small living room, and a back porch with a view of the city and a tiny backyard that was neglected and overgrown. I liked the architecture with its angular features and its ornate square bay windows running the height of the building and even the dull blue with yellow trim that it was painted. It made me feel a part of the old city, the part that had survived the 1906 earthquake. That was the way I liked to think about myself, as part of a great tradition.

Most of all I appreciated the incredibly high ceilings. This Victorian was the only building I found where I could raise a basketball backboard and hoop to the regulation ten feet. For me, the only real game in the world was basketball and to play it indoors I needed high ceilings and an entire house to myself.

26

It also had a good-sized kitchen with some pretty ancient appliances that still managed to function. I cooked. But always something simple and never more than two things together so I could make sure they were done at the same time. The refrigerator I kept well-stocked with Henry Weinhard's beer in bottles for me. A beer from a can is almost as bad as a wine cooler out of anything. But I couldn't convince the Chief, for whom I always kept a six-pack of Budweiser on ice. For Mickey it was a bottle of chilled white wine.

Mickey passed in front of my door, a clear glass coffee pot full of water in one hand.

"The Chief never does it," she said from his office where the coffee was brewing.

"Not since he put four tablespoons of coffee per cup," I called on cue. We had the game cum routine down pat.

"Ha! The male pretense of incompetence to avoid drudge work," Mickey said as she thrust her head into the doorway.

"And he's not here yet anyway," I noted and changed the subject. "Did you see the late news last night?"

"I was exhausted. Went to sleep at eight o'clock."

"Did you see this morning's newspaper?"

"Not yet. What is this? A current events quiz?" Mickey paused and considered. "Are we finally on to something?"

"Maybe."

"Wait 'til I get the coffee." She disappeared again.

Tired of the routine P.I. grind, which kept us out of the red, and not always impressed by our occasional unprofitable lapses into social work, Mickey wanted the kind of case that would put her back in touch with her Midwestern police roots. She had come from Ohio where after two years at Ohio State she had said goodbye to Columbus to become a policewoman or policeperson or whatever they were calling female cops that year. It was going to be her career until she got booted off the force after a proper internal review hearing for appearing—one photo only—in a *Playboy* pictorial on "Women in Blue." According to the police department brass she could no longer stand for morality, decency, and the law.

It was true, however, that she was not dressed in blue or much of anything in the quarter-page photo.

Not surprisingly, after seeing all of her, the Ohio boys in blue didn't agree with the brass and were sorry to see her go. There had even been a petition to keep her on the job but to no avail. She was out on her beautiful bare bottom.

She told me all about it when I interviewed her a year ago for the job at the St. John Detective Agency. She said that sometimes she was sorry she did it; that posing nude was unprofessional and unliberated. Then she grinned wickedly and said that it was fun once she overcame the initial embarrassment of being naked in front of a stranger with a camera. And the pictures made her look good.

"Every woman should pose nude at least once in her life," she said. "I didn't think I could look sexy without clothes."

"Sort of gives you a new perspective on yourself," I responded. I was trying to be as professional as possible.

"You learn the difference between naked and nude."

"Which is?" I never got an answer.

"So now you know why I was fired," she said.

She had the job. All very professional. But I still never mentioned why she got fired to Nadine, the woman I was involved with at the time.

That afternoon I spent three hours wandering from used bookstore to used bookstore trying to find a copy of the right back issue. It was impossible to find. Probably every cop in Ohio had at least one copy. I finally located one across the bay in downtown Oakland by Jack London Square. For more than the original cover price I became just another dumb male ogling a glossy air-brushed perfect nude woman. I wondered how Mickey would react if she knew I had a copy.

Probably use her karate on me. They trained you well on the force in Ohio.

That first day when I told her about the Chief she asked me not to say anything about the picture. I promised not to mention it to him. Ever. Of course I myself kept it hanging inside the door of the eight-foot gym locker that I used for storage space upstairs in my combination basketball court and training room.

Mickey came in with two full mugs. We both took it black.

"My name's in the newspaper," I said.

"It's about time." Mickey sat on the worn couch that took up a corner of the room. She balanced her mug on one of its arms. Then she looked up at the elaborate design swirled into the ceiling plaster. She crossed her legs and tugged at the hem of her skirt with long elegant fingers. She blew across the top of her coffee cup, then took a very careful sip. She left a thin line of red lipstick on the edge of the glazed ceramic mug. It looked like part of the design.

"Will it bring us more and better clients?"

I put my mug down on the plastic desk blotter and said, "Smartest thing I ever did. Get you on the profit-sharing plan. Keeps you involved, interested and alert."

"We could use some more to share. And we could use some hi-tech equipment around here."

"You keep the books. We're not doing so bad."

"Jeremiah, sometimes you give away the store."

"Look," I said, showing her the headline.

"Which drug attorney?"

"Our prominent drug attorney of course. You were the one who took the message yesterday that sent me over there. Listen to this. 'Richard Silverman's body was discovered by Jeremiah St. John, a private investigator employed by the attorney.' "

"Who did it?" she asked as she leaned forward on the couch.

"That's the same question the police asked me."

"Give me that paper," she demanded.

I passed it to her and opened up the Sporting Green section.

"The paper says an unhappy client is suspected . . ."

"Unhappy might be an understatement," I said.

" 'Orlando Gomez, a convicted Colombian cocaine smuggler currently out on bail, is being sought for questioning. Gomez was a client of Silverman's,' " she read.

"*Coqueros* kill. When Colombian cocaine cowboys pay they expect results. If Gomez gave Silverman a million bucks it was to win, not lose. Try explaining your million dollar fee to a *coquero* client on his way to San Quentin. If somebody pays that much, half is supposed to be for the judge. That's what someone like Gomez is used to in Colombia."

"Maybe he didn't get a chance to pay Gomez back," Mickey said.

I didn't say anything; Mickey had some more reading to do. She read silently for a few moments.

Then aloud: " 'The body was discovered by Jeremiah St. John' and so on. Yeah. This is some recommendation. Go with St. John and you're a dead client."

"We don't do bodyguard work," I said.

By now Mickey was at the bottom of the front page.

"What is this? What is this?" she asked excitedly.

She was tearing through the newspaper, looking for the continuation of the story on the inside. She was about to get to the good part. "A half-million dollars in a plastic garbage bag? A half-million dollars? And Silverman still owes us money?" She paused. "Well?"

"What do you mean 'Well?' It was evidence. It was A MOTIVE for murder. A motive for me. I had to let it be."

"Damn you, Jeremiah. You've got two partners. If I don't kill you now the Chief will when he gets here." She got up and slammed down the paper. "I hope he scalps you. I'll even help him."

"I don't think he'll require your help." The Chief mostly did what he wanted to do without interference or assistance from anyone.

Idiotically, I hadn't anticipated Mickey being that upset. Now was not the time to say anything about the fee I had collected. It didn't seem like anything more than loose change compared to the amount in the bag. Mickey was beating the couch with the rolled up newspaper. I was next.

"You're overreacting."

"I need a cigarette," Mickey announced.

"You gave up smoking."

"What's it been? Two weeks? I'll give it up again tomorrow."

She took out a pack of Virginia Slims and a disposable lighter from her purse.

I pointed to the sign on the wall: a burning cigarette within a red circle with a red line drawn through it. In case a client could only read Spanish, Vietnamese, Chinese, Japanese, Polish, Italian, etc. Or couldn't read at all.

"I've seen it," Mickey mumbled through the smoke drifting up around her face.

"Well? I'm allergic to smoke." When I had hired her a year ago Mickey had agreed to give up smoking. Since then she had given it up numerous times.

"Don't talk to me. I don't want to talk to anyone who can't recognize the difference between stealing and murder. It wouldn't even have been stealing . . ."

"Smoke ages your face you know. It makes it like yellow parchment. Have you ever seen papyrus rolls?"

"Jesus. You told me that a hundred times." Mickey took a deep drag. "What kind of P.I. are you anyway?"

"The new breed. Spenser doesn't smoke."

"He doesn't leave bags of money when he's owed."

"Moot. Anyhow you don't have the full story, Mickey," I said, knowing there wasn't that much more.

"All right." She took a final drag, coughed, and dropped some ash. "You should have an ashtray."

"You could use the plant." I pointed to a palm in a blue Mexican ceramic pot in one corner of the room.

She put the cigarette out in the dirt. "What is the full story, Jeremiah?"

"Wait for the Chief. You really should quit for good."

"What I should quit for good is this partnership."

"You could always try the San Francisco P.D.," I suggested.

"You know they'll just check with my department in Ohio."

"Maybe they'll send the photo over the wire."

"Damn you. Nothing like that would have happened to a man." Mickey caught her breath and coughed. "I'm not ashamed of that picture."

"You have a print for me?"

"Go to hell, Jeremiah." She stalked out of my office, a beautiful angry ex-cop.

"Or for the Chief?" I called after her.

I waited for about sixty seconds then buzzed her on the telephone intercom. She picked up the receiver.

"What'll I do without you?" I asked.

"Go crazy talking to the Chief."

"I'll miss your cough."

Mickey coughed. "All right. I'm starting my second year with you. I'll never smoke another cigarette. I swear. Just to show you."

"Just remember money isn't everything," I said as I disconnected us to have the last word.

From the other room I could hear her slam the phone down. I got up and looked out of the window at the row houses across the street. There was still no sign of my other partner.

# 4

It was mid-morning when a groggy Chief Moses finally turned up. From the start he had warned me that he didn't go by clocks but by the cycles of nature. There was more chance of the gravitational pull of the moon awakening him than an electric alarm clock.

In reality I had two Chiefs: one was mythological and the other was only slightly larger than life. And there were times when you couldn't pull the two figures apart.

In his mixture of Native American, Floridian, and Biblical mythology Chief Moses was a Florida Seminole—although in reality he had a hard leanness that suggested other bloodlines as well—who had grown to six feet seven inches mainly on a diet of catfish, alligator steak, and Everglades frogs' legs. He carried three hundred pounds with ease on his large frame. He claimed that when he was younger—it was hard to tell his age and the Chief also viewed chronological time with disdain—he used to wrestle gators for tourists at an alligator farm and serpentarium off the Tamiami Trail west of Miami at the edge of the Glades. The Chief had a photograph in his office of the front of the place showing him standing between a green stone alligator and a pink stone flamingo. Whenever he showed it I asked him how many flamingoes did he wrestle at a time.

The Chief also claimed that he was named Moses because the Indian family that raised him found him floating in a picnic cooler on the Tamiami Canal. Moses among the sawgrass blades.

When the Chief lost his taste for gator meat, catfish, trailer living and redneck bar brawls, he left South Florida for L.A. He thought he could make it in the movies but found out that he didn't fit any white director's image of an Indian. So like everyone else he pumped gas. But unlike everyone else he worked on cars instead of just parking them. Which was good considering the Chief's driving skills. He was just too big to fit comfortably behind any steering wheel that wasn't custom built.

After L.A. he started back east with a stop at Vegas. He worked his way up from casino security, or bouncer, to running KENO games, Nevada's version of Bingo. Unfortunately, the Chief liked to gamble a little too much himself and he got into trouble with some bookies who suggested he get out of town. It was time to move on anyway. So he headed back to South Florida.

Chief Moses took what he learned from the Vegas casino operation and parlayed it into consulting for Indian tribes setting up Bingo games on reservations. The work paid well. Chief Moses was connected with some of the largest operations in the southeast.

I got involved with the Chief three years ago when he came to Mendocino County in Northern California to work with the Pomos and their Bingo game. There were problems and not the usual ones that the Chief could solve by himself. So he got the number of a P.I. from the San Francisco phone book—mine.

I had just left the personal liability firm to open a one-man agency with the money I had made in my one year there. I was down in the Mission District, in an old building that was waiting to be condemned. I was willing to go anywhere for a case and this one had a paying client, so a hundred miles north up to Mendocino was fine with me. I didn't bother to mention to the Chief how raw I was in the business.

As it turned out I uncovered the Indian accountant who was cooking the books at the reservation Bingo game. After the Chief and I collected our fees we left the embezzler to the Indians whose version of justice was suitably biblical.

During that investigation we ended up in a deadly bar fight when the accountant fingered us as DEA men to a group of local pot growers. He had hoped they would take us out of the picture for good. But instead we took care of a half-dozen growers, one angry bartender larger than the Chief, and one Mendocino bar. All I suffered was a broken nose. Chief Moses came out without a mark on him. After that I knew I wanted the Chief with me.

Fortunately for me he had grown tired of setting up Bingo games and was ready to join the St. John Agency. I offered to add his name but he preferred anonymity. He did insist that we move into a building that wasn't collapsing, and that was when I found the converted Victorian, formerly an attorney's offices. I enjoyed the irony of that. The Chief helped me with my custom modifications and took up second floor basketball with me, which gave the house a better structural test than the earthquake it had survived. Last year we decided we needed an addition to the staff. Mickey the beautiful ex-cop turned out to be perfect. Not only could she investigate with the best of them, she could type, keep books, and was a hi-tech whiz. The latter skill sometimes left her frustrated with our office equipment and our investigative techniques.

The Chief was standing in front of me scowling. In his huge right hand he carried a copy of the *Chronicle*.

"You are in the paper," he said, moving the gravel of his voice along his throat.

"I thought you didn't buy newspapers, Chief. Something to do with offending the tree spirits."

"I was reading the front page at Blind Benny's newsstand. When I saw your name I decided to blow the quarter." Chief Moses slapped the folded paper down hard on my scarred wooden desk.

"So Silverman is dead." The Chief ran his right hand through thick black hair that he had once grown out into a long braided ponytail. Nowadays Chief Moses had it cut at a discount stylist for

35

seven dollars. His profile still looked like it belonged on a buffalo nickel.

He was quiet, too quiet.

"This country has too many lawyers," I said. "Now there's one less."

"And too many white men," he added.

I got up from the desk. "Do you have a complaint? I have the complaint box right there." I pointed to the familiar box with a slit in the top on the windowsill. "Mickey uses it all the time."

"I observe," the Chief said.

"I know. You've mentioned it before. Like the hawk in the Everglades. You people are very poetic."

"This hawk would like to know why it was you left the bag of cash."

"Just what Mickey asked," I said.

"Where is she?"

I shrugged. "Powdering her nose."

"She and I have a mutual interest," Chief Moses said.

"Yeah. Money or having me scalped. She mentioned both of them."

"Scalping," Mickey said as she suddenly entered the room. I wondered if she had been listening outside the door, waiting for the right line to come in on.

I started humming the Beatles song "Money Can't Buy You Love."

"No comment," Mickey said.

My sports jacket was hanging on the coat rack under Mickey's straw hat. The money from Silverman's trash bag was still in its pockets.

The Chief moved to the window behind my desk and looked out into the tangle of brown vegetation in the small backyard. I sat back down at my desk and Mickey took the one client's chair in front of it.

"Your backyard is a disgrace to the land," Chief Moses said.

"Feel free to invite the water spirits any time," I said.

He sat on the edge of my desk. "What do you have for me today? I don't want to follow another unfaithful wife from motel to motel."

"Don't you like taking the pictures?" I asked.

"No."

"And *I'm* tired of sitting in a rented car watching an empty house, hoping a teenage runaway will show up. That's man's work," Mickey added.

"Why?" I asked. "The runaway's a girl."

"Because a man sitting in a car can pee in a paper cup."

"True," Chief Moses said.

"If we had a video camcorder we could set up a hidden camera for a ten-day surveillance," Mickey noted.

I got up from the desk. "I know we're all down about that drug money." I took my jacket from its hook, pulled out the two short stacks of bills, and fanned them out like two decks of playing cards for my partners to see.

They both looked with grave eyes at the ragged money.

"You took this money from Silverman's bag!" the Chief said and grinned.

"I took what was owed me. With a bonus."

"Why didn't you tell me before?" Mickey asked angrily.

"It was going to be a surprise for both of you. I wanted to see the looks on your faces."

"Like hell," she said.

I didn't comment. I didn't want to say it was basic psychology: get them to think there was nothing so the twenty-five hundred wouldn't look so bad. Actually it didn't look too bad.

The Chief waved the bills in a fan in the air.

"Put it down, Chief," Mickey said as she began to count out the money and divide it into three stacks. When she was about halfway through, the telephone rang in the front office. Mickey always turned off the answering machine when she came in.

"The phone's ringing. Aren't you going to answer it?" I asked her.

"I'll lose count," she said.

"We don't want her to do that," Chief said.

Picking up the phone, I said, "St. John Detective Agency."

It was Sam Fan, Silverman's partner. "I've got to talk to you," he said. His voice had a peculiar quality to it, almost as if he were trying to imitate Humphrey Bogart.

"I'm listening," I said.

"Not on the damn phone! Nobody talks on the phone!"

"What do you want?"

"Will you come down to my office?"

I'd never worked for Sam. All of my work had been for
Silverman who always kept a number of P.I.'s in his stable. Fan
handled the more mundane felony cases and a lot of negotiated set-
tlements, diversions to various rehabilitation programs, and plea
bargains. It wasn't glamorous work but it was necessary. And it
kept Sam out of court most of the time. He never handled the
wealthy and dangerous drug clients of Silverman. But then Sam
hadn't bothered to learn Spanish. In general, Fan didn't have
much use for private investigators. He felt all he needed was a client to level with him and he would have all the facts he needed to
cut a deal. The way he ran his end of the business he was probably
right. So up to now Sam had never gotten around to using my services.

"Just come down here," Fan insisted.

"It'll cost you, Sam."

Chief Moses nodded his head and Mickey said, "All right!"

"I'll buy your time," Fan said.

"Portal to portal?"

Fan hesitated for a moment. "Okay. From the time you leave."

"When?"

"When?" Fan echoed. "Now."

"Everyone'll be alive when I get there?" I asked. "I don't want a
repeat performance."

"Cut it," Fan said.

"Should I use the fire door?"

"You're wasting time."

"I'll be there," I promised and hung up.

Mickey and the Chief were looking at me expectantly. "So
maybe we'll add Sam Fan to our client list," I said.

Mickey handed me a stack of bills. It was a lot lighter than what I
had last night.

"I'm going to see Fan."

"And us?" Mickey asked.

"You have a house to watch. The girl will show up today. She's
desperate by now."

"Not as desperate as I'll be."

"Chief, you've got a woman to follow. Get some good shots this time. Include her face. Okay?"

"He needs a better camera," Mickey said.

"Not today."

Chief Moses snorted and Mickey scowled.

I picked up my sports jacket and went out through the line of offices. Outside it was already hot. After two cool summers in the Victorian, it looked like a mid-August heat wave had settled on us. I decided it would be worth it to buy a window fan for my office.

Only I'd have Mickey and the Chief in there all the time. Which wouldn't be half bad.

# 5

This time I came up the elevator and used the double doors inside the building.

Since he was Silverman's partner, I always expected something more elaborate for Sam Fan than the rather stark office that reminded me of mine. The first time I was in it about a year and a half ago I thought Sam was waiting for new furniture. Then during the course of working for Silverman I was in Sam's office a few more times and nothing ever changed. I finally realized there wasn't going to be any new furniture.

For visitors there were two oddly curved blue-striped chairs. Sitting in one of them, I found that the sculpted curve of the chair hurt my back. The only way to get comfortable was to climb out of the deep depression of the cushion and sit on the edge.

At least the office was air-conditioned.

Behind his large desk Sam Fan sat as tall as he could get himself to be. He had the face of a swarthy elf with full cheeks, weak chin, and sharply pointed earlobes. His ears sprouted long strands of hair that rose up to blend with the fringe of hair left on his head. He wore the fringe long and it curled at his neck and over his ears. His eyes, in contrast to the rest of his face, were hard, expressionless. Like they had seen a lot. I estimated that he was about fifty, ten years older than his late partner.

Silverman had been amused by the fact that Sam Fan had changed his name from Fanucci to Fan. Silverman used to rib him about going after an Asian clientele.

Next to a nameplate on the desk were pictures of weddings, clambakes, children, more children, and some that had to be grandchildren, all signs of Fan's extended Italian family. I wondered how many family members had also changed their name to Fan.

The display of pictures contrasted sharply with the single photo of an adolescent boy in Silverman's office.

Sam Fan tugged at the dark striped tie he wore to match his dark blue summer-weight suit. The man was dressed for mourning.

"*You* wanted to talk," I reminded him.

He took out a cigar from a humidor hidden by all the pictures on the desk.

"If you don't mind," I said, as I made a small clearing-the-air motion with my hand at invisible smoke.

"Huh?"

"The cigar."

"Jesus," Fan mouthed as he put it down. "It's an expensive cigar."

"I'm allergic," I said.

"So you don't want me to smoke in my own office?"

I nodded my head.

"Fuck you, too," Sam said but he still stuffed the cigar back into the glass humidor.

"I appreciate it, Sam."

Fan leaned back, thinking. Finally he said, "I want to hire you, St. John."

"Why?"

"You worked for Silverman."

"He hired other P.I.'s."

"You were involved at the end."

"Not exactly involved. I just found the body."

"And a shitload of money," Fan said.

"Don't remind me, Sam."

"I need protection."

"I don't do bodyguarding."

Sam Fan spread his arms out and grabbed on to the edge of his desk as if he were going to try to move it. Some pictures fell over but he didn't notice or care.

"I don't want a bodyguard."

"You said you needed protection, Sam."

"I'll get it when you find out who killed Silverman."

I watched the small man fidget behind his pictures and his desk. "Explain." I needed some help with his attorney brand of logic.

"You find out who did it and we stop them from coming after me."

"Why would someone want to kill you?" I asked.

Sam Fan shook his head slowly in disgust. "How the hell should I know? Why'd they kill Silverman?"

"Don't play games with me. Because he was a drug lawyer who was into all kinds of shit. You never took any of those cases. You didn't learn Spanish like Silverman so you could deal with the Colombians. You were the DWI man."

"Thanks."

"So what's the problem?"

"What if it wasn't a drug case?" Sam asked. "There are a lot of other reasons to off a lawyer."

"Try a few out on me."

Fan leaned forward and stared at me.

"Don't you think there was something else?" he asked. "If the killer wasn't there for the money."

"Sure. In specifics. Silverman was killed for whatever was in the safe," I offered. "But the killer got that. He doesn't need to kill you for what he already has."

Fan smiled. "Good answer. Both parts. But I'm not so sure about your conclusion. Besides I got to put my mind at ease. And the family's worried." He indicated his collection of photographs. "You know what a pain in the ass families can be."

"So?"

"So are you going to take the case?" Fan had picked up a pen and was rolling it under his palm on the desk. It made an irritating clicking noise.

"The police are handling it," I said. Sam didn't look reassured.

"Like hell," he said.

"I can't be interfering in their investigation."

"Since when? What kinda P.I. are you anyway? You guys. . ."

"The new breed," I interrupted. It was my new stock answer.

Sam's look was a lethal weapon. "You guys are always interfering in police investigations."

"On TV. In reality we try to keep it down to a minimum," I explained. "Saves on license suspensions."

Sam Fan got up and walked to the window behind him. He looked out through the half-closed blinds down at Montgomery Street.

"If you're really worried I wouldn't stand by the window," I advised.

Fan moved away but not very quickly. He shifted his shoulders uncomfortably in his suit jacket.

"The cops don't care who killed Silverman. They despised him. They'll pin it on a Colombian drug client and clear the case. That's all they care about." He paused. "Well?"

"And just when I was planning to go on vacation," I said.

"Cut the crap."

"All right. Let me get this clear. All I have to do is find out who killed Silverman?" I asked. "No bodyguard work?"

"Yeah, St. John. That's all." Sam Fan sat back down. "Real simple."

I got up.

"Okay I'll take the case. But you tell me what did Silverman have in his safe? What did the killer get?"

"I don't know."

"You were his partner," I pursued.

"I don't know."

"You sound like one of Silverman's clients on the stand."

"I don't know what was in there. Silverman did his own thing. He had his own door to the goddamned street."

"That's what got him killed."

Sam Fan had nothing else to say. We settled on a daily fee, plus expenses, which were purposely on the high side. Incredibly, Sam didn't object. Everyone back at the office would be happy. Knowing Fan's reputation, I got a substantial advance in cash.

Fan got up and we shook hands. His palm was wet.

On my way out I smiled at the twin blondes, Jennifer and Jeanine, at their twin desks and at Victoria, the beautiful receptionist I couldn't get anywhere with. Not even up to bat much less first base. The law partners had good taste in personnel.

I stepped into the third floor hallway. By the elevator a tall attractive woman was reading the names on the floor directory. She smiled at me with teeth that reminded me of Chiclets.

"Do you know where Farr's office is?" she asked me. "I seem to be lost."

"Fan's office?" I asked. "The lawyer?"

"No, Dr. Farr," she said a little too loudly. "The dentist."

"Those perfect teeth don't look like they need one."

"Oh? Are you a dentist?"

I gave her a business card.

"A detective?" She made it sound about at the level of the oldest profession.

"You never know when you might need one."

She put the card in her purse.

The elevator came and she got in. It went up. I wondered if it would take her to Dr. Farr.

# 6

Move one: Try to find out what the police knew about the Silverman murder. I knew it wouldn't be easy from my interview with Detective Chang. The case was still in its crucial first twenty-four hours after the murder when most cases are solved or at least solid leads are established. It was the worst time to try to learn anything from the cops. But at least I had a contact on the force.

I started up the black Thunderbird, along with the Corvette one of the two true American sports cars. Only it was hard getting the three-person agency packed into the two front seats. I got a lot of complaints about that. And the odometer was broken so I wasn't sure how many miles were on it, but thanks to the Chief and his auto mechanic skills it ran smoothly.

At the precinct house I was lucky to get an empty visitor's parking space. Probably because it was getting on to evening. Usually they were all taken up by illegally parked police cars.

Downstairs, in the lower depths of the building, next to the Narcotics Division, was Vice. The sergeant with the beer belly who always gave me a hard time about private citizens in restricted areas wasn't around to hassle me. In the squad room I found the man I was looking for, Johnny Dajewski, at his desk typing a report. I was on a roll.

Johnny was using one finger on each hand to strike the keys. He hit one letter hard with an extended middle finger. Then he looked up. When he saw who it was he went immediately back to typing. I knew he was wishing that I would just go away. That's what happens when somebody owes you. They think you're always there to collect. Plus interest. Most of the time they're right.

Dajewski was a big-boned blond Polish cop with boyish good looks that made him look like a grown-up Dennis the Menace. Everybody called him Johnny D., including his Mexican wife, who after five years of marriage could still barely speak English. Maybe that was why they got along so well.

"I knew you'd be glad to see me, Johnny."

"Huh?"

"Am I interrupting anything?"

"Yeah."

"Go ahead and finish," I said.

I sat down in the wooden chair next to the desk to wait.

"You're not gonna go away are you, Jeremiah?" he finally looked up to say.

"Not yet."

"Do I still owe you?" he asked.

I shrugged, one of the favorite when-in-doubt responses of all of the St. John Detective Agency staff. Johnny D. in fact owed me for locating his wife's baby brother who had run off to Tijuana to set up as a drug trafficker and sometime pimp. I wasn't sure if it was legal but the Chief and I brought the boy back over the border against his will under the noses of the border patrol. Since then, after a stint in a drug rehabilitation program in Oakland, he was teaching Spanish in a private school in the East Bay. And Mrs. D. loved me for it. But it was a favor I had called in chips on before. By now Johnny was almost sorry he had asked me to help.

"All right," Johnny said. "But I've gotta finish this damn report."

"Bust another adult bookstore clerk?"

"Wish I had. But this is an Officer Discharging His Weapon Report that I gotta file. Damn thing went off by accident. Never happened to me before."

He pounded the keys for about ten more minutes then looked up as he yanked out the form from the typewriter.

"Well?"

"It's confidential, Johnny."

He led me to a coffee vending machine and started digging in his pockets for change. What I really wanted was something cold to drink but I got out two quarters and two dimes for two paper cups of hot coffee. I took the coffee out from behind the little plastic door and burned the tips of my fingers.

I looked into the cup: "It's thick. Like soup."

"Want your money back?" As Johnny sipped at the rim of his cup, steam rose up to his nostrils.

"Where can I get rid of this stuff?"

"Over there."

I dumped the liquid down a sink.

"We use it to open clogged drains," he said.

"Where can we talk?"

"In an interrogation room." He swung a door open. "Where else?"

It was an interior room with no windows. There were a table and a few uncomfortable chairs. The lighting was dim but at least there were no naked bulbs. The walls were institutional beige decorated with large dark stains the source of which I didn't want to know. The room smelled of smoke, sweat, and urine. Together the stink and the heat almost made me gag.

"A kid pissed his pants before," Johnny D. said as he sniffed at the air. "Take this chair. It looks the same, but that one," he said indicating the chair at the end of the table, "is for the alleged perpetrator. It's the pits. Every joint is loose. You can't move without feeling it's going to fall apart. Sit in it long enough and you'll talk just to get out of it."

Johnny D. sat down on one of the good chairs and put his feet up

49

on the table whose every square inch was pockmarked with burns and scratches.

"Okay. Shoot," he said.

"I'm working on the Silverman murder."

"Why? It's a day-old homicide. It's an open investigation."

"I'm getting paid to do it."

"It's Chang's case. I'd stay outta the way of that cop if I were you."

I leaned towards him as though we were not alone. "My client figures it won't be open long."

Johnny D. brushed away a fly that had somehow made it into the windowless room. The bluebottle circled up to the light like a moth.

"What do the cops have?" I asked.

"I'm in Vice."

"Silverman is vice. Silverman is drugs."

"Not when he's dead. Then he's Homicide."

"Come on."

"Hey, it's in the papers. We're lookin' for a drug dealer named Orlando Gomez." He paused. "But if you ask me he's back in Colombia."

"My client doesn't buy the Gomez theory. And I work for him. I need a different lead."

"Just between us I don't have one," Johnny said. "I hear it's Gomez open and shut."

"Some other angle on it. Come on, Johnny."

Johnny D. was tilting his chair precariously. "Why don't you talk to McCurdy in the DEA?"

"Are they involved in this one?"

"Yeah."

"How?"

"I'm not sure. They don't give us anything. We don't give them anything. That's how the system works. It's called interagency co-operation."

"What's the line on McCurdy?"

"They call him Big Mac."

"What am I supposed to do with that?" I asked.

"You can call him Big Mac and tell him Johnny D. sent you."
"What'll that get me?"
"I don't know. Maybe out on your ass. Or worse."
"You've been a big help."
"I try," Johnny said.
"What does McCurdy do exactly?"
Johnny D. thought about that one for awhile. "Used to work undercover shit. I don't know right now. He's been in on some stings in the past that I heard went sour."
"Anything I'd recognize?" I asked. I remembered that Chief Moses had a friend or two in the DEA and maybe I could get some help there if I had to.
"I don't have any specifics; it's just what I hear."
"I'm going to talk to McCurdy," I said.
"Lotsa luck."
"It was your idea. You got any better ones?"
He swatted at the large fly as it buzzed past his ear.
"Here. Give McCurdy my card. It'll help. He owes me a little. But make it believable. And take along your beautiful secretary. That'll help."
"She's my partner," I said as I took the card and smiled.
"Whatever you want to call her."
"How long until there's an autopsy report?"
"Talk to Homicide," he said. "I got my limits."
"Thanks, Johnny."
We walked back to his desk.
As I turned to go Johnny D. said, "Next time you come across a trash bag full of small unmarked bills give me a call." I had been waiting for Johnny to mention the money and I wondered what took him so long.
I went out of the squad room without asking him.

# 7

In the Wednesday afternoon newspaper there was a statement from a group identifying itself as PAL—People Against Lawyers, terrorists who were taking credit for the elimination of the "drug demon" Silverman. A photo of their typewritten message ran next to the text. There were several typewriter key peculiarities which affected the formation and position of a few of the letters. These idiosyncrasies could be used like fingerprints to identify the culprit machine. Most obvious were defects in the "t"s, the "m"s, the "g"s and the upper case "P"s and "R"s. But the newspaper copy wasn't clear enough for me to be certain about such an analysis.

The statement began by quoting Shakespeare's famous put-down in *Henry VI, Part II*—"The first thing we do, let's kill all the lawyers." Then it talked about Bay Area lawyers who were only interested in beating the system, winning on technicalities, letting murderers and rapists and drug traffickers go, and making cases longer, more complex, and costlier. Silverman was the kind of San Francisco lawyer PAL was dedicated to eliminating. No money-grubbing Bay Area attorney was safe, the group promised.

Rick Silverman killed by PAL to keep legal fees down in the city. That was hard for me to buy.

I called Sam Fan. I didn't want to see him yet but I thought I'd have to, given his phone paranoia. Victoria answered in that deep sexy voice and I tried, as usual, to get a conversation going with her.

"Hold, please," she said. So much for conversation with Victoria.

While I held I was treated to a Muzak version of "All of Me."

Until Sam broke in. "What's up, St. John?"

"Did you see the afternoon paper?"

"Did I see the afternoon paper? Yeah I saw the afternoon paper. I can't believe you're calling about that kook group."

Apparently, now that I worked for him, Sam was willing to talk with me on the phone.

"How kooky can it be if it wants to cut the number of lawyers in the Bay Area? I thought you'd support that, Sam. As long as you're not one of the dead ones."

"You're not telling me the PAL killed Rick. I'm not buying. I'm not buying a group that takes the same letters as the goddamned Police Athletic League."

"Neither am I, Sam."

"What're you telling me, St. John?"

"The PAL may not be as dumb as it seems."

"It's a joke! It's a hoax!"

"I've got to investigate every angle."

"So?"

"So I'll check out the PAL," I said.

"It said in the newspaper that this is the first anyone ever heard of a PAL. There's no such organization known to the FBI. It's a bunch of kooks."

"Kooks can be dangerous. Just like Colombian cowboys, Silverman's *coqueros*. They've been known to shoot people. Dead."

54

I heard heavy breathing at the other end of the line. "Got anything else?" he asked.

"The police are convinced it's Orlando Gomez."

"Good for the police. But I know better."

"Do you have any proof, Sam?"

He hesitated. "I got a gut feeling. For proof I hired you."

"All right. I need a list of Silverman's close relatives. Names, addresses, telephone numbers. Anyone who had anything to gain. Anyone who could be in his will."

"The asshole died intestate," Sam said.

I was silent for a moment.

"Tell me, Sam, you got a will?"

"Kiss off."

"Names and addresses, Sam."

"I got his ex-wife's address. She lives with their kid. That's it."

I thought of the boy in the silver frame.

"Silverman's from back East. Anybody there?"

"Nobody."

Sam gave me Mrs. Silverman's address. He didn't have the phone number. It was unlisted, particularly to Silverman and anyone who had anything to do with him. She had changed it three times in the past year.

"I got a client waiting," Fan said. "You got anything more to tell me?"

"What happens to the half-million?" I asked.

"It was $627,000."

"Who gets it?"

"It's been impounded."

"When it gets unimpounded."

"Silverman's ex-wife is claiming it. I've already heard from her attorney."

"And you know who'll get most of the money?"

"Her leech lawyer when it's all over," he said.

"Have you ever thought of joining PAL?" I could tell by the curses he let fly that Sam Fan didn't think that was very funny.

# 8

Rita Silverman lived in a restored turn-of-the-century hotel on Powell that had been converted into an elegant gingerbread apartment building. I parked on an angle under a tree on Powell just in time to get out of the way of a climbing cable car, its bells clanging as it passed through the intersection, coming towards me. I walked down the steep sidewalk and turned on the cross street to go up to the front of the building. A long curved awning ran from the outside door to the curb.

The unusual heat wave continued but it was past five o'clock in the afternoon and the temperature was dropping. I stood in the shade of the awning and straightened my silk rep striped tie and brushed the shoulders of my camel blazer. When I left the D.A.'s office I gave away all of my three-piece attorney suits to the Salvation Army. I replaced them with blazers, slacks and loafers. I felt more comfortable and the blazers, along with an occasional tweed sports jacket, were cut to give me enough room to wear my shoulder holster.

I opened the door and pushed the button marked Rita Silverman. A pleasant female voice came over the intercom, asking me to identify myself. I had rehearsed that.

"Jeremiah St. John. Special investigator working on your ex-husband's case."

"Special investigator? Aren't you the P.I. who discovered Silverman's body? And the money?"

Of course she had read the newspaper article. It was a little strange to hear her refer to her dead ex-husband as Silverman. And even stranger to be talking about the case over an intercom.

"There's no reward," she said.

"I'm not looking for one. I just need to talk to you."

The buzzer went off and I opened the inner door. She was up two flights. When I knocked on her door she opened it about half the length of a nearly worthless security chain. I saw dark brown eyes, bright red lips, and a narrow rectangular suggestion of her body between door and jamb.

She studied my I.D. as though it were a contract full of fine print, and then she strained to check me out through the narrow space. "I'm not going to talk about money," she said. "You can talk to my attorney about that."

"I've heard too much about the money already. Especially about why I left it there. I just want to get some information. Please, Mrs. Silverman, may I come in?"

She shut the door and undid the chain.

When the door opened I saw a short slim woman of about forty with hips and bust appropriate for someone larger. Her body looked put together from the best parts of two female types, the boyish and the matronly.

She was wearing a T-shirt and tight slacks. The T-shirt was faded and read: A WOMAN'S PLACE IS IN THE HOUSE. THE WHITE HOUSE. I assumed she didn't mean as First Lady.

"Call me Rita, Mr. St. John." She stepped back carefully on very high-heeled open-backed shoes.

"It's Jeremiah." I smiled.

She smiled. We stared at each other.

She led me into an elegantly constructed room that had a faded grandeur. It was off a hallway done in white Italian ceramic tile. The floors were covered with beige plush carpeting and the walls with flocked wallpaper. A bank of bay windows overlooked Powell. An elaborate crystal chandelier hung over a sunken area where there would ordinarily be a dining room table and chairs.

Instead of a dining room set there was a typing table with an old Underwood and a phone on it. The couch in the living room was leather and looked no better than the one in my office. There was a torn fabric chair across from the couch that clashed with the threadbare drapes and a makeshift coffee table of bricks and boards. There was a wet bar against the wall. Another touch of incongruous opulence.

"Please sit down," she said.

I sat on the old leather couch, which was comfortable if nothing else.

Rita Silverman sat down on the fabric chair across from me.

She ran her hands through black hair that had been turned into a helmet of curls. Her eyes were almond-shaped, with irises that had a gold cast. She was carefully, but not obviously, made up. She didn't look like she needed a facelift yet.

Rita Silverman crossed her legs and toyed with the back strap of one shoe.

Overall I found her very sexy.

"You're wondering why all this junk furniture in this expensive apartment, right?" she asked.

That wasn't exactly what I had been thinking right then but I nodded my head in agreement.

"The reason I have such *schlock* around is that I got the apartment in the settlement. But just the apartment. I got cheated out of all the furniture, the drapes, and of course the paintings. I'm surprised he left the wallpaper and the carpeting. You're looking at what a forty-year-old woman reentering the job market can afford in San Francisco."

"You needed a better lawyer."

59

"I've got a better lawyer. Sam Fan's heard from him already."

"Mrs. Silverman. . ."

"You were going to call me Rita, Jeremiah. Remember? And by the way who hired you?"

"Sam Fan hired me."

"Of course. That damn wop." She stared at me with those dark brown eyes. "You're not Italian are you? You don't look Italian. Not with those blue eyes. And not with a name like St. John."

"I'm not."

"I hope I didn't offend you. Sometimes a good ethnic slur is the only way to express how you really feel."

"Sam Fan can be a pain."

"That's putting it mildly. He's giving me grief over whether the bag of money is part of Silverman's estate. I just got a pretty damn unpleasant telegram about it."

Sam had fired off a response after he heard from Rita's lawyer. No one was wasting any time.

Rita pointed to a Western Union envelope lying beside the old manual typewriter.

"You don't see many typewriters like that around," I said.

"Except in antique shops."

I wanted to talk about Rick Silverman, not typewriters. "I'm sorry about your ex-husband. . ." I began.

"You're in an exclusive club. You're the only member so far. I would have loved to kill the bastard."

"Don't say things like that in a murder case."

"Look at the money he had!" She got up suddenly. "Yet he begrudged me my alimony payments. And even child support for his son!"

The only sign of a teenager was the same picture as Silverman had in his office. Only in a wooden frame on the makeshift coffee table, not a silver desk.

"How old is your son?"

"Richard is fourteen."

"Richard." I pondered that for a moment. She looked amused. "How did you meet Rick?"

"At a party. Back East. When he got out of the army in '68."

"I didn't know he was in the army."

"He never talked about it. Never."

"Was he in Vietnam?"

"Yes. That's all I know except that he was an army lawyer."

That seemed to have potential but Rita didn't have any other details. He had kept that part of his life a secret from his wife. A lot of men handled the Vietnam war that way. I switched us back to the present. "Where were you when Rick. . ."

"Call him Silverman. Everybody does. That's what I called him half the time." She went over to the wet bar.

"Where were you when Silverman was murdered?" I asked.

"You are subtle. How about a drink?"

"A beer?"

"I have three jugs of wine. Red, white, or rosé?"

"I'll have some of the house white," I said.

"Good choice."

Rita poured two glasses of white wine out of a large green jug, which she took from the small refrigerator. When she brought them over she put two paper coasters down on the boards that served as the top of the coffee table. Old habits die hard or never die at all.

With both of us sitting again, I got down to it. "Have you got an alibi for the night of Silverman's murder?" I took a sip of wine, which was sweeter than I expected it to be.

"I don't have to talk to you about it. You're not the police." Rita kicked off her shoes and tucked her legs under her. She took a long swallow of her wine. "If I killed him I wouldn't have missed the money."

"Somebody missed it," I said.

"Besides you?"

"I didn't miss it. I just left it."

"I appreciate your virtue, Mr. St. John, I really do."

"You're about the only one."

Her voice rose an octave. "Why would I kill him?"

"You've given me a few good reasons already."

"So? What does that prove?"

"Do you own a gun?"

"I did," she answered. "But it disappeared a month ago."

"That's not very convincing. But it's convenient."

"Mildred, my cleaning lady, collected anything she could put her hands on. I had to fire her. I would have anyway. I couldn't afford her on a secretary's salary."

"Could I have her name and an address?"

Rita went into the kitchen and came back with a scrap of paper. I put it into my jacket pocket.

"What kind of gun was it?"

"How am I supposed to know. It shot bullets. Silverman was the gun fancier. He bought it for me when we were still married. But he's the one who took it to the firing range."

"Did he ever take you?"

She shifted her weight.

"Once or twice."

"Did you shoot?"

"Yes. And I hit the target too. It was set in the chest area of an outlined figure. I imagined I was shooting Silverman in the heart."

She was baiting me but I didn't bite.

"Did Silverman keep a gun at the office?" I was convinced the bullet in the spine of the law book had come from Silverman's gun.

"Probably. We never discussed it."

"You have no idea what kind of gun it was?"

"No."

"But I bet it was silver."

Rita laughed. It was a nice laugh.

"When were you divorced?"

"Two years ago. Do you want to know why?"

"He wasn't the perfect husband?"

"We had some good times in the early years. He loved Richard when he was a baby. But something happened. I don't know what. I don't think I'll ever know. He started running around on me. At the same time he started doing coke. Our lives were falling apart."

"How much coke?"

"What does that mean? Enough to destroy himself."

"Who was he having an affair with?"

"I don't know. And I didn't want to find out. I wanted him out of my life and Richard's life."

I looked at her without saying anything.

"I didn't kill him. I've got an alibi."

"Which is?"

"I was having dinner right here with my son."

I settled the wine glass down on the paper coaster. The glass was sweating.

"What did Richard think of his father?"

"He won't let anyone call him Rick or Junior. He's Richard." She paused. "He hates . . . hated him."

I wondered how much of that hate he learned from Rita. Still, from what I knew Silverman could earn his own hate without much help from anyone.

"Do you think I can talk to him?"

"No."

"If he's your alibi. . ."

"He's back up north. At a tennis camp in Sonoma County. He was just in for the evening, then he took the bus back."

"When did he find out about his father?"

"I called him as soon as I heard."

"When is he coming back to the city?" I finished my wine as I waited for an answer.

Rita picked up both glasses, refilled them, and brought them back. Instead of answering my question she went into a high-pitched litany. "I don't want him around all of this ugliness. This investigation. Newspapers. The police. The reporters."

I lifted my glass from the coffee table. The old coaster clung to its underside like a large barnacle. Of course her alibi was also one for her son. These days fourteen wasn't too young for murder.

"When will he be back?"

"Two weeks. Then he's leaving for prep school."

"I'd like to drive up and see him."

"I told you he was with me when it happened," she half shouted.

"Rita, I'd like very much to see him. It's important, I think, to you. . ."

She slammed her glass down.

"Richard and I were together."

"I still want to talk to him."

"I won't tell you where he is."

"I'll find him."

"He's under a phony name."

"You're not that devious."

She poked me in the chest. "Leave him out of this. Leave him alone. You want to talk to somebody talk to Silverman's clients. The ones he didn't get off. Or better yet, talk to some of the victims. Silverman was more than a drug lawyer. Thanks to him and his technicalities we have killers, rapists, child molesters walking the streets. Talk to the victims. Talk to the families."

I stood up and held her shoulders.

She broke down. She nestled up against me. We just stood there, with her sobbing.

When she regained control of herself she moved back gently, just enough to be under my chin. I could feel her breasts pushing below my chest.

"Thank you," she said in a whisper.

"For what?"

"For holding me when I needed it. Now do me one more favor. Don't try to find Richard."

I didn't know what to say. But I knew what I had to do.

"I'd better go."

Rita nodded her head. The tears had streaked her mascara.

"You have an unlisted number?"

"You know I do."

"Can I have it?"

I had memorized the number from the telephone but I wanted it from Rita.

She hesitated.

"Rita, I might need to call you."

"What the hell."

She told me the number. I wrote it down next to her former cleaning lady's name and address.

As I left I decided I had acted like a professional with Rita. Just like with the garbage bag full of money.

Behind me I heard the security chain slip back into place.

# 9

I hit the horn of the T-Bird twice as I waited Friday morning in front of Mickey's apartment in the Embarcadero, just north of the Ferry Building. She lived there alone with a panoramic view of the bay and the Bay Bridge.

Five minutes later Mickey swung her long legs into the passenger seat. "Why did you keep blowing the damn horn? It's early in the morning."

"Only twice," I said. "Besides there are fog horns on the bay all of the time."

"That's different. They're romantic, especially at night."

I pulled away from the curb and started along the waterfront for the drive to Sonoma County and Richard's tennis camp.

Mickey had her honey blond hair pulled back into a ponytail, which emphasized her high cheekbones and those large green eyes. She was wearing a peach polo shirt without a logo and a crisp khaki skirt that revealed a lot of bare thigh. I noticed a light down of blond hair several inches above her knee at the line where she stopped shaving her legs. She had tied a white sweater around her shoulders.

"You look terrific."

"Jeremiah, will you watch the road."

"I got distracted."

"I noticed."

"How do I look?" I asked.

"Oh just terrific."

"I mean do I look like a member of a management consultant team evaluating the profit performance of the California State University Summer Sports Program?" I was wearing a striped rugby shirt with a logo and cotton slacks. It was the only polo shirt I owned. I had a vast collection of T-shirts, sweatshirts, warm-up suits and jackets from my college days: Chico State, Sacramento State, Sonoma State, and then Cal and finally, after graduation, Bolt Hall for law. I had done a lot of moving around in those days before settling on Berkeley and I still had all of my souvenirs. But none of them seemed appropriate for this role. My gun was locked in the glove compartment. I didn't think I'd need it at a tennis camp.

"What matters are the I.D.'s we have," Mickey said.

"Got 'em in the attaché case behind us. We are the most authentic management consultant team in California. It's believable and just intimidating enough. We just want to evaluate the rate of return for the State University. During the summer it rents out its sports facilities to private programs in tennis, basketball, football and soccer. The University is always looking to increase revenues from these rentals. The tennis camp administrator will understand that bottom line."

"Would you translate for tennis?" she asked.

"Triples matches instead of doubles. You can increase productivity and profits by 50 percent. Think of how many more kids you could jam into each court and multiply that by the fee for the camp."

Mickey punched my arm. We crossed Van Ness and started up Franklin Street where trucks were prohibited and the traffic was always lighter because of the steep hills. I turned west on the flat stretch of Lombard and headed for the Golden Gate Bridge.

"Let me see that picture of Richard again," Mickey asked.

"It's in the attaché case too."

She reached into the small space behind us and put the case on her lap. As she unsnapped the locks she asked, "How do you think the Chief will do in that fishy case we got yesterday?"

Chief Moses was going undercover in a fish processing plant in South San Francisco. "The owners believe hundreds of pounds of fish are being stolen. 'Right under their noses.' That's a quote."

"He was worried that he'd end up smelling like a fish but he couldn't stand peeping into another motel room," Mickey said.

"You can't say we don't have options in this business."

"Well, at least I'm off that stakeout."

"I told you the girl would show."

"It would have been easier with a hidden camera," Mickey said as she opened the case.

"With a camera you wouldn't have been there to talk to her."

Mickey stared at the picture I had gotten from Sam yesterday, minus the silver frame, to help us identify Richard once we located the right tennis camp. "Nice looking kid," she said.

After I briefed Mickey and the Chief on the Rita and Richard situation yesterday, she and I spent most of the morning calling and recalling the too-numerous tennis camps in Sonoma County with different approaches. The direct approach failed every time. The camps were reluctant to give out any information to anyone, no matter who you claimed to be. When we tried calling as parents the camps were concerned that we were divorced parents without custody who were out to kidnap our own children. And then there were identification codes such as "Give your mother's maiden name." Just like the banks. And then the camp spokespersons kept talking about their legal liability and how they could barely afford to operate now because of skyrocketing insurance costs brought on by the increases in litigation. I thought warmly of PAL.

Finally we hit on the right routine. It got us answers but not

Richard until one of the last calls. I convinced whomever I spoke to at the Cal State camp that I represented California Special Services, which was investigating the improper spending of welfare money on such luxuries as a tennis camp.

The person on the phone nearly choked. "Mrs. Silverman? On Welfare? On the state dole?"

"It happens in the best of families."

Regaining her composure, the administrator said, "I assure you this tennis camp is not a luxury. We concentrate on fundamental skills. The basics of the game. It is hard work. We turn out some real professionals."

"I'm sorry. Despite that admirable goal tennis camps don't meet the state-mandated standards for job retraining of welfare recipients. I've got the official list. Tennis pro is not included."

She wanted to know what this meant to the camp. I wanted to be sure I had the right Silverman.

"You may, particularly if you don't cooperate, have to reimburse the state, with interest, and there could possibly be a fine."

"Why?"

"Deep pockets," I said, tossing one of the Trial Lawyers Association's sacred money cows at her. "If the defendant can't repay us, in this case the Silverman family, then we find an entity that can pay. And you're it."

"I don't understand."

"Are you going to give Special Services the information we require for an accounting to the taxpayers of this state or do we have to take legal action."

"Of course we'll be glad to cooperate." She sighed.

"Thank you. Now to confirm our information. This is Richard Silverman, age fourteen. Mother's name Rita; father's name Richard. San Francisco address."

"Yes. A real tragedy, about the father. Poor kid."

I hung up before she could say any more.

The heavy morning traffic was thinning out. Ahead of us was the Golden Gate. The fog was so thick that only the orange tips of the towers were visible. The steel seemed to float, suspended in the early morning sky, turrets without support. Across the bridge in Marin County the sun had already burned off the coastal fog. The summer hills rose soft, round, golden and dry as tinder on each side of us. It was mid-August and as usual there hadn't been any real rainfall since the end of March.

"Wake me up when we get to Sonoma County." Mickey dropped the seat into a reclining position, stretched out as much as possible, and closed her eyes.

North on 101 the valley began to widen and the road became more level. Hills of dry grass rolled by endlessly. Brown and white cattle stood gathered under trees or spread out, like scattered chess pieces, on their grazing land. Less than half an hour out of San Francisco, California had turned rural. It was the same Redwood Highway I took up to the Mendocino reservation when I first worked with Chief Moses on the Bingo case. We'd come quite a way since then.

We crossed the county line, leaving Marin. It was marked by a green highway sign and a drive-in movie theater that showed X-rated films. The marquee offered women free admission on Monday nights. The huge curved screen faced away from the highway to protect motorists from getting distracted.

I read the highly suggestive erotic titles of the two feature films out loud.

That woke Mickey.

She read the marquee. "Are we going to be here Monday night?"

"Sorry. We're going to get the job done today."

"Too bad."

"You like these films?" I asked.

"At least men and women are equally nude in them."

"I never thought of it that way."

The air was getting ripe with the smell of fertilizer and Mickey rolled her window up.

Twenty minutes later I took what I hoped was the right exit. We drove past an enormous suburban shopping center marked by a three-story-high revolving sign. It was hard to believe that we were at the edge of the wine country of Northern California.

We had to double back, but a little more than an hour after we left the city we drove up to the entrance of the State University and tried to buy a parking permit for seventy-five cents from a recalcitrant machine. After three slaps to the side of the ticket dispenser I gave up on it and started to look for a parking space.

I thought of triples again as I parked my car without a permit in a lot across from the tennis complex under the blazing sun.

There were two rows of six courts, each court running north-south to minimize the disturbing effects of that sun. We went over to an entrance and looked in. On this side the campers were no more than ten or eleven.

"Walk tall. Let's look like we know what we're doing," I said to Mickey.

"Take your own advice, Jeremiah."

We strolled over to some metal stands at the end of the row of courts and sat down. I took out a small notebook and began to doodle in it. After five minutes of not being noticed by anyone we went over to the second row of courts and sat down again in the stands. This time Mickey doodled. This time we were noticed.

"Can I help you?" The questioner was a tall slim man of about sixty dressed in tennis whites. He had very large hands and a very bald head. Every exposed square inch of his skin was deeply tanned.

"Maybe," I said.

"Are you parents?"

"No. We're not. We're looking for the camp director."

"You've found him. I'm Lenny Carlton, tennis pro and camp director."

We gave our real names and shook hands all around. Then Lenny looked blankly at us until I said, "We're from MEC, Management Evaluation Consulting." I handed him two business cards which he looked at suspiciously. "We're evaluating all the summer contract programs at the University," I said very cheerfully.

"What for?" His eyes narrowed.

"To decide whether to recommend, based on revenue generation relative to potential, the current contractor, such as yourself, for next summer. We want to weed out those who aren't generating profits up to capacity."

70

"I've been here for years," Lenny said, bewildered.

"We know that. But we must follow procedures. We'd just like to mingle today. Talk to some of the camp participants. Get some of their feedback on the program. We're looking for the ROS. Rate of Satisfaction. A high positive indicates that you can charge more without losing campers, clients, students, whatever."

"Oh?" Lenny didn't look too pleased with the ROS concept.

"Next week we'll be up to audit your books. And we'd like to see your application statistics. Including percentage of returnees."

"My books are in order. I can get those statistics you want put together over the weekend. . ."

"We'll call first. Don't make too much of it," Mickey said.

Lenny relaxed just a little.

"Now if we could talk to some of the kids," I said.

Lenny looked at our cards again and then at Mickey. "I guess it's okay."

He brought us over to a group of players that had just come off the courts and introduced us as University officials who just wanted to ask a few questions. These campers were all pre-teens. I signaled to Lenny to give us some privacy and he muttered something about checking the radar equipment used for timing the speed of serves.

We quizzed the kids about food, rooms, and general satisfaction with the tennis camp. Most of the complaints were about the food. By the time we were done Lenny was back hovering unhappily.

"We would like to speak to a few of the kids individually. Off the record." I said.

"Mr. Carlton, I'm sure in your case this is all a formality," Mickey assured him.

"I guess it's all right." He walked off reluctantly.

I looked around. I still hadn't seen anyone who looked like Richard. But some new players were just coming out on the courts. These were older kids.

"There he is," Mickey said pointing to the last court.

We hurried along a green-screened fence to that court. We walked out to the net. A ball flew by. Richard returned it with a solid backhand down the line.

I signaled to the instructor operating the ball gun to hold it up and told him why we were there. He introduced us to Richard and explained our presence. I looked at him, Mickey looked at him; reluctantly he left.

"You want to ask me about my experience at this tennis camp?" Richard looked at us with dark eyes just like Rita's. Quite naturally, he was on his guard.

"Can we get to some shade?" I asked.

He hesitated, then said, "O.K."

He led us off the court to the shade of a grove of trees behind the complex fence. A swarm of players descended on the vacated court. From what I had seen so far Lenny Carlton ran a tight tennis business.

The three of us sat down on the soft grass. Richard glanced at Mickey's legs then quickly averted his eyes.

"We're not consultants, we're private investigators," Mickey said.

"Huh? You mean you used that consultant line to get past old man Carlton? Those your real names you gave him?"

"Why not? No sense complicating things," I said. "And we wanted to be straight with you."

"Sure. Just like you wanted to ask me about my tennis camp experience."

"You got any complaints? I'll pass 'em on to Carlton," I promised.

"You kidding?"

"No."

"Anonymously?"

"Sure. We talked to plenty of kids here already."

"Okay. They use tennis balls until they're fuzzless and dead. They pack the courts with too many kids at a time. We don't get enough singles practice like this."

"Noted. I'm serious. I'll see if I can help."

Richard bit his lip. "What's the catch? What do you want from me?"

"Just to talk to you," Mickey said.

He thought it over. "Let me see your real I.D.'s."

I showed him my license.

"I guess you're for real. Okay. I'll talk to you. It's about my father isn't it?" Curiosity had gotten us our "talk."

"In a way," I said.

"What do you mean?"

"Let's talk about your mother," I said.

"Why?"

"We're interested in protecting her. We need to corroborate her statements about the evening your father was killed."

"You mean she needs an alibi."

"We're on her side. We want one established."

"Did she hire you?"

I avoided a direct answer by saying, "It's part of the overall case we're investigating. Now that Monday night you had dinner with your mother?"

"Yes."

"Do you go into the city often by bus?" I asked.

"About once a week. Usually on Mondays."

"Why Mondays?"

"We work hardest on the weekends. Monday is kind of down time."

"Do most of the kids leave camp then?"

He hesitated. "No."

"But you do?"

"Yeah. I'm leaving for prep school in September. I'm not going to get to see my mother much."

I resisted asking him what prep school. "What time do you get into the city?"

"Between five and five-thirty. Depending on the traffic."

"And on that Monday?"

"I'm not sure. My watch battery went dead."

"How was the traffic?"

"Not too bad. I wasn't real late or anything."

"But you could have been early."

"Maybe just a little. I don't know."

"But you do know that you spent the evening from about six o'clock on with your mother?"

"Yes."

"And the bus station is downtown. Close to Montgomery."

"And to Powell where my mother lives. What are you driving at?"

"Look. We're trying to help your mom," Mickey interjected. She would be the good guy. I hoped I didn't have to be a very bad guy with a fourteen-year-old who seemed like a nice kid.

"Details are crucial, Richard," I said.

"When exactly did my father uh . . . die?"

I didn't have an official time of death but I estimated, "Between six p.m. and seven p.m."

"That's when my mother and I were eating dinner together."

For a vulnerable fourteen-year-old who had just lost his father he was holding up remarkably well. I looked at Mickey. She knew what I was thinking.

"You know your mother's gun is missing, Richard?" I asked.

"Gun? What gun? I didn't know she owned one."

"Well she did. And now it's gone."

"What're you saying? That it's the murder weapon?" He was angry, defensive.

"No. But she did have a gun. It's something the police are aware of too. We're checking it out. There's a possibility that it was stolen some time ago."

"Please believe that we're on your mother's side," Mickey said.

"Why? She didn't hire you. Who are you working for anyhow? You avoided my question before."

"You know that's privileged information," I tried.

From the look on Richard's face he wasn't buying it but wasn't going to pursue it.

"She couldn't kill him," he said. "She couldn't kill anyone."

"I agree. But would she think you could?"

Richard stood up and walked away from us. He stood with his back to us for a long time. I was afraid I'd gone too far. Finally, he came back and sat down.

"Did anything happen between you and your father?" Mickey asked gently. "Anything that would worry your mother."

"The last time I stayed with him he brought out his damn coke. I threatened to call the cops and he started slapping me around."

74

"What'd you do?"

"I threw some wild punches and missed. Then I picked up something—I think it was an ashtray—and threw it at him. I ran out of there."

"Was he all right?"

"Sure. He came out into the street after me."

"Where'd you go?"

"Back to my mother's."

"Did you call the police?"

"My mother wanted to but I wouldn't let her. I wasn't going to call the cops. I just wanted him to put that shit away. He was sick. Messed up. Maybe Vietnam did it to him. I don't know."

"We understand," Mickey said.

Richard looked at her with appreciation.

I could see she wanted to put her arm around him but thought better of it.

"I don't have anything else to say."

We thanked him and let him go claim his court. He was a likable kid with a lot to absorb. I hoped he had nothing to do with his father's murder.

On the way out I told Lenny that we had found the camp very cost-effective but that he could get the ROS up if he did things like provide new tennis balls more often.

"But the bottom line?"

"Hey. You improve the ROS and you can charge more. It's an investment. Like increasing singles time a bit for the players." I smiled at him.

Lenny started to object when Mickey interrupted, "We've been impressed by the camp's performance. I don't think we even have to come back."

"What about the books? The application statistics? Procedures?"

"We're the consultants. We write the procedures. But don't let this get around. I think your situation is unique." I winked at him.

Lenny winked back. He would keep quiet. He knew he was in for next summer.

When we got to the parking lot we found a ticket for parking without a permit stuck under a windshield wiper.

"I've never been able to get a ticket fixed in my life," I complained.

Mickey was preoccupied and just shrugged.

It was just after noon and the traffic south on 101 was light. In a few hours the northbound lanes out of the city would be in their inevitable gridlock. We stopped at a small restaurant that looked like a greenhouse and sold only vegetarian lunches. We each ate something buried under heaps of sprouts. Something alcoholic would have helped it go down. We made do with carrot juice.

Back in the car Mickey asked, "What do you think about their alibi?"

"It bothers me. It isn't all it's cracked up to be. What if the bus had been early? Rita could suspect her son. What if Rita hadn't been home when Richard arrived? He could suspect his mother. I have to work on Rita again. There's a narrow window of time when either one could have done it. They're covering for each other."

"Maybe the window will open a little more."

"I hope not," I said. At least not for them. But that window of time was undeniably there.

"Richard had a violent confrontation with his father," Mickey said.

"I know."

"You didn't tell us that much about his ex-wife."

"She didn't have a violent confrontation with Silverman that I know of."

"She wouldn't have told you."

"That's probably true."

"Is Rita Silverman very attractive?"

"Yes."

"That's your problem. Right there."

"I'll try to overcome it."

"Men! How can they be good cops? They're suckers for appearances."

"That lunch wasn't bad." That changed the subject!

Mickey and I got back early enough to stop at the address Rita Silverman had given me for her former housekeeper Mildred. It was an old run-down apartment house off 19th Avenue in the Sunset. I found Mildred's surname on the mailbox under 3A. Mickey had suggested a plan that included her doing all of the talking. It was fine with me.

Apartment 3A was on the west side of the building, the outside door only a few steps from a small parking lot and the garbage cans in back. We expected and got a cautious woman protecting herself behind a combination of locks and chains.

"Congratulations," Mickey said.

"For what?" the voice said through the door.

"You've been randomly selected to receive a cash prize," Mickey explained.

"What do I gotta do?" the voice asked.

I looked at Mickey who smiled and said, "You just have to listen to the new sound of San Francisco's newest FM station KVRO. The station that pays its listeners. We are so sure of our format that we're willing to pay you to listen for a week. We believe by then you'll be hooked on us."

"I hate rock and roll," the voice answered. "I mostly watch the TV."

"You don't know KVRO. We're the mellow music of the fifties."

"How much?"

"Fifty dollars. What else?" Mickey said as I waved the bills.

Mildred undid the locks and chains and opened her door. She was a heavyset blonde closing in fast on fifty. Her hair was done up in a thick bun that emphasized her full cheeks and square jaw. She was wearing a housecoat and slippers. Somewhere in the room behind her the TV was on.

I didn't know how well she did for Rita or anyone else but Mildred wasn't much of a housekeeper at home. The small living room that she led us into looked as if it hadn't been cleaned in months. Everything, except the TV, had either newspapers or dust all over it.

She turned the TV off.

"When do I get the fifty?" she asked.

"You just have to answer a few questions," Mickey said.

She cleared some newspapers from a reclining chair so she could sit down. "Sorry about the way the place looks. My boyfriend moved out. Temporarily."

She didn't offer us a seat, which was fine with me.

"Well?" Mildred asked.

"First question," I said. "Where's the gun you took from Rita Silverman's apartment when you were working there?"

"What the hell is this?" Her face was flushed with anger.

"Take it easy," Mickey said.

But the woman wasn't about to. "You're not from any radio station."

"We're investigating a murder," I said.

"You cops?"

"No. Private investigators," I said.

Her eyes narrowed. "If I answer your questions do I still get the fifty?"

"You get the fifty," I promised.

"I knew you weren't cops," she said. She was smiling now, softening the harsh jaw.

"How?" I asked.

"Because the police got the gun. If you were cops you'd know that."

"Why do the police have it?" Mickey asked.

"My boyfriend used it to rob a liquor store in the Haight. Only he got caught at the scene. The damn place had been hit three times in the past month. So they set a trap. There was a cop in the store pretending to be a customer. Now the gun is evidence." She looked around at the mess and said, "I've let everything go. Even myself. I really miss him."

She asked if we could do anything to help her boyfriend get out on bail before the trial. It turned out he couldn't make bail because he had jumped bail twice before. I told her there was no one in the business who would take a risk like that.

"Thanks for the information," I said as we started out.

"My fifty," Mildred said.

I paid her fifty bucks for information I could have had from Johnny D. for the price of a phone call. But what the hell, I would charge it to Sam.

"Hope your man comes back," Mickey said.

It was illogical but I felt that way too. Come home and maybe rob a gas station this time and get away with it.

As we stepped outside I heard Mildred laugh and say, "The thing of it is I don't even own a radio!" She slammed the door behind us, bolting, locking and chaining it.

Mickey and I looked at each other.

"That was still a nice touch. Fifty bucks for fifties music," I said to Mickey.

"That's what a radio station would do."

"I think it was the clincher."

"Next time we should give away a radio too," she said.

We both laughed.

As we walked towards the car I said, "So Rita Silverman was telling the truth."

"About *that* gun," Mickey said.

"Are you trying to complicate this case."

"You need a devil's advocate."

"I have the Chief already."

"One's never enough."

# 10

Saturday. Five days after Silverman's murder.

On my desk I had a file containing a list of Silverman's clients over the past year. Sam had provided the names, addresses and phone numbers. Cold facts. Which weren't enough. I buzzed for Mickey. When she came in I said, "We need to see what we can come up with from the newspapers on Silverman."

She looked at the list of names in the file.

"This is all Sam could provide?"

"That's it. At least the charge is listed under the name."

"Murder one. Rape. Drugs. Drugs. Drugs. Nice crowd. What are we looking for, Jeremiah?"

"I don't know. A lead. See what hits you while you're going through them."

"You mean I've got to spend this beautiful day in the library?"

Mickey rapped the edge of the file on my desk as if she were cutting meat on a chopping block. Then she sighed in surrender. "I'll give it a try."

"Don't be cranky. I remind you it's all on microfilm. And make copies for all of us to go over."

"I remind you that the new machine they have for that process is hi-tech. Meaning I need some petty cash to make the copies. Technology costs. As you always say to me."

"There is no petty cash in this office."

"Call it what you want," she said as she took all of the bills from my wallet.

"There should be some change," I said as she left.

The Chief checked in from a pay phone and said he was close to breaking open the case at the fish processing plant. He and his red pickup truck had fit right in. The thieves were even going to use it to transport some of the stolen goods.

"It's going to cost the client extra to get the smell out," Chief Moses warned.

"Add it to the bill."

I took a legal pad and made a list of suspects. The list was absurdly short at this point: Orlando Gomez, Rita and Richard Silverman. I crumbled the page into a ball and tossed it into the wastebasket with a nice hook shot.

I stared out of the window. The neatly spaced plane trees that ran up each side of the street in front of the two-story row houses were lush with dark green leaves. Everything was bursting with life. Except Silverman. Which seemed to be just fine with Oscar Chang and even Rita Silverman. I wasn't so sure about Richard.

When Mickey got back with the newspaper articles we could get a fresh start. Hopefully, she would come up with a lead worth pursuing.

A break, I rationalized, might give me a new perspective on things. I locked the front door, put up the closed sign, turned on the answering machine, and went upstairs to my gym. First I lifted weights, running through three sets of my usual workout with the barbell and the dumbbells. Then I moved out on to my parquet court. The old wooden floor was polished and looked like the Celtics' court at Boston Garden. I pounded the leather basketball on the floor—the answering machine didn't complain.

After an hour of shooting layups, jump shots, and attempting 360-degree slams, I was exhausted. I took a cold shower. Wrapped in a towel, I went into my kitchen and made myself a liverwurst and onion sandwich on dark rye. I washed it down with two Henry Weinhards. I dressed and went downstairs. I felt better.

I took down the closed sign and checked the answering machine. No messages. I took a fresh sheet of legal paper and wrote Orlando Gomez at the top.

Silverman had just lost a big drug case for Gomez in Judge Peter Troutvelter's court before he was killed. If Gomez had paid a fat fee up front he would be looking for a fat refund. And Silverman had called me to be the delivery boy. But someone had beat me to it. Someone who didn't care about or didn't see the bag of money. Someone who had to have another motive. Revenge possibly. Gomez angry because Silverman had failed to buy off the judge. On the other hand, using the limitless resources of the Colombian *coqueros*, Gomez got out on bail. Money he forfeited when he disappeared. But that didn't mean that Gomez wouldn't have demanded and taken the attorney fee money from Silverman. Money which apparently Silverman wanted to return to him. Sam Fan could be right that the killer wasn't Gomez. It was someone who didn't know about the bag of money and only wanted what was in the safe.

I spent most of the afternoon talking to Fan, trying to talk to Victoria, talking to the twin legal secretaries, trying to get someone to remember something about that day. But the day was so unremarkable it was hopeless. Sam insisted he didn't know what his partner had in the safe. I went back to the office and listened to the messages on the answering machine. Calls to be followed up that might lead to a few new cases.

Mickey came in after five-thirty with a collection of photocopied clippings that could have filled a scrapbook. "If I didn't get it, it doesn't exist," she said.

"Any change?" I asked.

"A lady needs her lunch."

We had just started looking through the stories on Silverman and his clients when the Chief called in from South San Francisco to report that he could name the thieves by early next week. I told him to bring an extra large Canadian bacon pizza for all of us. We had some work to do. The Chief and the pizza arrived sooner than I expected. The smell of cheese and tomato was overwhelmed by the cologne the Chief had on to cover the fish odor.

"Fighting the fish spirits?" I asked.

"The brown soap didn't work."

I went upstairs and got some Bud, some Henry's, and the bottle of white wine. We ate the pizza while we looked over the pile of clippings.

"He got a lot of coverage," I said.

"Especially when he died," the Chief added. Cheese was running in a long string between his mouth and the table. Mickey told him that he was disgusting.

"This is not my natural cultural food," Chief Moses explained haughtily as he licked the cheese from his fingers.

"Prefer French cuisine?" I asked.

"Your culture will kill us Indians yet. Pass the red pepper and the firewater."

I tossed him another can of Bud.

We went over the copies of the clippings in earnest. We found a lot of possibilities, a lot of clients and a lot of victims to interview, but no clear-cut leads.

After we exchanged ideas for another half-hour the Chief announced, "It is Saturday night and I've got a date." He drained the last can of Budweiser then tore off the aluminum top with one hand like the ex-jock on a TV beer commercial and got up. The Chief had a steady supply of attractive females who all liked to wear his Florida State University Seminole T-shirts. He ordered them by the dozen—with different numbers. I wasn't exactly sure what the women saw in him, his jerseys, or his pickup truck. But there was definitely something attractive there. As he moved to the door he said, "Too bad the white man is ruining casual sex."

"It was the gay man, Chief."

"Same thing." The Chief went out.

Although we hadn't found a real lead, work was over on Silverman's clippings for now.

I came over and sat by Mickey on the couch.

"Do you want some more wine?" I asked.

"No," she said.

I put my arm around her. She took it away, gently but firmly.

"I'd better go," she said.

"Why? Give us a chance."

"I'm not ready to Jeremiah."

I let her go without an argument.

I called the numbers on the answering machine and lined up some appointments. I wasn't sure what they were about—nobody is specific on the phone—but hopefully we'd end up with a few new cases.

I finished with the last number. I didn't have Mickey but at least I still had Nadine. I looked up her phone number in my black, actually blue, book, called her, and asked her if I could come over. I had trouble remembering telephone numbers. Rita Silverman's, which had a very simple sequence, was one of the few I was able to memorize immediately.

"Now?"

"Now."

"Ask nicer."

I asked even nicer.

Nadine's was only a short walk from my office.

Nadine was a sexy divorcée I had met while I was in the D.A.'s Office. She was the nurse the police used to conduct the exams and collect the necessary scrapings and fluids from rape victims. A few years ago we ran into each other at a party. She told me she had grown sick of opening Rape Evidence Kits and filling them with the detritus of the crime.

"I'll never handle another 'Pubic Hair Collection' for as long as I live," she had sworn. She was now working at the U.C. Medical Center in the city.

We started seeing each other. She lived with her ten-year-old son, Anthony, Jr., whom I liked. Usually I brought him a gift but tonight I wasn't going to take the time. Nadine's major character flaw was talking about her ex-husband Tony after we'd made love. She had the ability to discuss his every past action ad nauseum and to review their former life together before falling asleep. Usually I fell asleep before she was finished. My dozing off in the middle of this diatribe often led to a quarrel which led to an even better making up session. Hell, no relationship is perfect.

Nadine buzzed open the security door. She answered her door wearing a terrycloth robe. Her thick brown hair fell in unruly waves around her full face.

I stepped into the living room. She had all of the lamps turned on. Nadine was a sun worshipper who liked lots of light all the time.

"Anthony's in bed," she said with a smile. We kissed with as much friendship as passion. I had never really clarified my own feelings towards Nadine. I was guilty of sticking my head right into a sandtrap and keeping it there. But then so was she. At least I thought so.

With the ease of familiarity, we went into the bedroom together. Like everything else in the apartment the bed was utilitarian but comfortable. Nadine was not the kind of woman who liked canopies overhead. What she liked was the light on. What I liked was to look at her and her tight elastic body with slim hips and breasts like small ripe fruit.

We undressed quickly, without ritual. When she was naked I reflected on how tan she had become or how long I had been away from her. Her body showed only the smallest amount of white unexposed flesh. She still smelled of tanning lotion.

"You look great."

"I've been going to Stinson Beach. I've been on vacation all week."

"You taste like it," I said with my mouth puckered on an aroused nipple.

"Good."

"Yes," I answered.

"That wasn't a question."

"So?"

Nadine was probably one of the few women in the city who made the putting on of a condom the most exciting part of foreplay. She switched to condoms at the beginning of the AIDS scare. It worked well with the position she liked: woman on top. She wanted her body to be seen and appreciated. I was glad to oblige.

We made love in her position of choice, not urgently, but tenderly, like a happily married couple. Then, momentarily spent, we lay under the covers, relaxing, casually touching each other. I ran my hand along the sleek contours of her body.

"Where did you learn how to make a condom so erotic?" I asked her.

She giggled and said, "From a prostitute who was in the hospital for an operation."

"Huh?"

"I asked her what she did about all those johns and the threat of AIDS. So she taught me. I showed all the nurses on the floor."

"Oh," I said, feeling less favored and hardly unique.

Nadine started to tell me about her ex-husband Tony's lack of consideration. Before she could get going I interrupted and started to tell her about Silverman instead.

"I read about it. You left the money."

"Yes. I did."

"That was dumb. And so was not calling me sooner," she said.

I was regretting not letting her go on about Tony.

"I was busy. You know I have odd hours."

She paused, then said, "Well it was about time you called."

There was a knocking on the bedroom door. It was so light as to be almost imperceptible.

"What is it?" Nadine called.

"Mom, can I have a drink of water?"

"If you can go get it you can have it," she said, shifting a little nervously.

Nadine rolled over on her side, her breasts lolling playfully together. I ran a finger down into the flesh where her cleavage formed. She reached for me under the covers.

"I don't wait around for you. I go out with other men."

I didn't say anything immediately, instead I stroked her hair, waiting to hear the door to Anthony's room shut. It took him a long time to get a glass of water.

Then I heard a toilet flush and a door slam.

"He likes you," Nadine said.

"He knew I was in here?"

"Sure."

That didn't make me feel very comfortable.

"Next time I'll bring a present."

"You know what? I'm dumb enough to believe you."

The silence was tangible between us. At any moment I expected it to land heavily on me.

"I don't expect you to wait for me," I said.

"I wish you did," she retorted.

"Are you sleeping with anyone else?" I asked.

"Monogamy is safer. As long as I can stand it."

It was an ambiguous answer but I didn't press her.

The silence returned. My eyes were closed and I was lying on my back on the very firm mattress when I heard her unwrapping a condom.

# 11

On Monday morning the Chief called in to tell me he was transporting the stolen fish in his pickup to San Jose. I told him I had reviewed the clippings again myself on Sunday and had selected the most promising of Silverman's clients to visit.

"Alone?" he asked.

"I'm not expecting any trouble," I insisted.

"I would like to come along," he said. "I like the case."

"You wrap up the great fish scam. I won't be alone. I'm taking Mickey."

"Don't cry for help," he warned.

"Only if I'm in trouble."

He hung up.

Mickey and I got into my car. We were both acting as if our exchange last night hadn't happened.

It was another bright warm morning, the fog already burned away. I was feeling optimistic, which is what a night with the remarkable Nadine did to me.

Despite my feelings we didn't have much luck with the first few clients on my list.

"The son-of-a-bitch was shot six months ago," we were told at the door by the landlady at the first place we stopped at, a row house in the Upper Market.

"How's he doing?" I asked her.

"He's dead."

"He's probably not involved," I said to Mickey as we went down the creaking wooden stairs.

At our next stop in the Castro we were met by a young gay dressed in leather and wearing one gold earring. He told us the man we were looking for had died of AIDS.

"But not from me, man. He got it getting his ear pierced with a dirty needle. 'Cause I ain't got it."

"Good luck," I said to him. The man was too thin, too pale, and too depressed.

After that dismal start I was sure it would get better. But a businessman accused of computer crime was out of town, a pusher was back in jail, Colombians were back in Colombia, a child molester had jumped bail, and the other clients we could find in the city wouldn't talk to us. Not exactly a productive morning.

"Maybe you should have brought the Chief," Mickey said.

"Why? For luck?"

We were driving on the edge of the downtown financial district when I saw the blue and orange umbrella of a street vendor selling hot dogs. I pulled up and got two with onions, mustard, and sauerkraut and two cans of Classic Coke.

"Diet Coke," Mickey called out too late.

We double-parked on a side street and ate in the car.

"This is delicious," Mickey said, devouring her hot dog. "I love *nouvelle cuisine*. Especially with onions and sauerkraut."

Then I drove to a hardware store on Vallejo where I stunned Mickey by buying a window fan for the office.

"It was in the suggestion box," I told her.

Unwilling to give up just yet, I decided we should keep going
down the list. We struck out twice more but at the third address
we finally found a Silverman client who would talk. Clifton
Gorman was an overweight laid-back kid in his early twenties who
had been arrested for growing marijuana in his backyard garden.
"What happened?" I asked.
"The judge threw the case out because a police helicopter had
flown over the area takin' photographs. They invaded my privacy! I
coulda been out there sunbathin' in the nude! I coulda been doin'
anything."
"Who do you think would want Silverman dead?" I asked.
"I don't know about that but I'll tell you Silverman is one sharp
lawyer. All he talked about were the technicalities of the law. If
you wanna beat a rap on a technicality he's a genius. . ."
"Was," I said. "Remember?"
"Oh yeah. That's really too bad. But lemme tell you he had the
judge eatin' out of the palm of his hand. The prosecutor couldn't do
shit." Then he paused; I could tell he was thinking. "You said your
name was St. John? You're the guy who found the body, right? I
read about you in the papers." Clifton Gorman paused again.
"Why d'ya leave the money?" He was shaking his head in amazement.
"That's what I wanted to know," Mickey added.
As I walked down the steps I called back, "I took the four other
bags."
Gorman suddenly became animated. "You guys want a joint?
Home grown. The best, and protected by law. More or less."
Mickey and I decided to pass.
We drove to an address on Leavenworth where we found an un-
kempt character in his fifties who answered the door in a T-shirt
and boxer undershorts. I identified myself. He was out on bail
pending an appeal of his conviction for burglary.
He led us into a room that smelled of cheap cigars and wine. The
mildewed furniture was covered with cat hairs. There was no cat.
"I'm on full disability. That's how I could post bond. I ain't goin'
nowhere," the man said without being asked. "I used to be a sanitation worker. 'Til the injury."

I knew where he got his furniture.

Mickey and I declined his offer of a seat.

"The judge threw the book at me."

"Which judge?"

"Troutvelter. What a bastard."

"Did you blame Silverman?" I asked, seeking another suspect.

"I blamed the judge. Silverman was right. The cops didn't have a warrant. The VCR's should have never been admitted in evidence. You wait for the appeal. You'll see. I'll beat it."

"The rules of evidence are changing," Mickey said.

"I got a good lawyer to deal with that."

"Who's your lawyer now?" I asked.

"Sam Fan."

"Good luck," I offered.

The disabled sanitation worker scratched his head: "St. John? Ain't you the guy that left the money?"

"Some reputation you've gotten for yourself," Mickey said once we were outside.

"I'm working on my image."

"Good idea. Next time take the money. It'll do wonders for it."

"I've got other ways," I said.

"I can't wait."


By four-thirty we were all back in the office. The Chief had the names of the thieves who were actually exchanging the fish for small bags of marijuana, which they then sold in the processing plant to the other employees. Everyone was in on it.

"Are they going to fire everybody?" Mickey asked.

"They would have to close the plant down. They're going to fire the men who brought the drugs in."

"Quick work," I told the Chief.

"I wanted to get out of there fast. Smelling like a fish is not appealing to most ladies."

"I have to agree, Chief," Mickey said.

"I'm trying a new cologne," he said.

"I liked the natural man better," I said.

"No more fish."

There was a message to call Detective Chang as soon as possible.
"Shit!" I muttered.

I got through to him fast, too fast for comfort. Something had to be breaking.

"We've had complaints. You're bothering people. People don't like it. This is a *police* case, St. John. Understand? Only the *police* can bother people."

"I understand. Only the *police* can bother people. They do wonderful work in that area," I said.

"Don't patronize me."

"Sorry. I wasn't."

"Just stay out of it, St. John."

I caught my breath and held on. I wondered if I had enough nerve. I decided that I did.

"Could you just do me one favor?" I asked very politely.

"You've got brass balls. What is it?" Chang didn't trust my tone.

"Just let me know when you've broken the case."

Silence.

I hummed while Chang considered his options.

"It's broken."

"What?"

"You heard me. We found the gun in the stash house the Colombian was using before he took off."

"The murder weapon?"

"Right. The murderer's gun."

"That should lock it up."

"It's locked up," Chang said as he hung up.

I told Mickey and the Chief what Chang had told me. While they began a game of stud poker, I called Johnny D. for confirmation. Chang was not exactly my most reliable source.

I got it.

"Chang told you?" Johnny asked.

"Yes."

"Chang told you?" he repeated.

"Yes."

"I'm hearing things. There must be something wrong with this connection." He hung up.

That made me more suspicious about what was going on. Chang would do anything to keep me off the Silverman case.

I looked at the cards that were showing in the stud game. Mickey bet a quarter on three low hearts.

"Let's go out for dinner," I said.

Chief Moses called her but Mickey had the flush.

"I guess you're buying," I said to Mickey.

"Do you think that hot dog vendor's still there?" she asked.

"I'm going to try to pin one last meal on Fan. Johnny D. confirmed Chang's information."

"Good. We can go somewhere air-conditioned," the Chief said.

I looked out the window where I planned to put the fan at my disgrace of a backyard. "Could you water the yard tomorrow. You are the custodian of the land, Chief. You and all the other red men. You told me so yourself."

"Get yourself an Asian gardener, white man."

"I've got a new window fan out in the back of the car," I said.

"For *your* office?" Chief Moses said.

It was time to go to dinner.

# 12

We sat in a plastic-upholstered booth at Original Joe's on Taylor Street, the only diner in America where the countermen and waiters wore tuxedos.

I had Joe's Special, a scrambled omelet with ground meat, spinach and onions. Mickey and the Chief had hamburgers with everything on French bread. We had compromised on a large carafe of house Burgundy.

"So it's over. Case closed," I said.

"Why do you believe Chang?" Mickey asked. "That's what Fan said would happen."

"You believe Chang and I have an island called Manhattan to sell you, white man." Chief Moses bit into his hamburger. Toasted bread crunched. Flakes of crust fell to his plate and to the table.

"That's why I called Johnny D. For confirmation."

"Exactly what did he say?" Mickey asked.

"McCurdy of the DEA found the murder weapon in the stash house where Gomez had been staying."

"I know some people in the DEA," Chief Moses said. "I'll check around."

"Don't be too conspicuous," I said.

"I'll go in disguise."

"Let's live it up while we can," Mickey said and ordered another carafe.

"I'll drink to that," the Chief added.

"For tomorrow I talk to Fan." And then I grinned at the both of them and said, "I can be the devil's advocate too."

"What do you mean?" Chief Moses asked.

"Chang wants me off the case too much. Something's very wrong."

Mickey and the Chief grinned back at me.

"Keep Manhattan," I said.


"So that's it," I told Sam Fan the next day.

Sam had removed a few of the small silver-plated pieces that no one would miss from his dead partner's office and transferred them to his own. They gave the place a little touch of class but not much.

"No. That's not it," Sam said. He wasn't convinced by what Chang had told me any more than I was.

"They've got the gun."

"It stinks in my nose," he said.

It was early afternoon. Sam had his jacket off and his tie loose. He was out of mourning.

"So what do you want me to do?" I asked.

"The cops they got it solved, right? Case closed. Case cleared. So they should be out of your way. Now you go and find out who really killed Rick."

"You got it." I didn't want to let go of the case. Not with Chang pressing me. All I wanted was Fan's okay.

I took a last look at Sam behind his desk with the few meager silver ornaments in front of him and wondered where he was going from here.

\* \* \*

96

I decided to talk to McCurdy at DEA independently of the Chief nosing around. Maybe between us we could put something together that would make sense.

I tried to get an appointment on Wednesday using my own name. No way. We would have to use Johnny D. And we would have to be plausible.

I called in the reinforcements. Mickey had a working relationship with a small weekly Marin newspaper that gave her credentials as a reporter. So I took Mickey to the DEA field office in San Francisco with her cover. I went along as her photographer, complete with borrowed equipment.

Mickey gave the suspicious secretary Johnny's card and said, "Mr. Dajewski would appreciate any assistance that Mr. McCurdy could provide."

The secretary scowled like an angry pit bull but took the card in to McCurdy. It worked.

Daniel Big Mac McCurdy was a Good Ol' Boy from somewhere in the deep south. The first thing that you noticed was his size, about six-two and probably two-fifty with big hands, feet, and a bull neck. Compared to the rest of his body Mac had a small head that seemed about ready to slip down and disappear into that massive neck. He had surprisingly bright blue eyes, a wide grin, and splashes of freckles under leathery skin. He had curly red hair that was thinning and receding. Big Mac had to be pushing fifty but I could imagine him as a barefoot boy fishing some southern river for catfish.

"Glad to do a favor for a fellow officer. Now what can I do for y'all?" he drawled to Mickey. His eyes hadn't left Mickey since we entered his office. I doubted if he knew I was in the room. I wondered what he'd do if he knew about Mickey's *Playboy* picture and hated myself for wondering.

She picked up Johnny's card and said, "My newspaper is very interested in the Silverman case. We understand you found the murder weapon." Mickey was on her way.

"I didn't know that was news already," Big Mac said.

"It's news. Old news," Mickey said.

"The cops around here talk a lot," Big Mac noted.

"They like to get in the newspapers," I said.

97

For the first time McCurdy noticed me.

"Who's that?"

"My photographer," Mickey explained as I held up my camera—with no film in it.

"No pictures!" he said.

"Okay. Okay." I held up my hands.

Big Mac went back to appreciating Mickey. Mickey pressed her advantage.

"Would you say that the gun makes Orlando Gomez the number one suspect?"

"I'd say it makes that boy the killer but don't quote me."

"It was in his stash house?"

"Yeah. That's where it was."

"What were you doing there?"

"We were raidin' the place. The garage was full of cocaine, automatic weapons, electric appliances. . ."

"Electric appliances?"

"They resell 'em in South America. They ship out four-wheel-drive vehicles too. We got ourselves one of those."

"This is where Gomez lived?"

"We've got positive I.D.'s," McCurdy asserted.

"And where was the gun?"

"In the bedroom that Gomez used."

"Very neat," I said. It was too neat.

"What do you mean by that?" McCurdy asked me sharply.

"Nice work," Mickey explained for me and McCurdy seemed mollified. She continued. "What kind of gun was it?"

McCurdy thought about it for a while.

"A Walther."

"Gomez's prints on the gun?" I asked.

"I don't know. The San Francisco cops got the weapon and they don't like to tell us anything. It's called interagency cooperation."

"I've heard about something like that," I said.

"Don't quote me," McCurdy said. "On any of this."

"You don't have to worry about that, Mr. McCurdy," Mickey said and smiled teasingly at him.

I knew Johnny D. would come through.

Back at the office the Chief was sitting in front of the window fan, shuffling a deck of cards and reading *The Wall Street Journal.* "I am ready to play," he said as Mickey and I came in.

"Go ahead and deal," Mickey said but then thought better of it. "Let me cut."

"What did you think of McCurdy?" the Chief asked as he dealt out the cards for stud. He was wearing a smug look.

"We got some facts if you can call them that," I said. "They tie up Gomez in a very neat package with a bow on the top. Unfortunately or maybe fortunately for them he really has disappeared into Colombia."

"What about extradition?" Mickey asked.

"No one wants him enough to drag him out of a South American jungle," I said.

Mickey looked at her hole cards.

"What about you?" I asked the Chief.

"Talked to a few of the possibles who called. Nothing for now."

"Good. We wouldn't want anything to distract us from the Silverman case or from your stud poker game. But that's not what I meant."

The Chief smiled his huge grin. Something sure was making him self-satisfied. I didn't think it was his cards even though he was taking in the small pot left when Mickey folded.

"I talked to a friend of mine in the DEA Office," he said.

This was what I was waiting for. "What did he say?" I asked.

"It was a she."

"Sorry. I should have known."

"She said McCurdy's been involved in a number of sting operations."

"And?"

" 'He's fucked them up royally.' That is a quote."

That was going further than Johnny D.

# 13

It was time, as Rita Silverman had said, to "Talk to the victims. Talk to the families." The one story that stuck with me involved a father who had threatened Silverman and his client in court. On Thursday, ten days after the murder, Mickey and I paid the family a visit while the Chief went to the fish processing plant to clear up a few disputed items in our bill.

Mr. and Mrs. Arthur Martin lived in a small house in Buena Vista across from a park and playground. There were children riding the swings and climbing the jungle gym in the park. We could hear their shouts and laughter. Leery about showing us in, Arthur Martin studied my I.D. for a long time. Finally he led us into a large, light and airy living room simply furnished with a combination of modern and antique furniture. The oak floor was covered with several exquisite oriental rugs. His wife Amy sat in a leather wing chair. He sat down in an identical chair across from her.

WILLIAM BABULA

The Martins were an attractive couple in their early forties who lived in a comfortable house in a well-to-do neighborhood. But it hadn't protected their daughter and they lived with very uncomfortable memories underscored by the playground noises.

"The police were here because I threatened Silverman and . . . and . . . that other animal. . ." Arthur Martin began to explain.

"He was held in contempt of court," his wife said, almost proudly.

Mickey and I tried not to look at the pictures of the little girl on the mantelpiece.

Slowly, painfully, Arthur Martin began to call up the memories. "Our only child Kara was sexually assaulted in the bushes behind the playground. While we were right here in the house. It's only across the street. You can hear the children playing." He got up and began to pace as he spoke. I could see him going over a range of possibilities for the thousandth time. All the What If's, including the crucial one to them: what if they hadn't let her go alone to the park? "It happened in the middle of the damn day!" His anger might have been new.

"What happened in court?" I asked.

Arthur Martin tried to compose himself and began again only to hurl the words out. "Do you know what that bastard Silverman did? He had some money-grubbing expert witness testify how the rape law under which his client was charged did not cover sexual penetration with a . . . foreign object, only with a . . . a . . . part of the body. And the judge bought it! I couldn't believe it! A child molester . . . a child rapist who used the handle of a screwdriver . . . walked out free into the streets because of the ambiguous wording of some law. I should have threatened the damn judge too. I'd like to kill them all."

"This is our criminal justice system." Amy Martin's voice was quiet but deadly. "That's why we need vigilantes out on the streets."

I nodded. "We have them."

"What do you really want, Mr. St. John?" Amy Martin asked.

"Kara's our only child," Arthur Martin repeated dully and sat back down, spent.

"I'm trying to track down Silverman's killer." I felt uncomfortable; I couldn't decide what to do with my hands.

"Why should I help you find Silverman's killer?"

"Can you?" I asked.

Arthur Martin got up again and walked to the window. He motioned us over. It looked out into a backyard surrounded by a high redwood fence. "That's Kara on the swing. She doesn't go over to the playground anymore. Actually she won't leave the yard. She's seeing a child psychiatrist. A specialist in the field of child victims." We saw a pretty girl in a soft floral print dress that evoked innocence. Only her eyes looked dead.

"She was such a happy child," Amy Martin added looking in the direction of the photographs of her daughter. There was no fear in the face of that child. And her eyes were alive.

We all sat down again.

"No," he said. "I can't help you. I told you I wanted to kill Silverman. But I didn't. I've got a quote 'alibi.' We were all up in Seattle where I was interviewing for a new job. I want to get us away from here. For Kara's sake."

"All our sakes," his wife added.

"I understand," I offered lamely.

"Do you?" Amy Martin asked.

There was a silence that carried the intensity of the family's pain within it. I wished I had never known Rick Silverman.

"We can't. Not really," Mickey answered for us.

As we moved towards the door I turned and asked, "Who prosecuted the case?"

Arthur Martin shook his head in a gesture of disbelief. "A Deputy D.A. named Howard Vorflagel." Martin paused. "What an asshole."

Amy Martin blushed, looked directly at us and said, "He's right."

Mickey and I had arranged to meet the Chief that night at Monday's for drinks and dinner. He was already there working on a Bud.

The restaurant and cocktail lounge was decorated like an old-fashioned tavern with comfortable leather-upholstered booths, wood paneling, and ceiling fans. The food was eclectic but decent. The basic menu was Italian but on any given night you could find selections that included blackened redfish, sauerbraten, snails, or the Indonesian rice specialty nasi goreng. The chef was a very creative Hungarian.

Since it was close to the courthouse it was a hangout for attorneys, clerks, legal secretaries and even judges. It was a place where you could often find Silverman if you were looking for him. Alive, I never was, although I had seen him having dinner here a few times. I looked around, trying to recognize a lawyer or judge.

"Looking for someone?" Mickey asked.

"A familiar face."

"Any particular reason?" the Chief asked.

"So I'll feel at home." Mickey and I were still shaken by our meeting with the Martins. In the car neither of us had said a word.

"I went with the Italian tonight. I ordered an antipasto for three," Chief Moses said. "Beer?"

I nodded. Mickey wanted a half carafe of Chablis. Monday's had a list of 150 international beers but the Chief stuck with Bud and I had a Henry's.

"When are you going to try something else, Chief?" I asked.

"It's a known fact that ethnic minorities have intense brand loyalty."

"That's why he puts up with you," Mickey tried to joke.

My mind was still on Kara and her parents.

"The fish company will pay the extra charges," Chief Moses said. "But one thing. No one at this table eats fish tonight."

Our antipasto came.

Mickey stabbed a piece of Italian salami. "Nothing but good news," she said softly. Then she told the Chief about our visit with the Martins.

"Some Silverman scrapbook we are collecting," the Chief said.

We sat there eating in silence. Finally I said, "There must be something in those stories. Something we're missing."

"A clue," the Chief said.

I looked over at the long dark bar. The TV set above it had on the

Giants baseball game. The bar itself was crowded with bodies wedged in all along its length.

"A fair amount of action," the Chief said as he followed my eyes.

"For these days." I finished my beer and said, "Come on, Chief, let's try and learn something."

We went up to the bar and pressed forward to where the bartender was putting celery sticks into three Bloody Marys.

The bar crowd made room for us, especially for the Chief. It helped that a couple was called to their table for dinner. We took over their vacated stools.

The bartender was Nelson Bittenbender, someone I knew. He had given me information a few times in the past. He was tall, well-muscled without being overly developed, handsome in a pouting, long-faced way, and very gay. He sported an 1890's waxed handlebar mustache, which looked good on him.

"Nelson," I said, keeping my voice down, "when was the last time Rick Silverman was in here?"

Bittenbender's eyes shifted to cover the length of the bar.

"I don't know, Mr. St. John. I can't remember," he said and turned away.

I tried several more times to get him to talk but something or someone had silenced him. I was going to have to come at him in a different way at another time.

We went back to our booth.

"How'd it go?" Mickey asked us.

"Don't ask," I said.

Our dinner had arrived. No fish.

"Man cannot live by rejection alone," the Chief said as he attacked his food.

"Ancient Indian saying?" I asked.

"Motto of my people." He moved his fork to his tongue.

I stayed up late in the office that night looking through the stories on Silverman that Mickey had found. With my feet up on the desk I thumbed through each one again, examining the pictures closely once more. A pool of yellow light spread out from my desk lamp in a round stain.

I was going through them a second time when something clicked. I shuffled through quickly for the piece I wanted. There it was staring me in the face.

Silverman's client in this particular case was another accused rapist who was acquitted. The paper played up the brutal tactics Silverman had used to destroy the credibility of the woman, a Veronica Coats. On the inside page was a picture of Ms. Coats's sister, part of an angry mob protesting the acquittal outside the courthouse. The name given in the newspaper was Victoria Coats. She was the woman who worked as a receptionist for Silverman, the woman I knew as Victoria Justice. She had slipped into the enemy camp with a new name.

And maybe she had lived up to it.

# 14

I went to Fan's office to ask Victoria out for lunch. At least now I thought I understood why she didn't want to have anything to do with me: I worked for Silverman. I was part of the operation she had to detest. "I told you, Mr. St. John. . ." she began in her usual formal way.

"This is business, Ms. Coats, I need to talk to you about your sister."

There was no outward reaction to my use of her real name. But the woman who called herself Victoria Justice accepted my invitation.

We went to a new Vietnamese restaurant on Sacramento where, I had heard, the food was good. The Turtle was small but charming. The tables were covered with green linen tablecloths that matched the plush carpeting. We sat at a table for two right by a wall of mirrors that gave the dining room an illusion of depth.

"What do you want to know?" Victoria asked in a neutral tone when we had some wine in front of us.

The direct approach with this woman, I thought. I put down my glass and asked, "Did you kill Rick Silverman?"

She looked startled, but only momentarily.

"No," she said.

"Why did you take a job in his office?"

"You know who I am. You must have figured it out. To get revenge."

"How?"

She hesitated. "I wanted to kill him. It was a frequent fantasy of mine." There was a long pause, then she said, "After the trial my sister committed suicide."

"I didn't know that."

"The untold story. Silverman made her out to be not much better than a whore."

"You still say you didn't kill Silverman?"

The waiter, a thin Oriental with long black hair, served us.

"Well?" I asked.

"I repeat, I didn't kill him."

"Why not?"

"Somebody beat me to it." She stared down at the slices of Imperial roll on a bed of rice noodles. "That's not true. I could never come up with the nerve to do it. Damn! I hate to admit it."

That sounded like the truth to me; the same kind of truth that I had heard from the Martins. That was why they so desperately needed the law to work.

I bit a curried prawn in lemon grass that the menu had indicated was hot. Just spicy enough.

"What happened the evening Silverman was killed?"

"I don't have an alibi. I was the last one to leave. Except for Silverman."

"So you had motive *and* opportunity."

"I would have taken the money."

"If you had seen it. There were people in the office who missed it. Hard as that may be to believe. What about Jennifer and Jeanine?"

108

"They went home early together. The cutesy twins do everything together. They both had headaches."

"Was he expecting anyone?" I asked.

"You. He told me you were coming."

"Besides me. I'm not trying to be a suspect."

"Just you."

"What else do you remember?"

"I remember locking up the front door and taking the elevator down to the parking lot. We have reserved spots. Mine was between Sam Fan and Silverman. I got into my car and backed out."

"That's it?"

"That's it. Then I drove home."

"There must be something else," I said.

She tried to remember that evening. "Sam Fan had left early. I saw him go. And his Porsche was gone from the lot. Fan loves that Porsche. He drives it everywhere. He must sleep with it at night." That was it.

We ate quietly for a few minutes then I asked, "You still work at Fan's office. Why?"

"I'm waiting to see what happens to Sam Fan. Maybe I'll bring him some good luck too."

"Don't you like Sam?"

"Love him. Almost as much as Silverman. His virtue is that he's not as good. He won't get them off like Silverman could."

I picked up some steamed rice with chop sticks.

"Do you belong to PAL?" I asked her.

I met the Chief and Mickey at the courthouse at two p.m. We were going to get a chance to watch some of the players in action. Fan was presenting his arguments in a trial of two former Miami cocaine manufacturers who had moved their factory into the Haight-Ashbury. The pair sat at the defense table staring vacantly up at the ceiling. Sam Fan was boring them and everyone else still in the courtroom with his defense.

Because Sam was arguing for a motion to exclude evidence, the jury had been removed from the courtroom. Fan's point was that the cocaine and chemicals seized when his clients were arrested were inadmissible as evidence in the case and should be excluded. The police, according to Sam, did not have a proper warrant to conduct the search of the premises that led to the discovery of the cocaine factory.

It was the kind of strategy drug attorneys relied on. If the jury was allowed to see the actual physical evidence the conviction rate was nearly 100 percent. Sam's only chance was to win on a technicality before the judge and exclude the cocaine as evidence. For him and his clients this was the most important part of the trial.

The Deputy D.A. was Howard Vorflagel—the asshole, according to Arthur Martin.

Sam Fan waddled back to the defense table and Howard Vorflagel slowly rose to present his arguments before the bench. Vorflagel was tall and gangly, built as if his arms and legs had not fit perfectly into the trunk of his body. The wing-tipped cordovan shoes he wore were at least size thirteens. His sports jacket hung loosely about him, as if it had been handed down from an older and larger brother. An incongruous touch was the red boutonniere he wore in his right lapel. Vorflagel shuffled papers on his table, ran his fingers like a rake through his brown wavy hair and adjusted his horn-rimmed glasses.

"Mr. Vorflagel?" the judge said.

"Your honor?"

"Please! Must I remind you the court is waiting." The judge was the honorable Peter Troutvelter.

As Howard Vorflagel made his arguments he became articulate, convincing, even compelling. He cited the latest Supreme Court decisions on search, seizure, and evidentiary exclusion, and generally overwhelmed Sam's awkward position.

Judge Troutvelter's ruling on Fan's motion was simple: "Motion denied. Recall the jury, bailiff." The jury would see the kilos of coke that had been seized. The odds had turned against Sam.

The dark heavyset female bailiff in a tan police uniform with a gun in a holster on her hip went off to open the door to the jury room. The eight women and four men filed silently back into the box. They looked like they were anxious to start weighing the evidence.

At his table, Vorflagel looked cheerfully confident. By contrast

110

Sam Fan didn't look so hot. Clearly, he was going to have trouble without Rick Silverman. Sam didn't have Silverman's edge. It was hard to believe this could be the same Howard Vorflagel who had prosecuted the Martin case. The Deputy District Attorney had apparently been transformed since then.

Judge Peter Troutvelter banged his gavel with authority. Although I knew he was near the retirement age of seventy, he was a trim imposing figure who looked a lot younger. He had a long chiseled face. His hair was steel gray and it was brushed upwards in a short military cut. He inspired confidence.

Sam Fan made another motion.

Angrily, Troutvelter denied it as frivolous.

Troutvelter, I had learned from the newspapers, had been a pain in Silverman's neck. I thought about some of Rick's comments in print attacking the judge: "He is riding roughshod all over the constitutional rights of the accused. He doesn't give a damn about individual liberties. All he wants to do is to put defendants behind bars."

Not necessarily a bad idea, I had thought.

It looked like it was all over for Sam and his two clients.

I nodded at the Chief and Mickey and they nodded back. Together we got up and left the spectator area to pass through the heavy oak doors out into the hallway, which was jammed with attorneys, clients, witnesses, spectators, prospective jurors and anyone else who happened to wander in off the streets.

I spotted Johnny Dajewski at the end of the corridor. I pushed past the small groups of two, three, or four that most of the people had formed. I followed in the wake of a tall, well-built woman who strutted through on shaky high heels. The groups divided into even smaller units to make way for her.

Once through the main throng I rushed past her and called, "Johnny, I want to talk to you."

Johnny D. started walking faster. I started to run.

When I caught up to him he said, "Look I've gotta testify. I need to use the john."

We were standing outside the men's room.

"Just for a minute."

"Is it about Silverman?"

"Yeah."

"I gotta go." Johnny D. swung the door of the rest room open and I followed him in.

"Was Chang really not bullshitting me?" I asked.

Johnny D. looked at the bathroom stalls. Except for us, the men's room was empty.

"They got a gun," Johnny said as he zipped up his pants. "Just like Chang said."

"What about ballistics? What about the autopsy?"

Johnny walked over to the sink and ran water over his hands. The dispenser was out of paper towels.

"Shit!" he said as he shook his hands. Then he ran them through his yellow hair.

"What about the autopsy?" I repeated.

"The gun in the stash house fired the bullet that hit Silverman in the arm and fired the bullet we found in the picture of the Rolls."

I looked at him. "What about the bullet that actually killed Silverman?"

"It was fired by another gun. The same gun that fired the slug into a law book on the shelf."

"Silverman's gun," I said. "Who knows about this?"

"Chang and as few others as possible. I know someone in the coroner's office. That's it, Jeremiah."

"Silverman had a gun and got off a shot at his killer."

"I can buy that," Johnny agreed.

"Then where's that gun?" I asked.

"Good question."

"Then the case isn't closed," I said as we came out.

"Accordin' to Chang it is. Gomez wounded Silverman with his gun then killed him with Silverman's own gun. Simple?"

"That's just a theory."

"It's good enough for Chang."

"Hell, it's his theory." Then I added, "There would have been some signs of a struggle. What did Silverman do? Just hand over his gun after he was shot?"

Johnny turned to the Chief and Mickey. He didn't want to hear any more from me.

112

"Hey Chief, you're lookin' good. Lost some weight, huh?"

"White man's food," Chief Moses said. "One hundred percent unnatural."

Then Johnny winked at Mickey. "And you're always lookin' good."

"Diet Coke. One hundred percent unnatural."

"Nice talkin' to you but I've gotta testify," Johnny D. said as he walked down the corridor rubbing his hands on the sides of his pants.

"Say hello to the wife for me," I called after him. "You teach her any English yet?"

"You crazy?" he shouted back. "She'll get to be like you and your partners."

# 15

I had my own theory or at least a portion of a working theory. It was time to pay another visit to the former Mrs. Silverman. It was just late enough for her to be back from work.

After leaving the courthouse, I dropped off Mickey and the Chief at the office and drove to Rita Silverman's apartment. This time I had to park in a garage two blocks away. As I walked towards the main entrance Detective Chang came out of the building. He stood in the shade of the awning watching me approach. His dark suit looked like it had just been pressed. He was his usual collected self.

"How are you doing, St. John?" he asked.

"Can't complain. And you?"

He tired of the formalities quickly.

"Mrs. Silverman expecting you?"

"Not yet," I said as I stepped away from him.

"The case is closed, St. John."

"Don't think I don't appreciate the information you gave me," I said and went through the glass doors. As I climbed up the stairs I wondered what Chang was doing here.

I found out from Rita.

"He's investigating you."

Rita sat on the couch, her bare legs drawn up tightly beneath her. Her loose silk blouse was carefully unbuttoned, just enough to reveal the white flesh of the top of her breasts. She wasn't wearing a bra. I wondered if Chang had been able to ignore her. I couldn't.

"What did he want to know?" I asked as I sat down.

"If you were bothering me."

"Am I?"

She shifted her legs.

"No."

"Thanks."

"But damn it, why did you talk to Richard? I asked you not to."

"I know. But you knew I had to."

"He's just a child."

"Not really. It was good for him to talk about it, Rita."

"You think you're a goddamn psychiatrist?"

"It turned out okay. He's more mature than you think."

"Thanks for all these insights into my child."

"He's not a child," I repeated.

"I don't know what to think anymore. I just want him to be left alone." Then she sat up straight and asked, "How about a glass of wine?"

"It's too early."

"It's well after five."

"Still too early."

Rita stared at me. "Is there anything unscheduled that you do?"

"Some things."

"Name one."

"Investigate."

"Oh, that's hilarious."

I forced a smile.

116

In the dining room the old Underwood was still on its stand. There were a few typed pages next to it and some more pages crumpled up in a wastebasket.

"You don't mind if I have a glass do you?" Rita asked as she got up.

"Go ahead."

I went over to the wet bar where she was pouring herself a large glass of white wine.

She drank most of the glass with a gulping sound. Her facial muscles relaxed but her eyes were fixed on me hard. She leaned back against the bar.

"You know I've got an alibi. I was with my son Richard. You checked it out."

"I know it gives each of you an alibi."

"So Richard's a suspect too?"

"When two people with a motive are each other's alibis. . ."

She didn't let me finish.

"Chang told me the case was closed. That the police are certain it's Gomez."

So he was here to reassure the widow that the police can do their job.

"Then why are you worried about an alibi?"

"Because you're still investigating me. And Richard now. Isn't that what you're doing here?"

I looked around the room. "I'm not sure."

She was struggling to keep her composure. "I didn't kill him. My son didn't kill him. . ." Tears were forming in her eyes. "Excuse me," she said as she ran off into the bedroom.

As soon as she left I took out one of the crumpled sheets of paper from the wastebasket. It had half a page of type on it. I smoothed it out. It was an unfinished letter to Richard. I put it in my pocket, and went to sit down in her old fabric chair.

"So what is it you want? Really?" she asked again when she came back into the living room. The tears were gone.

"I want some people with personal reasons for killing your ex-husband."

Rita sighed.

"Besides me and my son?"

"Especially."

"But we're still on your list," she said.

"I can't help that. I'm looking hard for some others. Sam Fan doesn't want Gomez and he has a point. Chang wants him too much."

Rita stretched. Her nipples stood out against the thin material of her blouse.

"Look for a woman. Look for the other woman. Find his latest bimbo. Or the last one he dumped."

"Do you have any names?"

"You've got to be kidding."

"I'll find them somewhere else," I said.

"You do that."

As I got up Rita came towards me and put her hands on my shoulders. She didn't say anything but her intentions were obvious. I hesitated for a moment and then pulled her hands away.

"Why'd you do that?"

"I don't know," I said.

"You're making me come right out with it, aren't you? Okay then. Sleep with me."

"I can't. You're still a suspect."

It didn't sound right.

"I know. Also, it's not on your schedule." She tossed her empty glass at me. It struck the wooden door and fell to the tile hallway where it shattered. The shards looked like the machine-made ice cubes that come in the shape of quarter moons.

As I closed the door I heard Rita beginning to sob. I stood there for nearly a full minute, listening. Mr. Nice Guy. I'm sorry, I said to the empty hallway.

# 16

Over the weekend I thought about calling Rita but instead stuck to business and lined up several new clients.

On Monday morning Mickey and I went to the offices of the evening newspaper that had received the PAL terrorist note. Mickey was going to play reporter again. She thought that an appeal to a colleague in the press corps would be the right approach. Her best hope was Red Pitcher, the reporter who wrote the PAL story.

"Leave your gun," she told me. "Security is very tight. Someone tried to smuggle in a bomb." It was good advice.

We went into the gray stone building, through a metal detector, and up to a reception desk that dominated the main lobby. A slim black woman with a short Afro and large hoop earrings sat behind the desk. Between her position and the elevator stood an armed security guard who looked like he had put in the full twenty years with the Oakland Police Force.

Mickey gave the receptionist our names, the name of the tiny weekly she was supposed to work for, and said, "We're here to see Mr. Pitcher."

"Do you have an appointment?"

"Not exactly. But I'm sure he'll see us."

The woman whose nameplate read Silvia Surrey dialed her phone.

Sixty seconds later we were riding the elevator up to the newsroom.

"How did you know he'd see us?"

"Sometimes it's just dumb luck, Jeremiah."

"I'm glad to hear that. I thought you knew something I didn't."

We were directed by a second receptionist to a bald male sitting at a computer at a desk in the middle of the room. We made our way through the maze that the crowded desks had created. When we got to Pitcher, Mickey put her press card down in front of him.

Red Pitcher had a flushed face, a pug nose, and enormous freckles on his bald head. He looked twenty pounds underweight. He lit up a cigarette with the one he was smoking.

"Saves on matches," he said.

Red stared at the press card until Mickey picked it back up. Then gradually his watery colorless eyes looked over the rims of his half-glasses, inspecting the two of us.

"You wanted to see me?" Red asked.

"I'm doing a story on the PAL," Mickey explained.

"The PLO?"

"No. The PAL."

"People Against Lawyers," I added.

"Who's this?" He ran his palm over his smooth crown.

"He's with me."

"I figured that," Red said.

"I need some help. I'd like to see the note that the newspaper received from the PAL taking credit for Silverman's murder," Mickey said.

"Why come to me?" he asked.

"It was your byline," Mickey told him.

He laughed and said, "I didn't think anyone noticed. But the police have it, lady. It's evidence."

"You must have kept a copy," I said.

"Sure. In Archives."

"Already?" I asked.

"Silverman was killed two weeks ago today. It's old news, mister. Like yesterday's racing form." He wrote out a message on a memo pad, tore off the sheet, and handed it to Mickey. "Take this to Archives. Downstairs. Give it to Mrs. Kivitz. She'll make you a copy."

"Thank you."

As we started to move away he said, "I've never heard of this newspaper you work for."

Mickey stopped and said, "It's in Marin." As if that explained everything.

"Does it actually get published?"

"Usually. Just once a week."

He shook his head and his glasses slipped to the very tip of his nose. Only its slightly bulbous end saved them from falling into his lap.

"I'll send you a copy, Mr. Pitcher."

"You should do sports," I suggested.

He groaned and said, "Never heard that one before."

"It just slipped out."

"Thanks for your help," Mickey said.

We went down to Archives where we found Mrs. Kivitz at a desk behind the long counter that separated the Archives and the Archives staff from visitors. Mrs. Kivitz was a lot younger than I expected. She had a delicate face with small features under a haircut that looked like a long crew cut. Oddly enough, it made her more, rather than less, feminine. Her hair and eyes were black. She was about 5′1″ and no more than a hundred pounds. I saw from the nameplate that Mrs. Kivitz's first name was Carrie. Behind her were racks of microfilm storage.

She took the note from Mickey's hand, squinted to read it several times, and looked at us suspiciously.

"Pitcher wrote this?" she asked in a surprisingly deep voice.

"Honest," I said.

"He thinks this is the public library." She sighed but surrendered. "Okay. It'll be a few minutes."

121

Carrie Kivitz disappeared into the storage racks. I looked for a place to sit but there were no chairs.

"Not too anxious for business," I said.

Mrs. Kivitz was back quicker than I expected. She handed Mickey a single sheet of paper. "It's a good Xerox. One copy. Right?"

"Perfect," I said.

"There's a two dollar minimum charge for all copying," she said sternly.

The smallest we had between us was a five.

"We don't make change," Carrie Kivitz said.

"Open an account for us and credit the three dollars," Mickey said and smiled. "You never know when we'll need your services again."

We left Carrie Kivitz holding the bill like a crumpled tissue.

Late that afternoon at the office Chief Moses and Mickey were crowding me as I inspected two pieces of paper. I was using one of the P.I.'s more sophisticated investigative tools: a magnifying glass.

"You're blocking the light," I said.

"Who?" the Chief asked.

"Both of you."

"Like an eclipse," Chief Moses said.

"Move. I'll give you each a turn." They moved.

On one sheet was the complete PAL statement mailed to the newspaper. On the other was the letter from Rita's wastebasket. I moved the magnifying glass from letter to matching letter.

"At least we could have two magnifying glasses," the Chief complained.

"This is Jeremiah's idea of hi-tech," Mickey added.

"The next time we get new equipment," I said to the Chief.

"You could get one in a box of cereal," he said.

The copy I had now was pretty close in quality to an original. I concentrated on comparing the same letters: the peculiar topped "t," the "m" that seemed compressed towards an "n," the truncated "g," and the broken verticals in the uppercase "P" and "R."

"Looks to me like the PAL note was typed on Rita Silverman's Underwood," I said.

The Chief and Mickey moved back to my desk.

"What do you think?" I asked, handing them the papers and the glass.

"No doubt about it," Mickey said. "Now which one sent it?"

"It doesn't matter. It means Richard and his mother weren't together when Silverman was murdered."

"That window of time you didn't want opened is wide open now, Jeremiah. No matter how attractive Rita is," Mickey said.

"What do we do now?" the Chief asked.

"We can scratch the PAL. We look for Rick Silverman's women. And we check Rita's alibi."

"Which is the son's alibi, too," Chief Moses noted.

"I've been saying that all along. Hasn't anyone been listening?"

"Of course not!" Mickey and the Chief said together.

"What fun would that be?" Mickey added.

I like a woman with a sense of humor.

# 17

That evening I took Mickey and Chief Moses to Monday's where I wanted to try and pump Nelson Bittenbender again. This time I was not going to let him get away so easily.

The Chief and I left Mickey sitting alone in a booth while we took up temporary residence on a pair of red-cushioned bar stools. It was early and the place wasn't crowded yet. The Monday night baseball game had just started on TV. Neither the A's nor the Giants were on.

"What'll it be, gents?" Bittenbender asked as he tugged at his huge handlebar mustache with the thumb and index finger of his right hand. He was treating us like strangers.

The Chief ordered a Bud and I ordered a Henry's. I paid for the beers and left a generous tip.

Nelson stared at the money.

"Keep the change," I said.

Nelson leaned forward on the bar. "What do you want?"
The Chief smiled.

I wanted Bittenbender to be intimidated by the Chief. Obviously Nelson spent a lot of time at his club working out on forty-five different Nautilus machines. The Chief, who had never lifted a weight he didn't have to, had little respect for the body-building males and females of today and no use for their toys.

"I just have a few questions," I said.

"Yeah?" Nelson asked as he looked warily at the Chief.

"About Silverman."

"What about him?"

"The women he brought in here?"

"Silverman didn't bring women in here."

"Never?"

"Never," he answered.

"Nelson, come on."

"Nobody in particular. Nobody I can remember."

"Did he come in much?"

"Once, twice a week."

"Alone?"

"Like I said, usually."

"What would he do?"

"Have a drink. Maybe eat dinner. Look around. What else do you do here?"

"Did he always leave alone? Or did he pick women up?"

Bittenbender gave me a funny look.

"Or men?" I added.

"When he came in alone he left alone. I remember that. He never bought at this meat market. Now I've got to take care of some customers."

At least his memory had improved. "You've been a big help, Nelson," I said as I rose from the stool.

As he moved away Nelson shrugged. I wasn't asking exactly the right questions but I swore to myself that I would be back. I knew I could wring more out of Bittenbender.

When we returned to the booth Mickey was fending off the not-so-subtle advances of a young man dressed in jeans and a pink polo shirt.

He looked up at the Chief and me.

"My escorts," Mickey said. "I told you I was with someone."

"Nice to meet you," he said. "The name's James. Thought she was alone."

"She said she wasn't," I said.

"Women lie all the time."

He was unperturbed as he drifted off in search of another lying woman.

"The singles bar still lives," Mickey said.

"Not for Silverman," I commented.

"Was James his first or last name?" the Chief asked.

"Who knows? Who cares?"

"Let's go," I said.

We left Monday's and walked up the steep hill to the office. It was warm in the old Victorian so I turned on the window fan. Chief Moses looked at the fan, shook his head, and said, "Not much security. Anyone could push it off the windowsill and get in here."

"Do you want to be safe or cool?" I asked.

The Chief took the client's chair, reversed it, and sat down with his arms resting on the back. Mickey kicked off her shoes and stretched out on the couch. She arranged her light skirt carefully over her legs.

"Right now I vote for cool," Mickey said.

"Good. Is everyone comfortable now?" I asked. "The investigation continues with a call to Johnny D."

When I reached him on the phone Johnny groaned, "Oh no. Not you again. Whaddaya want now for Christ sakes?"

"A name."

"I got lotsa names. You got something particular in mind?"

"The woman Silverman was involved with."

"When?"

"When he bought it in his office."

"You've got other cases. Can't you get yourself into one of them, Jeremiah?"

"This one has the most to chew on. Maybe if you sent me some of your more interesting overflow business."

"We're cheaper," Johnny said.

"You get what you pay for."

"Jesus, Jeremiah, you're overworking my debt," Johnny D. shouted.

"Don't hang up. Humor me. Just give me something."

"I oughtta. . ." But then Johnny reconsidered. "Is there a tap on you?"

"A tap? No way!" I stated flatly.

Mickey started tapping the floor with her heel.

"I think I hear a tap," Johnny D. said.

"It's our device to monitor the lines. We're hi-tech here at the St. John Agency. This is a sterile environment. Now about Silverman's women?"

"What women?" Johnny asked.

"That's what I was hoping you'd tell me."

"Do your own investigatin'. If Chang ever found out I've been helpin' you it'd be my ass."

"Come on, Johnny."

He caught his breath. "I only got one name: Evelyn Moss."

"Moss. Like on a tree?"

"On the north side."

"You have an address?"

"Look in the Marin phone book. Under E. Moss."

"And that's it?" I asked.

"This was about a year ago, though."

"So can't you bring me up to date?"

"That's just it. Nobody since then."

Chief Moses got up from his chair, moved Mickey's feet, and sat down on the couch.

"Hey," she complained mildly as she rearranged herself to take up less space.

"Now can I get back to work?" Johnny D. asked. "I've gotta go on a stakeout."

"Some people just love their work," I said.

I expected a curse or two from Johnny but instead he said, "I've gotta put in for a transfer."

"Homicide," I said. "You'd work with Chang and you'd have to dress better."

"Why don't you just give this one up. It's good advice." He hung up.

Not as long as Sam Fan was paying the bills. And not as long as I was unconvinced that the police solution to the murder was the right one. And not as long as people kept telling me to give it up. It's part of my Taurus personality. Or so I've been told by my horoscope.

I turned the fan up to high and an intense whine filled the room. It was a painful sound. Mickey sat up straight and covered her ears. Next to her the Chief had fallen asleep, his eyes closed, his dark head nodding down towards his chest.

I couldn't resist clamping my hand over my mouth.

"Cute," Mickey said. "Hear no evil. See no evil. Speak no evil. The perfect emblem for the Jeremiah St. John Detective Agency."

"So far unfortunately on this one you're right," I admitted as I moved the palm in the ceramic pot near the window where it would trip an intruder.

The three of us spent Tuesday morning dividing up work on some of the minor cases we had let slip in pursuit of the Silverman solution. There were some background checks on prospective jurors that had to be done immediately. We all worked on those in the morning for one of our biggest law clients.

But by mid-afternoon I was free to try to reach Evelyn Moss. There was only one E. Moss in the Marin phone book and she readily agreed to see me even after I told her what it was all about. She said, "Why not? I'm bored out of my goddamn skull."

Evelyn Moss lived in an expensive house with a spectacular view of the bay. Evelyn Moss looked expensive too.

She had long frosted hair and long manicured nails. The kind of nails that would make simple tasks difficult or impossible to perform. She was still beautiful but her age was beginning to show in the lines of her face. If she was like everyone in California she would be visiting a plastic surgeon soon for a variety of lifts and tucks whether or not she needed them. She wore a red dressing gown and didn't have on much beneath it.

She led me out on a redwood deck that hung in space. Beneath us was a vertical drop and in the distance the bay. The sun was slipping behind the hill to the west and the shadow of the crest covered half the deck. Most of the bay was still in sunlight but a narrow tongue of fog had penetrated the Golden Gate to lick at the sharp edge of the city. I sat down on a wrought iron chair in the shade.

"Drink?" She indicated the wet bar that was built-in on the deck.

I thought about a beer but said, "I'll have white wine," feeling like that was the Marin thing to do.

She made herself a tall gin and tonic and poured out a glass of white wine. She brought the drinks over and I put mine down on a glass-topped table. She stood against the wooden railing in front of me. I saw her, the bay, and San Francisco all at once.

"Great view," I said ambiguously.

"Thank you." She smiled. Her upper body was in sunlight. The material of her dressing gown shimmered about her.

"I have my late husband to thank for all this." She came over and sat down in a chair directly across the table from me. "He actually died before he could divorce me. More or less you can say he died trying." She laughed. "It was his third marriage. I was younger than him. Much younger. The children from his first marriage hate me." She paused. "Well, you didn't come out here to talk about me."

"That's not exactly true. Tell me about your relationship with Rick Silverman."

"I had an affair with Rick. It ended over a year ago." Her tone was soft. She didn't exhibit any of the hatred shown by Rita.

"Any bad feelings?"

"No. Neither way."

"How long had it been going on?"

"Three years."

"That's a pretty long time," I said. "Who broke it off?"

"It just died. Rick changed."

"How?"

"This drug lawyer stuff. By the time we broke up it was already getting too big. Out of control."

"When did it all start?"

"He was just getting into it when we got involved. And it grew as his coke habit grew."

"How big of a habit?"

"The kind that gets you tangled up with Colombian dealers. And worse."

"Was Rick taking his fees in drugs from these people? Was he trafficking himself?"

Evelyn hesitated. "I don't know. I just had this sense that something really bad was going on with Rick."

"And you didn't want to be a part of it?"

"No. I didn't. I was scared of those people."

"Was Rick?"

"He couldn't be. But he should have been."

I looked down at the deep shadows on the bay. The east was still afire with a mirror sheen of sunlight. I sat quietly for a few moments.

"So you let it die?" I finally asked.

"There were other reasons. The drugs made him more than a little kinky."

"How?"

"Mr. St. John, you don't think I'm going to talk about it with you?" She smiled. "I hardly know you."

"Touché. I ask too many questions."

She drained her glass. She crossed her legs and her robe opened. Her legs were long, hard, and tanned. She didn't bother to close the flap that exposed her thighs.

"Did he find someone else?"

"I don't know. I really didn't care. It was one of those things that was just over. I stopped thinking about him. People I know would talk to me about him sometimes but I didn't really think about him until I read that he'd been shot."

At least she didn't remember that I was the one who had discovered the body. And was stupid enough to leave the money. Maybe my fame was finally going the way of all earthly things.

"What did these people you know say about him?"

"I hardly ever listened. I don't remember. Really."

"Do you know that he apparently hadn't been involved with a woman since you two broke up?"

"I don't believe it."

131

"I've had it from some pretty reliable sources," I said.

Evelyn Moss stood up and walked over to the railing. She turned her back to me and looked down over the railing to the darkening bay. I got up and joined her.

"He probably discovered celibacy. I told you he was kinky."

"Is that kinky?" I asked.

"It's the ultimate these days. Especially in a hot tub."

"I'll have to remember that."

As I started to go she said, "I do remember what one attorney friend of mine said about Rick just a month ago. He said his case success rate with drug dealers this past year had been phenomenal. Like he had some kind of 'edge.' That was the word he used. He couldn't believe it."

"Maybe celibacy works," I said.

"I doubt it," she shot back at me with a hard appraising look.

"Or maybe because he spoke Spanish."

It was time to leave Marin.

I left my card with her.


I had on my hands a somewhat kinky live ex-girlfriend and a kinky dead lawyer whose career had been headed to the moon. I suspected Evelyn talked a lot more kinkiness than she performed.

I drove into the city against the outgoing flow of rush hour traffic. As I watched the cars gradually move towards gridlock I decided to ask Mickey for a date. We would start all over again. After a workout with the barbells and a half hour alone on my parquet court, I called her from the private phone in my bedroom. If she turned me down I had the last Travis McGee for consolation. Some consolation.

"A date?" She sounded like she didn't understand the word.

"Just a date. It's a dying art."

"That's what I've heard."

"What do you say?"

"Tonight?"

"Tonight."

"You don't give a girl much notice. . ."

"I'm sorry."

"I wouldn't want you to think I'm always available."

"Wouldn't dream of it. What do you say? Is it a date?"

"I'll try it," Mickey said.

"Great."

"By the way, how was Ms. Moss?"

"A little to the north."

"Of what?"

"Sodom and Gomorrah."

# 18

The memory of Mickey's goodnight kiss and the two bottles of Napa Zinfandel we had shared with a rack of lamb lingered pleasantly on. The kiss had been deep and good but still innocent, telling me that we still had a long way to go. But that didn't mean I was in any less of a hurry to get there.

After all I possessed her image, like some shaman with an idol. But it wasn't the same. It wasn't anything. What the hell was the circulation of *Playboy* anyway? I couldn't tell if her photo in the magazine turned me on, made me jealous, or turned me off. Probably all three.

It wasn't my fault. It was cultural indoctrination. We were all exploited victims, including Mickey for posing for the picture. So I had some distance to go with Mickey and I still had too long a way to go in my investigation of Rick Silverman's murder.

I decided to bring my suggestion of a new tack to take over to
Sam Fan. I needed his approval and his bankroll. Mickey and
Chief Moses were concluding the jury investigation today for an
attorney who needed the results tomorrow morning.

I dressed quickly and drove the Thunderbird over to Fan's
office. When I got inside Victoria was at her customary post. Her
smile was friendly. She obviously knew I wasn't going to give her
away.

"Still stuck in the same old job?" I asked her.

"It's not the job, it's the people that keep me here," she said.

Sam Fan himself actually came out to show me in. He led me
past the desks of the blond twins Jennifer and Jeanine who were
wearing identical clothes today.

The reason Sam came out to lead me in was obvious; he had
moved to Silverman's office. Most of the permanent silver touches
remained the same but Sam had picked up the motif of an Oriental
fan. His name was printed on a large fan spread out on the silver-
plated door and there were about a half-dozen fans spread out
around the room. One was a calendar, another a letter opener, another contained a digital clock. It reminded me of those children's
books where you are supposed to find the hidden animals or faces
or whatever in the picture. Sam snapped open a pen that spread
out into a tiny fan.

"I missed that one," I said from the comfortable client's chair.

Sam chuckled. "Guess how many fans I got in this room?"

"Too many."

"Don't you like it?"

"You use the same decorator as Silverman?"

"No. This was Victoria's idea," he said.

"Her talents are wasted at the receptionist desk."

"She's not just a receptionist."

"No argument there."

On the wall, replacing Silverman's Rolls, was a silkscreen of a
Junk. It seemed appropriate. It had to have been Victoria's idea of
a joke of course, but it did go with the collection of fans. They must
have cleaned out a souvenir shop in Chinatown.

"Well," Sam said, "you didn't come here to talk about the decor."

I sucked in my breath. "What if I went to Colombia?"

Sam Fan bit on the fan pen in his hand. "Why?" He rolled his eyes up to the ceiling. All I could see were the milky whites. The dark irises had dissolved.

"I'd like to talk to Gomez."

This time Sam didn't hesitate.

"You out of your fuckin' mind? You'll never find him in the jungles down there. And if you do find him he'll kill you. If he kills you I don't learn anything. The only winner is the P.I. business in the Bay Area."

"So you won't pay for the plane ticket?"

"I know what this means, St. John. It means you can't get a damn lead in the city. That's what it means."

"How do you know it wasn't Gomez?"

"Why don't you call him long distance and ask him? It's cheaper. Call after 11 p.m. and I'll spring for it."

"Do you know how many Gomez's there are in the Bogota phone book?"

"Use the Yellow Pages. Look under Drug Dealers." Sam spun his chair until he was showing me the shining back of his head. There were ringlets of dark hair curling damply at his neck. His seemingly disembodied voice said, "The Colombian would've taken the money."

"What does that prove?"

"You're a *schmuck*. Gomez has a brain."

"You hired me."

"Look, St. John, do you got somethin' or you just wastin' my time fishin' around here?"

"I've got some leads."

"North of Colombia?"

"Yeah. North of San Jose. But I have these annoying questions. Gomez was convicted. Everybody, the cops, the judges, the prosecutors figure he had paid Silverman big money to win. And Silverman lost."

"Rick got him out on bail for the appeal. Rick had it set up for Gomez to skip. Gomez flew PSA to San Diego and a private plane dropped him over the border. He got his money's worth."

"Maybe. Did they give him a parachute?"

137

Sam Fan swung back to face me. He glared at me.

"Who was Rick Silverman seeing after Evelyn Moss?" I asked.

"Evelyn Moss? You've been working. I'm almost impressed. You're up to last year."

"I'm getting paid."

Sam Fan toyed with his fan letter opener.

"He didn't talk about anyone after her," Fan said.

"That was over a year ago."

"Right when things turned fantastic for him. When the drug cases started falling into place one after another. He couldn't lose."

"Until Gomez," I reminded him.

"I told you, the man was free."

"And how did things turn for you?" I asked.

"For me? Hey, I was his partner."

I left that alone for now.

"You know what Sam? I don't believe Rick Silverman suddenly took a vow and became a monk."

"He was Jewish."

I ignored Sam's comment and said, "More likely he bought a gross of latex condoms."

"Hey, when the Surgeon General talks straight. . ."

I interrupted and said, "I want to go through Silverman's town house."

"What for?"

"I don't know until I go through it."

"You're a P.I. Break in."

"It's a hell of a lot easier with a key, Sam."

"Everyone's been through it. Now it's all part of the estate. I don't got a key."

"But his things are still there?"

"Unless Rita the Bitch ripped them off. Which I wouldn't put past her."

"She have a key?"

"Sure she's got a key."

"I think I'll skip the Colombia trip."

I blew Victoria a kiss as I left.

I didn't even look back to see her reaction. Maybe I wasn't in love with her anymore.

* * *

I waited until after six before going over to Rita's.

"About the other day I'm sorry," she apologized. "I was upset."

"Maybe it was the wine."

"What do you want?" Her tone was no longer apologetic.

"The key to Silverman's town house."

"No."

I reached into my blazer pocket and pulled out the sheet of paper I had taken from her wastebasket and the copy of the PAL letter.

"Where did you get that?" she asked angrily.

"That's not the point." I explained to her the similarities between the pairs of letters from the two typed pages. "The PAL note was typed on your Underwood."

"You're accusing me of sending that note to the newspaper?"

"Where's Richard?" I asked. "Still in Sonoma?"

"I moved him."

"Why?"

"To keep him away from you."

"Your alibi's worthless."

"So what. It's the goddamned truth."

"Then why doesn't your son believe it? Why does he send PAL notes to the newspaper?" I asked.

Rita collapsed on one of the odd pieces of furniture in the living room.

"Bastard," she said angrily. "Richard didn't type that note. I did."

"Why?" I asked.

"Because Richard arrived early. The place was a mess and nothing was ready. So I gave him money to go out to a movie."

"Or anyplace he wanted to go. You can easily walk to Silverman's office from here." I paused. "So you were both alone when Silverman was murdered?"

"That's what it comes down to."

"So either Richard or you could have killed him."

"He's just a boy!" she shouted.

"Who hated his father. That's what you told me."

"Don't get us tangled up any more than we are in this. Everybody hated Silverman. Not just his family."

"Sometimes your family is the hardest to please."

"I didn't kill him. Richard didn't kill him."

"How did Richard act when he came back from the movies?" I asked.

"Perfectly normal. He talked about the film he saw. He didn't act like someone who just murdered his father."

"You know something? I believe you. I don't think either one of you is capable of it. The only thing is you should believe each other."

"Maybe you're right," Rita said in a voice that was barely audible.

"Can I have the key?"

"Why not?" She got up gracefully and went into the kitchen. The key was hidden under the knives in her cutlery drawer.

"That's the first place a burglar would look," I warned her.

"Anyplace I hide something somebody says that's the first place a robber would look."

"No, a burglar. Not a robber. There's a difference," I said.

"Whatever. But there's only one first place to look. And a hell of a lot of second places."

She was right.

Rita smiled and dropped the key into my open palm.

"Thanks."

"Don't look for Richard." I couldn't tell if it was a threat or a plea.

"I won't."

She looked at me skeptically.

"Unless I turn up more than this PAL note."

"You won't."

"Good." I paused then added, "Don't you trust me?"

"No."

"Well then I hope you have an inventory of the contents of the town house."

"Damn right I do," she said as she slowly closed the door behind me.

# 19

By mid-morning Thursday we sent off the juror investigation reports to our clients by messenger.

"It's not the best kind of work," Mickey said to me.

"No. It's not. It gives the edge to the side that can afford to buy it. But everybody's looking for an edge."

The phone rang and the Chief took it. He said, "Yes," and then said to me, "I must go." And he was gone.

"Like the wind," I said to my other partner and added, "Turn on the answering machine. We're going down by the water."

The town house was on Marina, across from the Green, near the San Francisco Yacht Club. It looked recently renovated. According to Fan, Silverman had bought the place within the last six months from a desperate client. He had practically stolen it. And if Fan said that . . .

There was a driveway that led to a garage under the house. I pulled into the driveway and parked; I had nothing to hide. I took the small bag of tools I always kept in the trunk. There might be stubborn little locks or other problems inside. In the bag I also kept a loaded Polaroid camera.

"What an ugly green," Mickey said.

The stucco front of the townhouse was a pale, seasick green. It was the kind of pastel color more appropriate to a tropical island. But it, along with shades of pink, salmon, and sand, was popular along Ocean Beach and the Marina.

"Very Caribbean," I said.

We walked up the steps to a small porch. There was no name on the mailbox.

I turned and looked northwest towards the yacht club. The row of masts that ran out from the restaurant and marina buildings sat as unmoving as pillars sunk in cement. I had never known San Francisco to be so still and so hot.

"It must be over a hundred," I said.

The street itself was noisy and busy. The traffic was beginning to back up at the red light a block away as I unlocked the door with Rita's key. We stood in the dark hallway for a moment. The place had the smell of a sealed vacation house. We walked around on the first floor, opening the drapes, letting the summer light in.

There were a living room, dining room, breakfast room and kitchen. The furniture for the most part looked like expensive antiques or at least good reproductions. Fan had said Silverman had bought the house and all its contents. Except the people, I presumed.

We started with the kitchen. While Mickey went through the cabinets I looked under the knives in the cutlery drawer. No telling where Rita had picked up the idea.

"What exactly are we looking for?" she called down from the chair she was standing on.

"We'll know it when we find it."

"You're a big help."

Dishes, utensils, pots, pans, dishwasher detergent, and even dishtowels; everything was there. You had the sense that

Silverman was only away on vacation and that he would be back any day now.

We found nothing in the kitchen. There were a few possible hiding places in the other rooms on the first floor and we went through all of those but came up empty. There didn't seem to be anything on this floor to shed any light on the case.

We went up the carpeted steps of a spiral staircase and found two bathrooms, a bedroom and a study. The den was a scaled-down reproduction of the way Silverman's office had looked before his death—except that here he had a painting of an enormous yacht hanging on the wall. I wondered if he had owned it. It had been done by the same artist who painted the Rolls-Royce. There was a silver letter opener, a silver ruler, and, of course, a silver telephone. I assumed the desk was locked and I reached into my bag of tools when Mickey started pulling out the drawers.

"It wasn't locked. Can't be anything of value in it," she said.

The drawers were full of neatly stacked papers.

"It's all routine personal stuff. Auto Insurance, Home Insurance, Leases, Time Share agreements, that kind of thing," Mickey said.

"You never know. Go through each pile thoroughly."

"Yes boss, but it's hot in here."

The windows had probably not been opened since Silverman's death. I opened one but it didn't help. It was hard to believe that the bay was only a few hundred yards away.

"There," I said.

"Swell."

While Mickey dug through the desk papers, I went down a short hallway to the bedroom. The bed was a king-size oval that was covered with an elaborate silk bedspread. There was a large mirror on the ceiling. I wondered if that was Silverman's own addition. At the head hung a nude portrait of a woman. It wasn't Rita and it wasn't Evelyn. The woman in the picture had remarkably translucent skin and red hair. Above and below. She was reclining odalisque-style on an ornately carved chaise longue. The painting, like the others, was signed Diego Hammond.

"Mickey, come here."

She came down the hall and stepped into the room.

143

"Wow!"

"Want to try it out?"

She laughed.

"I think that's what we're looking for." I pointed to the picture of the nude at the head of the bed.

I got out the Polaroid, adjusted for the light, depressed the red button, and the camera flashed and whined. The portrait was so detailed and realistic it could have been mistaken for a photograph. As the first Polaroid materialized, I adjusted the light setting and then shot the rest of the film. The pictures weren't great but they would do.

Mickey contemplated the picture. "She has nice tits."

"See that mirror up there," I said, pointing to the ceiling.

"Yeah. What about it?"

"Just in case you missed it." Then I shifted back to the painting and said, "I hope it's a recent work."

Mickey walked over to it and touched the woman's bare feet. She ran her fingers along the toes. I would have selected another part of her anatomy. "It can't be too recent. The paint's dry."

"That's about as good as carbon dating," I said.

"I try."

"Let's go where we can breathe."

# 20

Back at the office we found the Chief waiting for us. We told him where we had been then I asked him about the call. He said it was from an Indian brother in trouble.

"Some white bookmaker threatened to break his knees. I had to make a better threat to the white man. He caught on very quickly. We have an understanding now." The Chief added, "We don't charge the brother a fee."

"Of course not," I said.

"And two more new clients came in. We have some more sleaze work, as you call it, Jeremiah."

"You've been busy," Mickey said.

"So have we." I took out the pictures and passed them to the Chief.

"Hold them by the edge."

"It is all the same picture," the Chief said.

"What do you think?"

"She has got nice tits."

"It's a picture of an oil painting," I explained.

"I can see the frame, Jeremiah," he said. Chief Moses handed me the Polaroids, got up, and stretched. He looked like a grizzly rearing up on its hind legs. The maroon and gold Florida State Seminoles T-shirt he wore was ready to split across his chest.

"It's still early. I'd like to talk to Diego Hammond," I said.

"What kind of name is that?" Chief Moses asked disparagingly.

"I wouldn't talk, Chief, if I were you."

"You're not. For which I thank the Great Spirit."

I got out the San Francisco Yellow Pages and looked under artists. Diego Hammond had a half-inch box in a single column that advertised "Portraits a Specialty." I copied down the address and telephone number. When I called the number I got a recording machine that told me the artist was at work now and couldn't come to the phone but if I left my name and number at the sound of the beep he would get back to me as soon as possible. I wasn't patient enough for that. I hung up before the beep.

"I'm going to have to pay Mr. Hammond a visit," I said as I got up.

"We," Mickey and the Chief said in unison.

Diego Hammond's studio was on Telegraph Hill. We parked at its base on the east side and started up the flights of wooden steps that led up to the top of the hill. Hammond's studio was three-quarters of the way up, nearly in the shadow of the great 210-foot hose nozzle known as Coit Tower that rose above the crest. Once mainly an artist's colony, the area was now an expensive and fashionable residential district.

Hammond's building was a holdover from less fashionable days. It was a three-story wooden structure. There were three separate mailboxes, indicating that each floor was a residence for a single family, with Diego Hammond occupying the top floor. On the doorway there was a neatly painted hand with a forefinger pointing up. Under the finger there appeared in carefully scrolled print the following: "Diego Hammond—Portraits in Oil—3rd Floor." The hand looked familiar to me.

"That's the hand of God," I said.

"Where?" the Chief asked, looking up at the perfectly clear blue sky.

"The sign. That's the hand of God touching Adam in the Sistine Chapel."

"If it's good enough for Michelangelo it's good enough for Diego Hammond," Mickey said. "I learned something at Ohio State."

"I should never have dropped out of FSU. Then I too could have recognized the hand of God. Hell, if Burt Reynolds could graduate. . ."

I interrupted him. "Don't believe everything you read."

With Mickey leading the way we went up three dark flights of stairs. On the top floor under a dim lightbulb was a sign on the studio door that read: "Artist at Work—Do Not Disturb." The three of us stood paralyzed on the hot indoor landing, staring at it.

"You should have respected his phone message," the Chief said.

The Chief had great respect for machines; especially those that talked to you.

"Well, we're here now. . ." I said feebly.

Mickey was ahead of me. She lifted the sign off the two hooks that supported it and turned it over on its flip side, which read: "Open. Please Come In. Artist at Rest."

She hung the sign back up with the invitation showing.

What else could we do but go in? I turned the doorknob and we stepped into a room bathed in light. It was like coming out into the sunshine after lunch in a dark barroom.

From across the studio Diego Hammond, artist at work and not at rest, began cursing vehemently at us.

A beautiful young girl with very pale skin and wildly curly black hair covered her naked body with the red drapery she had been posing on. She said something in a language I didn't understand but I got the drift. Then she just sat there, wrapped in red velvet, glaring at us with dark startled eyes.

Diego Hammond shouted at us: "Didn't you see the goddamn sign? Why do you think I put it out there? So fools like you can ignore it?"

Diego Hammond had flushed skin, long brown hair, and light

brown eyes; he also affected an outrageously long and thin Salvador Dali mustache. With his paintbrush dripping red, he came marching across the room in a frenzy. He brandished the brush at us as if it were a bloody weapon. He didn't seem to notice or have any concern for the size of the Chief. I wished I hadn't ignored his phone message.

He stopped for a moment in front of Mickey and looked her up and down.

Mickey didn't flinch. "The sign said 'Open,' " she said in her best injured-party tone.

The Chief was looking the draped model up and down.

Hammond marched past us through the door and out to the landing. When he saw the sign he screamed down the stairs, "I own this building. I could kick you out on your asses."

"Damn kids," he said turning back towards us. Then he slammed the door behind him. I wondered if there was anyone downstairs to hear him.

The model, who didn't look to me to be any more than sixteen, sat completely still under the Chief's scrutiny.

Diego Hammond walked back to his easel, put down the paintbrush, and said, "Go, Asha. No more today."

I thought Asha suited her.

Asha got up, walking awkwardly within the folds of red velvet. She opened a door at the back of the studio and disappeared.

Hammond seemed to shrink as he calmed down and I realized what a tiny man he actually was. Not only was he extremely short but he had a very small bone structure that gave him an aura of bird-like fragility. On his small face the Dali mustache was an incongruity. His hands, however, with their long thin fingers seemed outsized for the rest of his body, as if an artist had consciously distorted them.

"What do you want?" he asked. He was studying us as if for a group painting. I noticed that a calmer Diego Hammond had acquired a slight Spanish accent.

Mickey, the Chief and I all exchanged helpless glances.

"Come," Hammond said as he started to lead us across the paint-stained floorboards. I was careful to step over a fresh blob of brilliant yellow.

148

There were just a few canvases in the corner of the studio, indicating either that he worked slowly or sold most of what he painted. I thought that the setup, rundown or not, indicated success for Diego.

Against the east wall I recognized the carved chaise longue that my—and Silverman's—beautiful nude had posed on. I saw that Mickey and Chief Moses had recognized it also. Diego Hammond did not make house calls, not even for someone like Rick Silverman.

Hammond opened a door directly across from the one Asha had disappeared through and led us into a small office. There was an air conditioner in the single window in the room and Hammond flipped the switch.

"It will take a few minutes," he warned.

In a kind of Musical Chairs we all found seats although the size of the room had us bumping our knees together. Hammond himself got behind a desk that was so small it looked like it was designed for a grade school child.

As he stared at us Hammond's light brown eyes darkened with anticipation. He said, "Her I would paint. The Indian I would paint. You," meaning me, "I do not find very exciting." He had turned up his accent.

"I could say the same about you," I said.

"Do not take it personally."

"I didn't. Now, Mr. Hammond. . ." I began.

"Diego. Please."

"Diego. Fine. We're private investigators. We'd like to ask you a few questions." I flashed my identification.

He was incredulous. "For a few stupid questions you interrupt my work. You are Philistines." His thin aristocratic nose twitched above his mustache. He licked the hair above his lip and tugged at each end of his Dali. I half expected it to come off in his hands.

"We just have a few questions," Mickey tried on him.

"For a few questions you need three of you?"

"We work together. We're partners," Mickey said.

I was glad she was there. Her voice had a soothing effect on him.

"All right. Let's get this over with," Diego said in unaccented English.

149

I took out one of the Polaroids and put it on the desk in front of him. "Your work?"

"You saw my signature if you took the picture."

"When did you paint her?"

"Six, maybe seven months ago. Why?"

"Rick Silverman hire you?"

Diego crossed his arms over his pigeon chest. "No more until you tell me what this is about."

"You read about Silverman?" I asked.

"I only use the newspaper to cover the studio floor."

"You didn't know he was murdered?"

Diego took a deep breath. "I do now," he said as he gave another tug at his mustache. I couldn't tell if he was lying.

The Chief leaned forward with a look of great impatience on his face. On his face impatience was intimidating.

"Silverman hired you?" I asked.

"I did work for him before."

"Other women?"

"No. Expensive obscene cars and expensive obscene boats."

"Did he own the yacht?" I asked.

"It was part of a complicated deal that fell through. By then the picture was finished."

"You didn't care much for Silverman?" I asked.

"He had no taste."

"Only money," I said.

"I thought you only did portraits?" Mickey asked.

"I will work on objects. Some people like their possessions in their portraits. In the background. I will do landscapes too. Did you ever notice the landscape behind the *Mona Lisa*? I use a landscape to reflect the soul of my subject." It came out like a parody but Diego meant it.

"In other words," the Chief said, "Silverman paid well enough for you to paint whatever he wanted painted."

"Yes he paid. I demanded an even larger commission than usual for the Rolls and the yacht. And he paid." His expression indicated that the Chief's point had hit home.

"What was her name?" I asked, pointing at the photograph on the desk.

Hammond focused on it. He didn't move a muscle as he spoke in a dull monotone. "She would come every afternoon exactly when I told her so we could catch the northern light. She would undress in the model's room in my apartment and walk right out, without a robe. Without embarrassment. She was truly beautiful. As beautiful in life as I created her in art."

"What was her name?"

"The picture is called *Portrait*."

"Of a lady?" I asked.

"It was Silverman's condition."

"What was?" I asked.

"That I not know her name."

"So you charged more," Mickey said.

"Of course."

"And this was six months ago?" I asked.

"About."

"Is this how she looks?" I asked.

"Of course. You know my work."

I looked at Mickey and Chief Moses; they didn't seem to have any more questions. We were not coming away with very much. But maybe, just maybe, we were off square one.

"Thank you, Mr. Hammond, for your cooperation."

Hammond ignored me; his attention was on Mickey. He said to her in a whisper, "I would like very much to paint you."

"I can't afford it."

"No money. No money."

"In the nude?" she asked bluntly.

"But naturally."

She looked directly at Hammond and said, "I'll think about it."

"You will be immortal," he promised as he handed her his business card.

I was glad to get her the hell out of there. A woman who posed nude for the camera would be tempted to pose nude for a Diego Hammond.

On the way out we passed the young black-haired model who had reemerged wearing a bright yellow silk robe that looked large enough for a heavyweight boxer. She sat in the chaise longue, eating a green apple and staring out towards the bay. One bare leg was drawn up to her chin. I would have liked to have a portrait of her but not at Diego Hammond's prices.

As we went back down the single narrow set of creaking wooden steps that ran up and down Telegraph Hill I said, "That girl must have been sixteen."

"Not even," the Chief said.

Mickey who was in front of us stopped abruptly and swung around to face us. "Did you look at the skin at the corner of her eyes?" she asked.

"No," we both said.

"Of course not. Men! She wasn't a day under twenty-five." Mickey's dress flared out as she walked down the hill.

# 21

After dinner Chief Moses and I drove Mickey to her apartment. We watched her go into the lobby of the eight-story building. She walked into a wash of bright yellowish light and continued towards the elevator.

"Are you in love?" the Chief asked. "Or is it moon fever?"

I looked up at the helter-skelter pattern of lights on in the windows of the apartment building. It reminded me of a huge illuminated Halloween pumpkin.

"I hope not," I said. But I was glad I'd kept my word about not telling the Chief about the *Playboy* picture.

I watched Mickey's apartment windows and waited for her lights to go on. I could see her moving through her rooms, pulling down the shades. No voyeur was going to get off on her.

As I pulled out of the loading zone I said, "It's a good time to catch Johnny D. Why don't we give him a chance to identify the woman in the Polaroid?"

"Why not? He'd enjoy it."

Only Johnny wasn't at his desk. At the station house we had to deal with the sergeant who didn't like civilians in his domain. I asked him where we could find Johnny D. He wouldn't tell us.

Until the Chief said, "There's a family emergency. Are you willing to take the legal responsibility if Johnny's not informed?"

He thought that over and then said, "What the hell. This is Vice, not Narcotics or Homicide. He's at the park on a stakeout of the men's room"

"Nice work," I told the Chief as we went out.

"The white man is not the only one who can speak with a forked tongue."

We started towards the park. It was the only one in Johnny D.'s precinct. It was two square blocks with a small duck pond, a softball diamond, two basketball courts with three broken rims on the backboards, and enough trees and bushes to hide several hundred rapists, muggers, and assorted thieves and junkies at any one time. Of course there were bushes for pairs of lovers too. And the still notorious Glory Hole Men's Room for one night stands of another kind.

We left the Thunderbird on the north edge of the park and proceeded cautiously on patrol into the area. There was a single light burning on the low roof of the rest rooms on the west side. The squat concrete building looked like a World War II bunker.

"Why don't they just lock up the damn place?" I wondered aloud.

"The queers break in." The Chief had little use for gays.

"Of course."

"You would think they had never heard of AIDS," he said.

"These are not your upscale gays, Chief. Some of them can't read or write."

The Chief shook his head in disgust. Then he peered into the darkness and asked, "So where is he?"

"Where do you stake out a john?"

We started stalking around in the bushes like deer hunters, whispering: "Johnny D.? Johnny D.?"

After twice going around the circle of bushes and trees that surrounded the john we decided that there were no police out in the field. Only two desperate straight couples.

"Must be," I said, indicating the rest rooms.

Chief Moses agreed with a nod of his head.

We went into the men's room. The floor was concrete with a rusty drain in the center. The greenish walls were covered with graffiti and telephone numbers next to names and promises of various sex acts if the numbers were called. Most of the names and nicknames were unmistakably male. Between the bent and scratched but unbreakable metal mirrors there were several crude but graphic anatomical drawings.

"Nice place," the Chief said with distaste.

The flushing handles on two of the urinals had been torn off. Where there had once been another urinal, there were now just capped pipes and gaping holes. I wondered about the strength it would take to tear out a urinal. It would have to be somebody like the Chief. Or kids with crowbars and determination.

I looked for vents. There had to be a vent. There were two over the line of stalls.

Chief Moses and I went into a stall right under one of the vents. I gave a whispered call: "Johnny. You in there? You old voyeur."

"Who the hell are you?" The voice did not belong to Johnny D. We had picked his partner's vent.

I led the Chief to the stall under the other vent and called for Johnny again. Louder this time.

"What're you doin' here? Are you crazy?" Johnny's voice was filtered by the rusty screen.

"The sergeant said it was okay."

"What line of bullshit did you give him?"

"Hello, Johnny," the Chief said. "We told him your wife was having a baby."

"Jesus. She's not even pregnant."

"He's kidding. We told him she suddenly started talking in English. It was a miracle; like speaking in tongues," I said.

From behind the vents both cops were cursing at us.

"Will you get outta here before I bust you," Johnny ordered.

"Keep it down. You want to blow the stakeout?" I responded.

155

"Whaddya want?" Johnny's voice had the desperation of captivity.

"I just want you to look at something," I said.

"I've been lookin' all night."

I stepped up on the black toilet seat and held one of the Polaroids up to the vent. "I thought I'd make your day."

"Shit," Johnny D. muttered.

"You seen anything better in here?"

"Do you get combat pay for this?" Chief Moses asked.

"What I'd like to get is a transfer. Even to Narcotics."

"Do you know her?" I asked.

"Nice tits."

"Yeah. But do you know her?" As I spoke the toilet seat was shifting beneath me. One or both of the bolts holding it on was broken.

"Hold it still," Johnny said.

"This damn seat keeps moving."

Suddenly the vent sprang open and Johnny D.'s hand came thrusting out. It was like a scene out of a grade B horror film. And it surprised me. It surprised me so much that I almost lost my balance. The Chief grabbed my sides as I struggled to keep my position.

"Now I know why I keep you around," I said.

Johnny D. slammed the vent shut.

"I don't know her. What is she? A hooker?"

"Silverman's last known woman."

"Why don't we just hang on to this. The scenery's pretty bad around here."

"And so is the smell," Chief Moses said.

We left the stakeout in time to chase away two white kids in black leather jackets who were trying to hot wire the car. I didn't catch the name of the gang on their backs. But Chief Moses did.

"The Redmen."

"They could give you a bad name."

The Chief scowled at me and said, "So could the Washington Redskins."

Each time we went back over the newspaper stories on

Silverman, Judge Peter Troutvelter stood out more and more as his
legal nemesis. Despite Silverman's impressive string of victories,
when he lost it was in Troutvelter's court. He was a man I had to
talk to. I had a hunch he could help identify the woman in the Polaroid.

It was the last Friday in August. That morning I called the judge
and spoke to his secretary who asked my business. I told her I was
a P.I. working on the Silverman case and she told me that there
was no way the judge could talk to me about a possible criminal
case. Still, she put me on hold and two minutes later, sounding
very surprised herself, she told me that his honor could see me today during the noon recess.

A little after noon I was ushered into his chambers. Behind his
desk Judge Troutvelter looked as impressive as he did behind the
bench. He took off his glasses and leaned back into a large executive chair. He studied me with eyes sharp as drill points. Close up I
confirmed my estimate that he was near seventy. He indicated an
overstuffed leather chair in front of his desk and I sank into it.

Behind the judge were bookcases of leather-bound volumes and
a coat rack from which hung his judicial black robe.

"We don't have much time, Mr. St. John." He glanced at an expensive watch on his bony wrist. His voice was as chilly as the air-
conditioning.

"I realize that, your honor."

He joined his hands in front of him on the desk and began to
knead his blue-veined knuckles. All of his fingers were slightly
twisted. They obviously were giving him pain.

"Arthritis," he said. He reached into the center desk drawer and
took a new bottle of aspirin out of a yellow box. "Damn," he cursed
at the child-proof cap as he tried to pop it open between his thumb
and forefinger. Finally in frustration he slid the bottle across to me
and asked, "Would you mind?"

I pushed up at the arrow and the white plastic top bounced on
the judge's desk. He picked it up with some difficulty and then
dropped it in a wastebasket.

"There," he said with satisfaction. "I keep telling my wife to get
the screw-top bottle. You'd think she was senile. And she's fifteen
years younger than me."

With a small penknife he pried out the cotton in the neck of the bottle. He dropped three pills into the palm of his left hand, put them into his mouth with a motion that looked like he was slapping himself in the face, and washed them down with the contents of a large ceramic mug that stood on the right edge of the desk. On the mug was printed: "Here Come De Judge."

He slammed down the aspirin bottle in front of a framed photograph of a handsome woman with silver hair who looked in her mid-fifties.

"Your wife?" I asked.

"Yes. My first wife knew how to buy aspirin," he added. He grinned at me. "Course I didn't marry Eleanor because she knew how to buy aspirin. She has other virtues."

"I'm sure."

"You wanted to talk to me about the Silverman case, Mr. St. John?"

I explained the investigation I was conducting.

"So?" He looked and sounded skeptical.

"You were Silverman's nemesis," I said.

"I give the law a strict construction."

"Unlike some of your fellow judges."

He stared up at the ceiling. "He won in my court, too. Sometimes the prosecution can destroy its own case. Let's get to the point, Mr. St. John. What do you want?"

Flexing my back, I said, "I appreciate this, your honor. You've been handling a lot of drug cases. From what you've seen of these cases with drug dealers, would you say that Orlando Gomez would have killed his own attorney?"

The judge rubbed the bridge of his nose then looked straight at me without expression. Finally, he asked, "Who are you working for?" Before I could say anything, he continued, "Sam Fan." It wasn't a question. "You realize this is all off-the-record speculation. I'm only basing a conclusion on how I've seen these individuals behave in the past. Remember Gomez was a Colombian drug dealer. A crazy cowboy *coquero*. He paid Silverman an exorbitant fee. Then he was convicted. Mr. Gomez could not have been a very happy man. In his country violence is the expected response. For *machismo*."

158

"With money like that you expect to buy the judge?"

"In Bogota."

"And in the city?"

"Not this judge," Troutvelter said coldly.

I was getting out of line but the judge wasn't throwing me out of his office. Instead he wanted to convince me that Gomez had killed Silverman; just as I had once tried to convince Sam Fan. We were both about as effective.

"There are other judges," I said.

"Of course."

"And Gomez was out on bail. He could skip the country and go back to relative safety in Colombia."

Judge Troutvelter sighed and glanced at his watch again.

"Damn it, Mr. St. John, the police are convinced that Gomez killed Rick Silverman. What exactly are you trying to do? Sometimes the police have been known to be right."

"Including a detective named Chang?"

"Especially Chang. What are we talking about, Mr. St. John? You must have some of your own evidence or at least a theory, something that suggests it wasn't Gomez, or you're wasting your time and mine."

I hesitated, then said, "What if Silverman was going to return the money to Gomez?"

"That's speculation," the judge said.

"He called me to make a delivery," I admitted.

"But was it the money? And was it to Gomez?"

"I don't know. He was dead when I got there. If the money was going to Gomez, why would he come and kill Silverman?"

"For his *Latino* honor."

"He left the money."

"Gomez didn't care about the money. It was probably easier to travel without it."

"Your honor, Silverman opened the safe. There was something in there that the killer wanted. I doubt it was Gomez."

"Do you know what was in the safe?" he asked.

"No."

The judge frowned. "Is this all you have?"

"So far. And this." I pulled out the Polaroid of the woman and showed it to him. "Do you recognize her? She was Silverman's woman. I'm trying to find her."

At first I thought my hunch was right. I saw a flicker of recognition behind the judge's eyes. He gave the picture careful, even intense scrutiny. But then the flicker became a dark shadow and he said, "I wish I did." Turning jovial, he added: "Nice tits."

"That's what everyone says."

The smile on his face was pasted on. He made a motion to dismiss me. "Now, Mr. St. John. . ."

"I understand." I got up. "Thank you for your time. I appreciate it."

He reached his thin right hand over the massive desk and we shook hands. Despite his arthritis the handshake was firm. I was careful not to grip too hard but found my own fingers being squeezed.

"Don't try to make unnecessary business for the courts. We have enough as it is."

"I know," I said.

"Good."

I took back the picture, thanked the judge again, and went out the side door into the corridor where the usual courtroom crowd was milling about at the end of the lunch hour. I knew that the judge had really told me nothing. In fact, he had elicited from me what I knew about the Silverman case. Now I understood why he had been so willing to talk to me. I had been put on the stand.

It was time to follow up on the Chief's information about McCurdy. My only access to the DEA man was through Mickey as star reporter and beautiful woman—not necessarily in that order. Back at the office she was examining the incriminating photos she had taken to wrap up a disability fraud case.

"It's unbelievable. The guy is playing tennis."

"Okay. But it's back to the Silverman case."

"What do I have to do?"

"See McCurdy."

Mickey was unhappy about trying out her game on McCurdy for a second time. Even with Johnny D.'s card.

"It can't work twice," she insisted.

I cajoled. I threatened. I promised to buy a video camcorder as soon as we had the money. She acquiesced albeit reluctantly. She would make McCurdy's day I assured her as I donned a pair of black-rimmed glasses, a false mustache, and a fedora.

Mickey thought I was hilarious. "You look like Groucho Marx," she said between giggles.

"I'm not that funny. Only to you because you know me."

"Why don't I get a disguise?" she asked.

"He's supposed to remember you."

"Good luck," she said.

I got the camera equipment and we drove to the DEA field office. We tried to use Johnny's card again. This time the pit bull secretary was adamant.

"No reporters. And no photographers."

"Just ask. And take in this press card too," Mickey insisted.

"I have my instructions."

"If he says no we'll leave. Otherwise we'll camp out here all day," Mickey said.

"How would you like that?" I added with a leer.

The woman took the cards and disappeared. I was sure McCurdy hadn't forgotten Mickey.

The secretary came back out and said, "All right. Go on in."

I opened my mouth to say something but Mickey punched me in the arm. I kept it shut.

The DEA man looked the same as he did last time, right down to the rumpled shirt and wrinkled tie. As we came in he made a show of shuffling some papers across his desk with his huge hands but his attention was really on Mickey. He barely glanced at me but that didn't mean anything. I still felt naked in my disguise.

Big Mac pulled out a chair for Mickey.

"Please sit down," he said.

She took the two cards back and sat down. I sat down too and I didn't remove my hat.

"I'm doing a follow-up story on the Silverman case," she explained.

"I didn't see the first one," he said. He was sitting on the front edge of his desk, clearly trying to get his body as close to Mickey's as possible. The extra weight at his waist bulged out over his belt in a classic spare tire as he leaned forward. The boyish freckled face was florid under his thinning red hair.

"Do you catch the *County Star*?" Mickey asked.

"No. Can't say that I do."

"It was a good story," I said.

"Is that the same guy as last time?" he asked with his drawl.

"No," Mickey said. "I'm breaking in a new photographer. The other one talked too much."

"I noticed that. But I told you no pictures."

"No problem," I said.

Mickey smiled warmly at McCurdy who was as close as he could get to her without falling into her lap.

"We just need to ask a few questions," she said.

"Fire away."

"I know the police position is that Gomez killed Silverman, but I've heard something else was going down." I said it quietly.

McCurdy reared up. "Like what?" he asked. His face hardened, the Good Ol' Boy was gone. He had humored us before, but this was getting serious.

"A sting, Mr. McCurdy," I said. "Isn't that your specialty?"

"The goddamn amateur hour is over," he said as he made his way past Mickey and me to the door. I thought he was going to take us hostage. Instead he said, "Y'all leave now. An' tell that Polack Dajewski to go to hell." His large hands were packed into menacing fists. Then he added to Mickey, "This sonofabitch talks more than the other one."

We left fast. Behind us we could hear him bawling out his unfortunate secretary.

"What do you think, Mickey?" I asked when we were back in the car.

"I think you talk too much."

"What about the sting?"

"There's something there."

"We just need a few more questions answered," I said.

"Don't we always."

162

In the car I took off my glasses, my mustache, and my hat. I put the camera behind my seat. I knew what to do to begin to tie this all together. We could start tomorrow. As we drove I explained our next move to Mickey. She had her doubts. Back at the office Chief Moses was much more agreeable.

I gave Sam Fan a progress report over the telephone. I wouldn't say that he was thrilled with it.

# 22

It was the last weekend in August. Mickey, Chief Moses and I were sitting at a booth in Monday's with a good clear view of the bar. I wanted to go a few more rounds with Nelson Bittenbender. Working a lot of angles we had gotten some very useful information about Nelson Bittenbender from a talkative, broke and sick ex-lover. For a Sunday night the place was pretty crowded but not so much with the courthouse gang as during the week. Everyone around us was discussing the unusual heat, and with September, the city's hottest month, still to come.

"The polar ice caps will melt," Mickey said. "San Francisco will be under water."

"That should cut down on the crime rate," I said.

"And on randiness," Mickey added.

"There goes the profit side of the business," Chief Moses concluded.

The cocktail waitress wiggled her way over to us in her tight mini-outfit. There was a run in her pantyhose which she had tried to repair with nail polish.

I ordered a Henry's, the Chief a Bud, and Mickey a glass of the house white. The drinks arrived in less than a minute.

Leaving the Chief as backup, I took my bottle of beer, went up to the bar, and sat on a stool in front of Bittenbender, who was slicing lemons and limes into quarters on a cutting board. He ignored me. I didn't care; I was prepared for him today.

"Hello, Nelson."

Bittenbender looked up, nodded his head at me in reluctant recognition, and went back to work with his knife. With the Giant game over, the TV was showing a tape of a Triathlon run last spring. As he cleaned the board Nelson watched the runners in the final marathon phase.

"I'd like to talk about Silverman," I said.

"Damn it, St. John, we already did."

"Let's try it again, Nelson."

"What do you want to know? Was he gay? No, he wasn't. I have it on the best authority. . ."

"You said Silverman hadn't been in here with any particular woman in about a year."

Nelson sighed. "That's what I told you."

"What about her?" One of the Polaroids materialized in the palm of my hand.

Nelson Bittenbender studied the picture. "That's a photograph of a painting."

"You get the brass ring."

Nelson bent down below the bar and began unpacking a crate of beer.

"Well? Have you ever seen her with Silverman?"

He put some beer into the refrigerator ever so slowly.

"I'm busy," he said and went to replenish some customers at the other end of the bar.

I waited until he was finished. "Now serve me."

"What do you want?"

"Another Henry's."

166

Nelson brought out a Henry Weinhard and put the dark brown bottle down on the bar with a glass.

"That's two-fifty."

I took out a brand-new twenty and held it on the bar. "Keep the change," I said without releasing my hold on the bill.

"So?"

"Ever seen her with Silverman?"

"No."

"Do you know her?"

Nelson hesitated.

"Come on," I urged.

"It's hard to tell without clothes. They all look alike without clothes."

"Dress her in this." I released the twenty.

"I don't know her." He left the money and walked away.

I stalked Nelson and told him in a whisper that I knew a certain father with connections who was trying to discover his identity. He blamed Nelson for turning their only son gay when he was sixteen. That was five years ago and now the boy was dying of AIDS.

At first he denied everything but then he wanted to know how I had found out.

"Snitches," I said. "There are a lot of desperate gays in the Castro."

"He wasn't sixteen. He was a consenting adult," Nelson whispered.

"Tell it to his father back in Kansas City."

Nelson was ready to talk. "I don't know her name. She comes in here once in a while to get picked up ever so discreetly."

I took a sip of beer.

"By whom?" I asked as I put the glass down.

"Do you want a list?"

"Yeah, I'd like that a lot."

"Get real, St. John. I don't know. Lawyers mostly. Maybe a judge."

"Names?"

"Believe it or not there aren't too many guys in here who like to give me their names."

"You never saw her with Silverman?"

"He avoided her."

That I found interesting.

"Hey, Nelson. . ." a drunk called from the end of the bar.

"The guy's had too much," Nelson said as he started towards the man.

"Where do I find her?" I asked.

He stopped. "Talk to Amos Billy."

"Where do I find him?"

"Wherever pimps gather."

I picked up my unfinished glass of beer.

At our booth Mickey was alone. "Where the hell did the Chief go?"

"He had to make a telephone call."

"Right now?"

"It was urgent. I ordered the blackened redfish for you. The Chief can stand to see fish again."

"Thanks," I said. "I'm glad he's cured."

"Where the hell were you?" I asked the Chief as he moved with surprising grace through the tables between the bar and the booth.

As the Chief slid in next to Mickey he said, "I had to make a call."

"I told you," Mickey said.

"Did our information help you with Bittenbender?" the Chief asked.

"Like a brain transplant."

I dropped the Chief off on a street corner he directed me to. When I asked him what he was up to he said that it was his personal Bureau of Indian Affairs matter. I didn't push him on it. Then I drove Mickey to her apartment; I parked in the No Parking Loading Zone in front of it.

"Are we getting anywhere?" she asked.

"How should I take that?"

"I'm talking about the case."

"Oh. Maybe we'll know something when we find Mr. Amos Billy."

Mickey swung her door open, scraping the curb.

"Sorry."

I ignored the unpleasant noise and said, "I enjoyed our date the other night."

She turned and looked at me, her face and hair shining under the interior car light, and said, "So did I."

"Let's do it again sometime."

"Sometime soon."

"Tonight?"

"Not tonight."

"Why not?"

"You'll never get a parking space here on a Sunday night."

"I'll take a ticket."

Mickey drew in her breath. "Jeremiah, I didn't like what you . . . we . . . did to Bittenbender."

"We had to get some kind of lead."

"I don't like to use a person's sexuality like that. Gays are so vulnerable."

"You don't sound like an ex-cop."

"Just remember why I am an ex-cop."

I remembered. "We had to break something open. It turned out to be Nelson."

"I know. I'm not blaming you. Not really."

Maybe not but the result was the same for tonight.

She disappeared into the lobby and I drove back to the Victorian where I lifted weights, shot baskets, and tried to read the rest of the Travis McGee. I finally decided to call Nadine. It was time to get serious.

This time I would take something for Anthony. Even though Anthony would be asleep, I wanted to have a gift there for him when he woke up in the morning. Sort of like Christmas. I found an all-night pharmacy on Polk that was more like a department store. It had what I wanted.

There was a schoolyard a block from Nadine's apartment where Anthony played ball. I had gone there a few times with him to shoot hoops on the asphalt courts. But a while ago some teenagers had stolen his ball. I bought him the best Magic Johnson simulated leather outdoor basketball in the store even though I couldn't think of a way to charge it to Fan.

"Gonna play a little night ball?" the clerk asked.

"You might say that."

Anthony was asleep when I got to Nadine's. I needed to make a decision.

"He'll love it," Nadine said as she took the basketball from me. Her slim body was lost under a large robe. She had cut her hair. It looked good.

"I like your hair."

"You noticed."

We sat down on the couch together.

"Anthony'll be sorry he missed you."

"Maybe it's better this way. Let him remember me by my gift."

"What are you talking about?"

"I don't think we can go on like this," I said.

"Why not?"

"Because it's not permanent."

"Why couldn't it be?" she asked.

"I have my reasons." All of them were named Mickey.

"What's her name."

"It's not just that. Anthony needs a real father."

"He had one and look what happened."

"It's over Nadine. It has to be."

"What about just living together? No marriage."

"No. Not now."

"So it's over," she said almost in a whisper.

There was a long silence as I waited to see if she was going to break down and cry. Maybe I was expecting too much.

She said, "I've been seeing a man. He wants to marry me."

She hadn't had her head very deep in the sand at all.

"Does Anthony like him?"

"Not as much as he likes you."

"But does he like him?"

"Yes."

"It's none of my business, but do you love him?"

"I'll work on it."

I got up and started for the door. "I'll never forget you," I said.

Nadine moved towards me. As she moved she slipped out of her robe. By the time she reached me she was out of her pink baby dolls as well. Her tan was even deeper then before.

"You bet you won't," she said as she started unbuttoning my shirt. "This is going to be a night to remember." When my shirt was off and my pants were unzipped she picked up the basketball.

"Let's get in the bedroom." I said.

We did.

Nadine stood naked before me and watched me undress. She ran her fingers through her hair, the movement drawing her small breasts taut. Between her knees she held the basketball.

"You know. He didn't even notice I got my hair cut."

"Who didn't?"

"The guy who wants to marry me."

As I pulled off my jockey briefs I said, "That's because he wants to do more than just jump on your bones." Before she could say anything I added, "What are you doing with that basketball?"

"I'll think of something. You know I'm handy with things in bed," she promised as she reached for a condom and started to roll the ball up my thigh.

# 23

It *had* been a night to remember and when I left just before dawn I regretted that it would be our last. Nadine had made me promise to come to the wedding, not for her sake, for Anthony's. I was sorry that in the frenzy of the moment I had agreed to go. I should have asked her if she was going to invite her ex-husband Tony as well.

I hoped Anthony liked his basketball. I know I did.

I woke up Monday morning to the sound of Mickey's typewriter. There were reports that had to go to our clients. I heard a door slam downstairs: Chief Moses moving through the office. I didn't need my digital alarm clock to tell me what time it was. There was enough sunlight flooding the room to make it past ten o'clock. Another door slammed shut.

"All right," I shouted from my bed. "I hear you. I'm getting up." I buried my head under a pillow to block out the noise from downstairs. Although I had had very little to drink I had a vicious hangover type headache. Maybe it was the exhausting sex. Maybe it was the wages of sin. Maybe it was the basketball. Probably all three.

"Could you hold down the noise?" I shouted.

Then I gave up. I kicked off the sheet I was using as a cover, walked to the bathroom, and started the water running. Once Mickey and the Chief heard the water rushing like a river through the pipes they would know I was really up. I shaved and showered, standing under the hot water until I had used so much of it that it began to run cold. I took a few seconds of the cold water and then quickly turned off the hard fine spray. I finally felt awake. My headache was gone.

As I come down the steps Mickey looked up from her typewriter and applauded softly.

"Was the typewriter too noisy?" she asked.

"Yes."

"A computer is much quieter."

"I'll move it up on my priority list," I said.

"Next to the video camcorder?"

"Right."

Past Mickey, in the next office, I saw the Chief at his desk, his lizard skin cowboy boots up on its scarred top. He was reading *The Wall Street Journal*. The Chief had recently decided to gamble in the market as well as at cards. Chief Moses had enough money socked away from his days as a consultant to gamble wherever he liked, from Wall Street to Reno. The only place he avoided was Vegas.

"Rough night?" Mickey asked.

I didn't know what to say to her. I finally decided on: "I did something that had to be done."

"I won't ask."

"It was business. Sort of."

I stared at her beautiful face. I felt nothing stir inside of me. I had mixed emotions after my last night with Nadine. Maybe I had made the wrong decision. But probably I was just tired. Whatever it was I was sure I would get over it.

I shrugged and went to the Chief's office. Mickey got up and followed me.

The Chief looked at me over the thin edge of the newspaper and over the tops of reading glasses I had never seen before. He reached for his telephone and said, "I've got to call my broker." I listened as Chief Moses placed a buy order for an over-the-counter oil stock.

He placed his hand over the mouthpiece and said to me, "Indians love oil."

"And firewater," Mickey added from behind me, "among other things."

"And the Great White Father in Washington."

"Keep up the good work," I said and left them to handle the clients who were scheduled to come in that morning.

It was now September, exactly three weeks after Silverman's murder. I was going to press the case.

The precinct house was not all that far from the office and I decided I needed the walk. It felt good to be out in the air even though any break we had from the heat had been brief. At the station I went downstairs to Vice without attracting any attention.

Johnny D. was sitting at his desk tapping out another report in his two-finger style.

"Stakeout over?"

Without looking up Johnny D. said, "We got our quota of fags." He took a deep breath and stopped typing. "I've gotta get outta Vice."

"That's what we all say."

"One of those damn queens could bite me."

"You'd probably poison him."

"All right, Jeremiah, what is it this time?"

"How do I find Amos Billy?"

"The phone book."

"I tried it. He's not listed."

"He moves a lot. Did you try information?"

"Come on, Johnny."

"Whaddya need a pimp for anyway? I thought you P.I.'s got all the gorgeous girls you wanted. For free."

"Only on TV."

Johnny D. walked around his desk, stretched and yawned. His

shirt and pants looked like he had slept in them. The cold butt of
his service revolver jutted from the shoulder holster under his left
arm. "Could this have anything to do with Silverman?" he asked.

"Bingo!" I said and thought of the Chief.

"I'm not supposed to do this kinda thing . . ." Johnny D. began
as he started to make his way through a maze of desks to a small
alcove set up against the far wall. In the alcove were a terminal, a
keyboard, and a chair. Next to it on a small table was a printer. He
sat down at the keyboard and began to type in commands. I could
read the name Billy, Amos on the screen. A few seconds later information about Billy began to print itself out in green letters.

"I heard these are bad for your health," I noted.

"Only if you're pregnant."

Johnny D. activated the printer and a sheet of green and white
striped paper began to come out like a huge lizard's tongue. When
the printer stopped, he tore off the paper at the line of perfora-
tions.

"That's everything we've got."

"How about a picture?"

"You want a picture? Go to an art gallery."

"Come on, Johnny."

"Christ, Jeremiah, you can't miss him."

"Why not?"

"Because he looks like a pimp."

I looked over the information on the printout. "He covers a lot of
territory. From street corners to call girls." I folded up the sheet
and said, "Thanks, Johnny."

"I think we're even," Johnny D. said under his breath.

"I hope not."

"How'd it go with McCurdy?" he asked.

"Didn't need your card." I didn't want to owe him.

"Sure," Johnny D. said and smiled.

As I came up to the main floor I saw Chang standing in an office
doorway. I tried to slip along the wall to the main exit but he spotted me and called out, "Hold it, St. John!"

I quickly shoved the printout into my back pocket. But that
didn't turn out to be the focus of Chang's interest.

He came up to me looking his usual sleek self, once again

demonstrating that Homicide cops dressed better than Vice cops.

"What are you? Some kind of cop groupie?" Detective Chang asked in a voice loud enough for half the room to hear.

"I never thought of it that way," I said as I moved quickly to the door, hoping Chang had no more to say.

"Keep your nose clean."

He could have said things a lot worse than that. He was certainly thinking them.

I took my gun and the Chief to the last address Johnny D. had for Amos Billy. The place was a seedy hotel in an unrestored part of the Tenderloin. There were three winos sitting on the sidewalk in the heat in front of it.

The Chief and I moved towards the entrance when one of the winos got up and lurched forward. I thought he was either going to throw up on us or panhandle. Instead, he grabbed a tarnished brass handle and pulled the door open for us.

He was a thin, wraithlike figure, with very short gray hair and about three days' growth of beard on his face. The stubble was the same color and as long as the hair on his head. His hand was shaking so violently that he had a hard time keeping the door open for us.

I pulled out all of the loose change I had and dropped it into his free hand. He smiled, revealing, to my surprise, a mouthful of yellowed teeth, and saluted. He was wearing the remnants of a doorman's uniform. He had on dark gray pants with a tattered black silk stripe running down the outside of each leg and a jacket from which the brass buttons and epaulets had been torn. His eyes in contrast were bright and alert. They seemed to belong to someone else.

The steaming lobby was early Victorian combined with late decrepit. The potted palms in the corners were brown and dying. The tiles underfoot were cracked and in some places actually crumbling. You had to watch where you stepped. The chairs and couches looked like they had gone through the San Francisco earthquake and fire. I didn't think the place would make it into *America's Hundred Best Hotels* this year.

On a ripped-up leather chair sat a man in his late twenties who was trying hard to look like a hippie. As part of his sixties costume he had tied a red bandana around his upper right arm. It was an eighties sign that advertised he needed a fix.

He looked up at us first with hope and then with hostility. He didn't take us for dealers or users so we had to be narcs. That meant no deal for him while we were there.

Across the room a tall black man in a tank top was making more gestures with his hands than the Giants' third base coach. Every once in a while he would make a motion as if he were cracking a board over his knee.

"Crack," the Chief said behind me. "That's what he's got to sell."

"Among other things," I said as I watched the black run his forefinger along the side of his nose.

Two women, one black, one white, passed behind us and started up the steps to the right. They were each at least six feet tall. The black one wore an enormous blond wig and the white one wore an enormous black wig. They were both dressed in evening gowns the color of red roses.

"Twins?" I asked the Chief.

"Guys."

Chief Moses was right. That was about the only thing that made sense of the situation.

We walked up to the desk where the clerk sat in front of the room key boxes sweating and reading the latest issue of *Penthouse*. The clerk was so transfixed by the gynecological photographs that he didn't notice us. The Chief slammed the desk bell with the open palm of his hand. It sounded more like a shot than a ring. The startled clerk looked up, closed the magazine, but didn't get out of the chair he occupied.

He had a crew cut, a smooth fat baby face, chubby neck, and matching body. I leaned over the narrow counter and saw that he was so short that his feet didn't reach the floor. There was a little stepstool behind the counter to get him up high enough to conduct business.

"What's your pleasure?" he asked us in an unctuous voice. "You two want a room?" He winked his right eye at us.

"I would rather sleep on the tracks," the Chief said.

178

"Fuck you and the pony you rode in on," the clerk replied.

"Little man lives dangerously," the Chief said as he reached for the clerk's collar.

"Easy Chief, remember why we're here," I said.

An unhappy Chief Moses released the clerk.

"I'm looking for a friend." I slipped across some of Sam Fan's more or less hard earned dollars to the lucky little man.

"What friend?"

"Amos Billy."

"Never heard of him," he snapped, cracking his knuckles.

I wondered if it was another signal and turned to look at the other occupants of the lobby. The hippie waiting for someone to respond to his own signal for a fix was in his own world. The tall black was sitting down—resting between innings. No one made a move towards us. The clerk was just cracking his knuckles and sweating.

"Where can we find some girls?" the Chief asked.

"Everywhere."

"I don't see any," I said.

"It's still early."

Chief Moses pushed me aside and got the clerk's fat neck in a stranglehold. There were lines of dirt in the creases of damp white flesh.

"Let us have some cooperation," the Chief said.

"You're choking me."

Behind us the black man and the hippie had vanished. They had to think we were cops. Who else but cops would come in and choke a desk clerk.

"You want girls? I know the man to talk to," the clerk coughed out.

Chief Moses relaxed his hold.

The little man rang the desk bell three times. He stopped and then hit it two more times.

Out from behind a door that had the word "Manager" painted on it stepped a very large Oriental male wearing a Hawaiian print shirt, black shorts, sandals, and mirrored sunglasses. Dead ringer for a martial arts black belt called forth to kick our faces in.

179

The Oriental extended one leg and one arm in a classic martial arts stance. He advanced towards me but Chief Moses stepped in between us. He threw a kick at the Chief and grazed his chin. I was seriously considering pulling the gun I carried under my blazer when the Chief put a shoulder tackle into the black belt's midsection. They both went down to the floor. Tiles cracked under their combined weight. Despite his apparent strength and skills, once under Chief Moses, the Oriental was rendered immobile.

I walked over to the bodies sprawled out on the floor and said, "We're looking for Amos Billy."

The man pressed under the Chief began shouting at us in what must have been his native tongue.

"What's he saying?"

"How the hell do I know," Chief Moses said.

"I don't think we're going to get much here."

Slowly the Chief extricated himself from the Oriental and they both rose and faced each other. I was expecting another round but instead they bowed from the waist to each other. I took a look behind the desk and found that the clerk had vanished. Must have had a trap door installed for just such occasions.

The Chief took my arm. "Let's go, Jeremiah."

As we came out onto the sidewalk the old ghost of a doorman grabbed me and pointed to a wino lying in a spear of sunlight by the front of the building.

"You gotta help him. He just collapsed."

The Chief looked at him in disgust. "He will sleep it off."

Against my better judgment I went over to the body. The man was breathing. I could smell the wine vapors from his mouth and nose. The wino looked at least sixty but was probably younger. His long stringy hair was soaking wet. I felt his forehead and nearly burned my hand. His fever was raging.

"The man's on fire. Call an ambulance."

Chief Moses cursed all winos but went back into the lobby for a phone. For my contribution I grabbed the wino by his coat, dragged him into the shade, and started peeling off his clothes.

He had on two jackets, two pairs of pants, and three pairs of socks. By the time I heard the ambulance coming down the street, weaving its way through the heavy traffic, I had him stripped down to his undershorts.

"Why's he dressed like that in this heat?" I asked the ersatz doorman.

"He's street. You live on the street you live in your clothes. What's he gonna do? Hang his winter clothes in a cedar closet? And most nights are cold. You dress for cold."

"You have a place?" I asked the doorman.

"I make out."

I palmed a five and asked, "Where can I find Amos Billy?"

The attendants were putting the wino on a stretcher. They moved quickly and efficiently, with the economy and grace born of experience.

"I know his corners," the doorman said.

"What do you mean?"

"Where his girls work. Their locations."

It was a start.

Chief Moses materialized beside me as the ambulance sped away.

"I've got an idea," I told the Chief as we drove back to the office.

"Ideas. Another one of the white man's burdens."

Some days it didn't pay to take your colleagues into your confidence.

# 24

"I've got an idea," I told Mickey.

"Put it in the suggestion box," she said.

The Chief thought that was very funny.

I ignored them both and started to walk around her, looking her over from a variety of angles.

"St. John, this is sexual harassment."

"And sexual harassment is not a compliment," I added for her.

"What are you doing besides the obvious?" she asked.

"Mickey, how'd you like to be a hooker for a night?"

"Are you insane?"

"It's all for the cause," I explained.

"Which is?"

"The Silverman case."

Mickey pursed her lips and crinkled up her nose. The Chief looked ready to kill me.

"What exactly am I supposed to do?" she asked.

"You get to be the bait," the Chief said. His tone wasn't pleasant.

"That's attractive."

"And maybe fulfill a woman's fantasy," I made the mistake of saying.

"What do you know about my fantasies?" she asked angrily.

"Not much," I admitted. "I was just kidding."

"Like hell," the Chief said as he swung his legs up over the wobbly arm of the old couch.

"Keep out of my fantasies," Mickey said.

"For now. I promise."

I wondered what her fantasies were? Posing nude in *Playboy* had been one. I also wondered if we would ever have another date.

"Oh, what the hell!" she said finally. "I always wanted to be an undercover cop."

There was one fantasy about to be fulfilled.

"Great!" I said.

"I'll need clothes to fit the part."

Chief Moses shook his head. "Women never have a thing to wear."

There was a boutique a few blocks from the office that according to Mickey sold the right kind of clothing—if you could call it that. The three of us descended on the place. We rummaged through the entire store while a chubby young saleswoman dressed like a discount house version of Madonna and equipped with orange and black hair pulled up into spikes hovered over us. She was all alone and clearly unhappy about it.

"Can I help you? Please?" she pleaded.

"What does your well-dressed hooker wear?" Mickey asked.

"Huh?"

Your well-dressed hooker in this case would wear a red low-cut cotton sweater that was at least a size too small, a short black leather skirt, and high-heeled black boots. In one of the boots there would be added a derringer in case she needed protection on the job. Underneath it all, so to speak, would go a lacy pushup bra to exaggerate her breasts, transparent bikini pants, a matching garter belt, and gray star-studded stockings. Except for the stockings, everything was black. Mickey had insisted on the underwear for authenticity. Chief Moses and I thought she was going overboard in the role but we lost.

"You don't need to be *that* authentic," I said. After seeing the accessories I was beginning to have second thoughts about my plan.

Mickey gave me a grin that exposed those beautiful white teeth. She tossed back her honey blond hair provocatively and winked at me.

"This was your idea." Then she added, "I want to have some fun too."

I didn't say a thing about fantasies and resisted asking how much she was planning to charge for a trick.

Much to the relief of the nervous saleswoman I paid with more of the cash I had earned from Sam Fan. We stepped out on the sidewalk with the Chief and I each carrying a single bag with the name of the boutique and a female silhouette printed on a pink background. The woman inside promptly locked the door and hung up an "Out to Lunch" sign.

"What did we do to her?" Mickey asked.

"The Chief scares women who dress like Madonna."

"We lowered her level of customer," the Chief said.

"Thanks," Mickey said.

"I did not mean you. I meant your pimp over there."

"I'm going to need a new outfit myself, man," I said.

When we got back to the office Mickey went into the bathroom to get dressed for the part. It took her forever but when she finally appeared it was obvious that the wait had been worth it. Against the tightly stretched material of the red cotton sweater I could see the dark shadow of her black bra and above that the full rounded bare tops of her breasts. She had teased her blond hair to exaggerated fullness and put on heavy makeup: powder, rouge, lipstick, eyeshadow and liner. Her face looked like a painted doll's. Her garter belt straps were visible just below the hem of the incredibly short leather skirt. It looked much shorter here in the office than at the boutique. Maybe this wasn't such a good idea. On the other hand I had never seen so much of Mickey revealed before in person.

"Is that the right size?" I asked about the skirt.

"Of course not."

"Now can we see what little is left to the imagination?" I asked.

"You haven't paid yet," she said as she struck a consciously awkward seductive pose. She had one hand behind her neck and pretended to chew gum.

"I think we better order in," the Chief suggested in deadpan.

We had Chinese food delivered in those little white cartons you never see anywhere else except when you buy a live goldfish to carry home.

When it was dark enough for some real action to start, we dropped Mickey off on the first of the corners that belonged to the girls of Amos Billy's stable. The plan was to move her quickly from corner to corner on the theory that a moving target would be harder to hit on. And sooner or later one of those girls would howl and sooner or later Amos Billy would appear to assess the situation on his corners and kick some ass around.

As we followed her in the Thunderbird things happened quickly. Mickey fended off an angry pair of black hookers, walked past a proposition from a sailor, and played deaf to three offers from would-be customers who pulled their late-model cars up to the curb to negotiate a deal for services. Mickey did a good job of moving quickly through the corners that Billy controlled.

Until a confrontation with a short stocky woman with olive skin and curly black hair. She was packed into gold hot pants that were ready to come apart at the seams. The woman was circling around Mickey, gesturing for her to go away, to go to some other corner, to get the hell away from there.

We had moved the car up the block into a parking space by a meter.

The woman in gold was screaming now in a mixture of Spanish and English. If she had been carrying a knife she would have pulled it on Mickey but her clothes were so tight there was no place for her to conceal a weapon. The usual place would be in a boot but she was wearing incredibly high gold spiked heels with open backs and toes. I wasn't sure if I felt any better knowing that Mickey had a small caliber pistol stuffed into her right boot.

It looked like the short wild woman was going to go after Mickey's eyes with her nails.

Instantly, the Chief and I were out of the car. Things were getting too dangerous for our hooker.

Just then a new electric blue Eldorado pulled in at the corner. A black man with a goatee was leaning over from behind the steering wheel, shouting through the passenger-side window.

"Hey, Mexi Mama, cool it!" he yelled out.

"Thees beetch. . ."

"There's enough fo' everybody. Understan'? So cool it!" The man got out of the Eldorado.

The woman in gold turned her back on Mickey and walked with an exaggerated wiggle away from her towards the man.

"Hokay. Hokay. Is cool."

The vanity license plate read BILLY. Nice of Amos to be so helpful.

Billy, dressed in a three-piece grape-colored velvet suit with a slouch-brimmed "pimp" hat to match, was coming on hard to Mickey when the Chief suddenly had him in a half nelson. Billy was struggling to pull something out of his belt.

"Stop fighting, Billy, or he snaps your neck. All it takes is a little more pressure and CRACK!" I warned him as I felt along his waist for a weapon. I found a switch blade. I expected there would be more.

Billy was shouting obscenities; his ugly vocabulary was impressive. Chief Moses shook him and a revolver fell free like ripe fruit from a pear tree.

I packed away his gun, got into his car on the passenger side, and pulled out my own revolver. Meanwhile the Chief deposited Billy behind the steering wheel. Somehow his hat had managed to stay on his head. Chief Moses got into the back seat.

Billy looked around in the car. He looked at the Chief, at me, and at the Smith and Wesson I had pointed at him.

"You the cowboy an' Injun been lookin' fo' me?"

Billy had heard from the midget clerk or the wino doorman.

"Not any more," the Chief said.

The short hooker was pounding on the side of the car with her fists. I locked my door. I saw that Mickey had the good sense to get half a block away from it all. Now she was supposed to get into the Thunderbird and drive back to the office and safety.

"Drive, Billy," I ordered. The motor was still running.

"Come on!" the Chief added.

Billy shifted into drive and pulled away from the curb, laying a strip of rubber down on the street.

"Easy Billy," I said. "We're not looking for attention."

"Nice car," the Chief said.

"If that Mexican broad went an' fuckin' dented it . . ."

I liked the way Amos Billy concentrated on the important things in his life.

"Real nice," I said. "With good air conditioning." The interior of the car was like a refrigerator. The Chief's favorite climate.

"Everythin' electric." With the accent on the first "e" in electric.

"I heard of uncooperative men getting their necks caught in electric windows," the Chief said.

"Or their dicks," I added.

"So don't break any more laws, Billy. Just drive," the Chief said.

"Where, man?"

"Take a left. Over to Geary."

"We're going to Golden Gate Park," the Chief said.

Billy began to sweat. The Park was the quietest and most convenient place in the city to murder a man.

"You don't wanna go to the Park," he said.

"No. You don't want to go to the Park," I said.

The Chief laughed.

Above the high white collar he wore, Billy's dark face was glowing with perspiration. He took off the purple pimp hat and put it down between us on the seat.

"You guys cops. Right?" he asked hopefully. "You just shinin' me on." He grinned at us.

"We are not cops," Chief Moses informed him.

"Then who the fuck are you?"

"Private investigators."

188

That shut Billy up. We drove west on Geary in silence.

"Turn left on Arguello," I said.

Billy turned his head towards me and said, "It's dangerous in the Park at night, man."

"We'll be with you. Don't worry."

"Look straight ahead," the Chief ordered.

Amos Billy snapped to attention.

I felt the wide brim of his soft grape hat. I wondered how I would look in it.

"I don't know nothin'," he insisted as he stopped at a red light.

"We haven't asked you anything," I said.

Billy hit the accelerator before the light turned green and shot the Eldorado out into the intersection. The Chief locked his arm around Billy's thin neck.

"That was stupid."

"No cops aroun' when you need 'em," Billy muttered.

"Obey the traffic laws, Billy," I said. "Or you could get hurt."

"I'm hurtin'!"

Chief Moses released his hold.

"Just remember who's in the back seat."

"No way I can forget, man."

"Turn into the Park."

Amos Billy turned in at Park Presidio.

"Pull over," the Chief ordered. Billy quickly obeyed. We sat in the dark with the motor idling and the air conditioning running.

"I don't know nothin'."

"You said that."

"Then what you want, man?"

"Where'd you get this hat?" I held up the grape hat.

"Huh?"

"Put on the interior light," I said.

Billy fumbled around at the dashboard until he found the right knob. Then he hit the cigarette lighter and reached for a pack of Marlboros wedged in the corner between the windshield and the top of the dashboard.

"No smoking," I said.

"Why, man?"

189

"I said so."

"Shee-it." He put the pack down. The lighter clicked and popped out at him. He made no move for it.

"I want you to look at a picture," I said as I reached into my pocket. I passed him one of the Polaroids.

His mouth seemed to twitch at the corners. His eyes opened just a little wider. Something was frightening Amos Billy, hard man of the mean streets.

"Nice tits," he said in a half-whisper as he tugged at his goatee.

"We know that. Who is she?" Chief Moses demanded.

"Never seen her befo' in my life."

"I don't believe you, Billy. Do you believe him, Chief?"

The Chief's arm clamped itself around Billy's neck again. His Adam's apple was ready to pop through the skin. Very little pressure had to be exerted. Amos Billy's tolerance of pain extended to beating up on his stable of women.

"Okay, man, okay. That hurts. Shee-it. I'd rather deal with the cops any day. They gotta respect your rights."

"We don't, Billy," Chief Moses said.

"That's the beauty of private enterprise."

"You ought to know all about that, Billy," the Chief said.

"About this picture?" I urged.

Billy tried to shake off the Chief's hold. "She ain't with me no more. She ain't been with me 'bout a year."

"Come on, Billy, don't jive us."

"She's back in your stable." I was going on the assumption that she had returned to Amos Billy after Silverman's death.

"She out on her own."

"You let one of your women go? A beautiful white woman? Just like that?" I asked. "I don't believe it."

"All right. I couldn't touch the bitch. She had herself protection. Had herself contacts."

"What kind of protection?" I asked.

"The right kind, man."

"What the hell does that mean?" The Chief applied some extr pressure to remind Billy of his presence.

"Muscle. The law."

"Names, Billy?"

"Don't got no names. Them kinda people don't leave their cards with no nigger pimp."

"What's her name?" I asked.

Billy hesitated, considering his options.

"Come on, Billy."

"Rhoda Bunney."

I turned and looked at the Chief. He shrugged.

"You better not be shining us on," I warned.

"I ain't. I swear. That's her name."

"Where can we find this Ms. Bunney?"

"In the Yellow Pages."

"What are you talking about?"

"She go with a fuckin' escort service. Body Heat, man."

We had everything we needed to get from Billy. I reached out and took back the picture of Rhoda Bunney from him. I told him to turn off the interior light.

"Get out," I said.

"Huh?"

"Get out!" I waved my Smith and Wesson at him.

He reached for his grape hat but I said, "That stays."

Amos Billy got out and I slid over into the driver's seat. He was standing next to the idling car, shouting, "Where you goin' with my wheels?"

I depressed a button and slid the electric window halfway down. Through the opening I said, "We'll leave the car on your corner. Just where we found it. In the tow-away zone."

"You rippin' off my car!"

"Just borrowing it."

"What 'bout my gun?"

"It's under the front seat."

"What I suppose to do?"

"Take a cab."

"Ain't no cabs out here."

"Have a nice walk," the Chief said.

"Have a nice day," I said as I put on Billy's purple pimp hat. The band still felt moist with his sweat.

191

"Ain't you 'shamed to be drivin' 'round in a car like this?" he shouted.

"I like it," I said. "Maybe you could lend me your suit?"

"Fuck you, Honky!" was the politest thing he screamed.

"Watch out for muggers in the Park," I warned as I shut the window. I stepped on the accelerator and shifted into drive simultaneously. The Eldorado almost flattened Amos Billy who was left wildly kicking at invisible objects with his purple suede shoes and tearing at his goatee. I took off the hat so I could see where I was going. Looking at the Chief in the rearview mirror I said, "I think I could use some Body Heat."

"Rhoda Bunney," the Chief said through a whistle.

"With the right kind of protection," I noted.

I parked the Eldorado in a tow-away zone at one of Billy's corners. A block away about twenty women, some muttering, some joking, were being herded by the police into a Hooker Wagon. And then I saw my Thunderbird.

"Shit! The car's still here. Where's Mickey?"

"The wagon?" the Chief asked.

We started to hurry towards the Hooker Wagon when we heard a stage whisper from an alley. We stopped as Mickey stepped out into the light. She told us that she just missed getting picked up in a police sweep of prostitutes.

"We were going to surround the wagon. Just like in the old days," the Chief said.

"You were supposed to drive the Thunderbird back," I said. "Not hang around the streets."

She grinned sheepishly. "I forgot the keys." Then she looked down at her outfit and added, "There was no place to carry them anyway."

"In your boot with your gun," Chief Moses said.

"Can we get the hell out of here? They might come back."

I got the car and picked up Mickey and the Chief. The two of them squeezed into the front. Mickey was in the middle over the drive shaft and the Chief was in the bucket seat. Mickey was trying to tug her skirt down but where she was sitting it was impossible.

"You ought to consider a new car with a back seat," she said.

"I love this T-Bird. At night, with the lights off, it's as invisible as a Stealth Jet," I said as I pulled away from the curb.

"So get another black car. I'm not complaining about the color."

Chief Moses said, "Get a Pontiac."

It was a familiar conversation.

The Hooker Wagon sped by us. Mickey looked at it and said, "I expect a bonus."

"Combat Zone pay," Chief Moses added.

"What else?" I agreed as we drove past the abandoned Eldorado. Amos Billy would wind up paying a nice fat fine to get his wheels back.

"Well, did you learn anything?" Mickey asked me.

I turned towards her and said, "Yeah. That you look great dressed as a hooker."

"I'll remember that for the P.I.'s Ball."

At the next red light I put on Billy's grape pimp hat.

"What's that?" Mickey asked.

"The spoils of war," I said. "Like taking a scalp." I grinned at the Chief.

"Don't blame the Native Americans. The white man started that practice for bounty hunting," Chief said.

"You look like a pimp," Mickey said. "Is that one of your fantasies?"

"I'm working on my image. Remember?" I smiled at her.

"How can you see with that hat on?" she asked.

"I can't."

I took the grape hat off.

# 25

I put on the office lights and hung up the purple pimp hat on the coat rack. I liked the way it looked there.

"What do you expect to learn from Rhoda Bunney?" Mickey asked. The question didn't sound serious coming from a woman dressed like a hooker.

The Chief grinned foolishly while I tried to look grave.

"Some new techniques?" he suggested.

I got out the Yellow Pages and turned to Escort Services. Every ad included at least one photograph of a woman's face or body. You knew whom you were getting. Or thought you were getting.

"I can't believe this," Mickey said. "Look at all these women."

"It must be better than walking the streets," Chief Moses said.

"These are not cheap ads," I noted.

Body Heat like all the other escort services promised you

"warm" young women who would fulfill your fantasies. "Your Satisfaction Guaranteed," the ad read. Under the line "All Major Credit Cards Accepted" it said, "Serving the Bay Area" and listed a 563 exchange.

"I didn't know you could advertise stuff like this in the phone book," Mickey said.

"Sign of the times."

"Isn't it late to call?"

"It says 24-hour service," I said as I dialed the number. After three rings a woman straining for a deep sexy voice answered and said, "Body Heat Escorts. Josephine speaking. Can you hold?"

I held.

"Can I help you?" Josephine finally asked.

"I'd like to engage an escort," I said.

I thought Mickey was going to gag.

"What are the particulars?" Josephine asked.

"Well, Josephine, I would like Ms. Rhoda Bunney for tomorrow night."

There was a long silence on the other end of the line. I thought we'd been disconnected.

Instead she asked, "Has Ms. Bunney served as your escort before?"

"No."

"How did you know about her?"

"By mouth."

"What?" she asked.

"By mouth."

"By mouth?"

"Word of mouth. A satisfied customer."

"I don't know what you're expecting, Mr. . . . . What did you say your name was?" Josephine suddenly sounded as stiff and formal as the Mother Superior of a convent school.

"It's St. John."

"St. John?"

"Do you have trouble with your hearing, Josephine?"

"Sorry." She cleared her throat. "Not everyone who calls this number is a serious client. Let's say we get our share of kinky calls.

196

Sometimes it's hard to tell. Especially late calls like this."

"I'm a serious client, Josephine. My name is Jeremiah St. John and I'm not a kook."

"So he claims," the Chief said.

"You asked what I was expecting. Your ad said 'Satisfaction Guaranteed.' I expect to be satisfied."

"I'm sure you will be," she said cheerfully, her voice modulating to a higher pitch. She was now a saleswoman about to close a deal. She cleared her throat again. I wondered how many cigarettes a day she smoked. "You know, though, our companions require you to provide references."

"Companions?"

"Well, isn't that what you're looking for?"

"If you say so."

"And Ms. Bunney is one of the strictest on that point. She will not companion without a bona fide reference or two. She pronounced the "e" in "fide."

"I have a bona fide reference," I said, pronouncing it the way she had.

"Who?" she asked.

"Rick Silverman, attorney at law."

She hesitated then said, "The man is dead."

"Would you please try it on Ms. Bunney. He hasn't been dead that long. Just three weeks tonight."

"I will have to call you back."

I thought the Silverman reference would make Rhoda Bunney curious enough to escort me if nothing else.

When Josephine called back she said, "There's been a cancellation. Ms. Bunney is available tomorrow night."

"This must be my lucky day."

"Oh, it is."

"Where do I pick her up?"

"I beg your pardon?"

"Where do I pick her up?"

"Oh no, Mr. St. John. We never give out an address. Ms. Bunney will meet you at the place of your choice."

"You sound charming yourself," I tried.

"I'm reservations. I don't companion. And I certainly don't give out addresses." And she wasn't dumb.

I didn't want Rhoda Bunney coming to my office. I had her curious but a P.I.'s office would make her too suspicious. I gave Josephine the name of a restaurant on Fisherman's Wharf.

She sniffed. I pictured her looking like a fifties telephone operator complete with headset and helmet hairdo.

"Are you a tourist?"

"No. Not exactly."

"From out of town?"

"Petaluma." Petaluma was a combination bedroom community and chicken farm above the Bay on the Petaluma River some thirty-five miles north of the city.

"That explains it."

We settled on the price—which was steep, and the time for the meeting at the restaurant.

"Have a nice night," I said as I hung up.

When I looked up, Mickey and the Chief were both grinning at me. So I got up and put on the grape felt hat and leered at Mickey who was still in her hooker outfit.

"It's a tough job but somebody's got to do it."

"Like hell," was all she said. Maybe she was getting jealous.

When I came downstairs the next night in my blazer and slacks, my new shirt and tie, and my polished loafers, Chief Moses and Mickey were long gone. I had asked them to wait after work to tell me if I looked like a tourist from Petaluma. They told me not to worry.

"Don't even try hard," Mickey said.

"Be true to your inner spirit," Chief Moses added.

They were right. I was perfect for the part.

I drove down to the wharf, anxious to be there early. I paid for a very narrow space in a lot across from the restaurant. I was nosed up to the brick back wall of a bakery. On each side of me was a delivery truck. I could barely open the door to let myself out. I wondered if I would ever get the Thunderbird out.

"That's our compact car space," the lot attendant who had directed me in explained. He was a little over five feet tall and didn't look old enough to drive. Maybe the space looked bigger to him.

"Just don't let anyone block me in from behind."

"Hey, don't worry. The lot's full."

I slipped him a buck to make sure.

I wondered how Sam Fan would react when he got the receipt for Body Heat along with my other expenses.

I went up a flight of stairs to the restaurant and took a seat at the bar. From there I could see everyone coming in. I was to recognize Rhoda Bunney by the rose she was carrying in a gloved left hand. Of course, I had other ways of recognizing her.

Two of the walls of the restaurant were solid glass through which I could see the Golden Gate Bridge, the island of Alcatraz, and the boats of the San Francisco fishing fleet, rocking in their berths at the wharf. I watched their bare masts gently rise and fall with the swells, their bone whiteness harsh and intense against the rim of orange sun.

I recognized Rhoda immediately, before I even noticed the glove and the rose. She was even more beautiful in person. I stood up.

"Ms. Bunney, I presume?"

"Mr. St. John?"

I nodded.

She put the rose down and pulled off the white glove.

"What would you like to drink, Ms. Bunney?"

"Please call me Rhoda." She indicated a small table in the cocktail lounge by the window and said, "Do you mind?"

"Not at all."

She moved towards the table, her light linen dress floating loosely about her.

I pulled out her chair for her. It was all part of the illusion that this was an ordinary date.

"I like to sit by the water," she said as she looked towards the Golden Gate where the bridge lights illuminated the falling curtain of darkness.

I signaled to the cocktail waitress.

"A vodka martini. Very dry. On the rocks with a twist," Rhoda ordered from the young Vietnamese woman who appeared at our table.

"The same," I said.

The waitress glided away. Rhoda studied the view. Her red hair was playing like loose fire about her delicate features. The picture had not caught the true color of her hair. Nor of her eyes. Which were like polished jade.

"Do you want me to call you Mr. St. John?"

"Call me Jeremiah."

"Fine." She ran her tongue over her lips. "Jeremiah, I've always found it best to get money matters out of the way first. They can make the evening tense."

"I agree."

"You said you wanted to use American Express?"

"Yes."

Her oversized leather shoulder bag was as big as a briefcase. And for a good reason. Rhoda pulled out a portable version of a device found in almost any store in America: the credit card imprinter. She unfolded the two halves and snapped them into place. People at nearby tables were staring. I looked around and smiled idiotically as I dug out my plain green and white American Express Card from my wallet.

Rhoda took the card and held it up between her thumb and forefinger.

"Sorry it's not gold or platinum."

"As long as it's good," she said as she checked the card number against the book of lost and stolen cards. When she didn't find mine listed she ran it through the machine with an expert forward and back motion. She handed me the charge slip to sign. I signed, noting that the price for the evening had gone up since I spoke to Josephine. This wasn't a time to haggle.

"You have a class operation," I said as I took my customer's receipt and the two carbons.

"I never leave home without it," she said as I tore the carbons in half and put them into the pocket of my coat. There were black smudges on the tips of my fingers. I wiped them off on the napkin.

The drinks came. As we drank Rhoda went into high gear as a

conversationalist. She knew Books, Cinema, and even a little Poli-tics. Her textbook was *Time* magazine out of *People*. I went along with her playing at first date. It was the only way I had a prayer of getting any information out of her.

We finished our drinks and were seated in the dining room where we got the last window table. I ordered another vodka mar-tini for each of us and then we shared a bottle of Chenin Blanc from a chateau in Sonoma with the broiled Mahi-Mahi steaks we had both ordered. After the coffee we had Courvoisier in large snifters. Just as I had hoped, the alcohol was beginning to make Rhoda wan-der from the straight line of *Time* conversation. By the second co-gnac she was on parties she had attended as a companion. It was after she finished describing a University of California alumni event at the Claremont across the bay in Berkeley, that she asked, "Why did you use Rick Silverman's name?"

"I was a friend of Rick's," I said.

She gave me a guarded look. "He never mentioned you."

"Well, he mentioned you."

"I don't believe you," she said.

"I could have used Amos Billy as a reference."

She gulped down the rest of her second Courvoisier. Her body was stiff with tension.

"How do you know Billy?"

"Let's say professionally."

She looked startled. "Oh?"

"You don't seem like Billy's type."

"I wasn't. Let's just say I graduated."

"To Rick Silverman?"

"It started as a way to work my way through college." She paused and waited as though she thought I was going to challenge her. When I didn't she said almost in a whisper, "Then I got to like the money." Rhoda said nothing more. Her face was flushed and her eyes were unfocused.

I signaled to our waiter for the check. When he came she said, "I'd like another cognac, Jeremiah."

"Another Courvoisier for the lady."

After the waiter left, she asked, "What are you? A cop?"

"No. I told you. A friend of Rick's."

The waiter returned, leaving the check with another cognac added on and the total recalculated.

"What do you want?" she asked.

"To find out who murdered him."

"Why?"

"So nobody else gets hurt."

She looked at me thoughtfully. I had reached her on some level. "What do you want to know?"

"What was your relationship with Silverman?"

"Sex."

"That's to the point. What else?"

"What else is there?"

"How'd you meet him?"

She thought that one over for a long time. I was sure she had a story rehearsed.

And she did.

"By chance in a bar." The words were slurred slightly.

"And you two just hit it off?"

"Yeah." She sipped her cognac rather sloppily.

"I don't believe you."

Rhoda sighed. "He was Amos Billy's lawyer and Billy owed Rick. I was . . . payment."

"Permanent?"

"That's how it turned out."

"Did Rick get you the job at Body Heat?"

She was fighting the alcohol, trying to keep her story straight. But it was too late. At least I thought so.

"Yeah," she finally said.

"So you've been working there for the past year?"

"Yeah."

"Did you have companions that Rick was interested in?"

"Why would he be?"

"Business reasons."

"Sometimes."

"Who?"

"I can't give you names."

"Why not?"

202

"Why not? I'm scared. Look what happened to Ricky."

I had never thought of Silverman as Ricky. I had never heard it used by anyone else before. It just didn't fit.

I tried my best but Rhoda Bunney would say nothing more about either Amos Billy or Silverman. Despite the alcohol I had the feeling she wasn't as incoherent as she wanted me to believe. She was still hiding the specifics of whatever operation she had been involved in with Silverman. What I needed to do was to find out where she lived. As it turned out, I've done easier things.

At first I thought there would be no problem when she offered, "We could make this a nice night." She had trouble saying "nice night." I assumed the proposition would get me to her place. But when I offered to drive her home she suddenly sobered up. "Your place," she said crisply.

"My brother's visiting from Nevada," I lied.

"So?"

"So. How about your place?"

"No."

"You don't want to drive all the way to Petaluma," I said.

"There are other options."

The argument went on a little too loudly all the way down the steps to the front of the restaurant. Finally she said, "Okay, get your car."

"Come on," I said, pleased that she had given in.

"I'm too dizzy to walk," she said.

I ran over to the lot for my car but I found it blocked in by a pickup truck.

"Damn!"

"Sorry about that, but I made him leave the keys," a new attendant explained. I had wasted my buck tip.

"Well, just get it out of the way," I said angrily.

"All right, man, all right." The attendant was at least six-eight but he didn't look like he weighed more than a hundred fifty pounds.

I turned to look back at the restaurant and I saw Rhoda getting into a taxi. I ran into the street to try and catch the cab's license number but missed it.

In the lot the attendant was still maneuvering the pickup truck, trying to get enough room for me to back out. I felt like slashing its giant black tires.

Rhoda Bunney had done a hell of a job on me.

I drove along the Embarcadero towards Mickey's place, wondering how she would react to a surprise visit. At her door Mickey checked me through the peephole and, after enough time passed to drive me crazy, she unbolted and unchained it. I stepped into an apartment that was ruthlessly Danish Modern.

As if reading my mind, Mickey said, "It comes furnished. It's functional."

"I didn't say anything."

"What do you want?" she asked. Mickey was wearing a soft blue robe that she held tightly drawn about her.

"To talk."

"Then sit down."

We both sat down at each end of the couch; it was like sitting on a board. She didn't object as I put my feet up on her teak and tile coffee table.

"Do you want a drink?" she asked.

I shook my head.

"How was Ms. Bunney?"

"It was strictly business."

"I know what kind of business she's in."

I just shook my head. "Believe me. I wouldn't chance it with a hooker. No matter what."

"What you do is your business," Mickey said.

"And you don't care?"

"No . . ." It was not a very firm no.

"I want it to be your business, Mickey."

I got up, offered her my hands, and pulled her up gently from the couch. She came to me easily and lightly as I took her in my arms and kissed her. I slipped the robe off her shoulders and it fell simultaneously open and down, revealing high full breasts and a light haired pubic V. I hadn't expected to find her naked under the robe. "I just got out of the tub," she said. Pressing against her warm flesh, I wanted my clothes off. More than anything I wanted to make love to her.

I placed my hands on her shoulders and stood back to look at her as if I were admiring a sculpture. She put her hands on her hips and smiled back at me. The robe was lying on the floor.

"Is that your *Playboy* pose?" I asked although I knew it wasn't.

"Men are all voyeurs."

"It's cultural conditioning. Women are all exhibitionists. It keeps us interested in each other."

"You want to see the pose that got me fired?"

"Love to."

She moved naked across the room to a rocking chair, swung her legs up over an arm of the chair into a tight but still revealing V as she sat down, and put her hands behind her head, pushing up her hair into tangles. She gave me a vacant, slack-jawed smile. I remembered it all very well. Especially since I saw it every time I opened the locker in my upstairs gym. I wondered if I would ever have the nerve to show it to her. Hell, I didn't have enough nerve to tell her about the vintage collection of hard-boiled detective novels I had up there.

"There I was," she said. "All of policewoman me. The photographer had to get down on the floor to shoot it at the right angle. I ended up showing more than anyone else in the spread. No pun intended." She grinned. "Really. I couldn't believe it when I saw it. Why couldn't I have been one of the girls with clothes on? Or at least I could have been posing demurely with a hand or two in the right places. Like art."

"I guess they liked all of you."

"I felt like a fool. Worse, now I still feel like a fool." She climbed out of the contorted position that she had taken in the rocker.

"You're beautiful," I told her.

"You should have seen the pictures they didn't print."

"Why? I've got the real thing."

The next morning I sat up in Mickey's hard Danish Modern bed. Sunlight pouring into the room had awakened me. The sheet and the blanket slipped down to my waist. Beside me, Mickey stirred.

"Will you move in with me?" I asked her although I wasn't sure she was awake. But she heard me. She sat up next to me with the sheet modestly pulled up to nearly cover her breasts.

"You snore," she accused.

"So do you," I responded.

"I'll think about it," she said as she slipped back under the blanket so far that her head disappeared. I went down with her—so to speak.

It took us over an hour to get out of the apartment.

In the car on the way to the office I repeated my question to Mickey: "Will you move in with me?"

"Not only do you snore, you take too long in the bathroom."

I sat in silence waiting for a red light to change.

"Does that mean no?" I asked as I shifted into first and stepped on the accelerator. We started up a steep incline.

"You're the private detective. You figure it out."

"That's what everyone says."

# 26

By the time we got to the office that Wednesday morning the Chief was already there. He looked at us curiously as we came in together but didn't say anything. Instead he asked about Rhoda Bunney and I told him what had happened. He resisted the urge to comment.

A half-hour later we had our case work sorted out. I was going to give Rita Silverman another try. Chief Moses said that I was spending too much time on the case and I agreed. But I was still going to see Rita. I called her office. They said she no longer worked there. I got her at home.

Rita and her son remained suspects, but they were long shots. I was more interested in trying to jar free a few of her memories of Silverman that could relate to his murderer. I just needed the right questions. I hoped.

When I appeared at her apartment she acted glad to see me. She seemed more relaxed. We sat down with mugs of fresh coffee.

"No work today?" I asked.

"I quit."

"Oh? How are you and Richard doing?" I asked.

"I've sent Richard off to prep school. You'll never find him."

"I don't want to," I replied to her challenge.

"And what about me?" she asked.

"I've got more likely suspects." Actually that wasn't true. But it wouldn't hurt anything to make her feel a little complacent.

"So it's a social visit. Nice," she said. "I quit my job because things are looking up. I'm going to get rid of all this *schlock*." She indicated the furniture. She started bouncing around the room. She was energized.

"This have anything to do with the infamous garbage bag of money? That tarnish on my image?"

"Right." She grinned. "It looks like it'll be part of the estate."

"Well, well." I wouldn't want to be the one to tell Sam Fan about this turn of events.

"I earned it."

"I'm sure you did."

She plopped down in one of the chairs she detested.

"Come on, St. John. Out with it."

"I still have very few answers," I admitted.

"Okay. Let's try it again. Maybe it'll come out different this time."

I cradled the mug of coffee in my hands and asked, "After he left you, did you see Silverman much?"

"As seldom as possible."

"But you did see him."

"Once in a while. When he came to visit Richard. Sometimes he was impossible to avoid."

"Did he talk about his law practice?"

"He bragged," Rita said grimly. "He bragged about his cases. His drug traffickers. His Colombian cowboys. How big time he was now. How he did things his own way. He made me sick."

"How was he doing before the big drug cases?"

208

She stared into her mug. "Not bad; not good. I don't really know. He was always running around on me and that costs. He didn't get his women for free. Not the kind he went after."

"When did the coke start?" I asked.

"I'm not sure exactly. But before he started making it big with the drug clients."

"So he gets into coke. And then at some point his life changes. He learns Spanish. He wins big cases. He has megabucks."

"You sound like him," she said as she put her empty mug down.

"Sorry." I paused. "Think about it, Rita. First the coke and then the clients and the acquittals."

"So?" she asked.

"He had something on a lot of people."

"Like what?"

"He had a blackmail setup."

"How, Jeremiah?" she asked.

"I'm not exactly sure. And I doubt that he set it up by himself." I didn't want to go into details I didn't really have. But whatever Rick Silverman had operated with Rhoda, he must have had another partner. Someone involved with Rick in this could have had the motive to kill him. "Did he ever mention anyone? Somebody tied to the cocaine?"

"No."

"He must have talked about someone."

"No."

"What about Rhoda Bunney?"

"What's that? Some kind of game?"

"A name."

"I don't believe it."

"Come on Rita. There must be someone. What about Vietnam? Did he ever talk about the war?"

"I told you. Never. He never talked about the war. He did talk about the law. And corruption. He talked about corruption in the courts. He would laugh about it. He would call them all fools."

"Who?"

"Everybody."

"Can you be more specific?"

209

"He was never specific."

"Everybody?" I half-whispered to myself.

So no leads from Rita, just half of her cold quiche for lunch and some small talk that had nothing to do with the case.

I could have kicked myself for letting Rhoda lose me last night.

I drove back to the office and spent the rest of the afternoon trying to sort things out with Mickey and Chief Moses. Whenever I had some kind of pattern established Mickey and the Chief demolished it. Hell, what else are partners for? Only Mickey wasn't just a business partner anymore. Looking at her made me ache to hold her and to make love to her.

At the end of the day when I thought I had enough conflicting elements in precarious balance I decided to go see Sam Fan. I needed his sledgehammer approach to things. And he expected a report. And my expenses.

Fan's office was already closed when I arrived but I got an answer when I pounded on the outside hall door. Sam Fan ushered me in and then carefully locked up behind us. He took me to the office that he was still trying to settle comfortably into.

"Working late?" I asked.

"Are you?"

He settled back into what had once been Silverman's chair. His briefcase was lying open on the desk.

"So what do you got, St. John?" he asked as he indicated a chair for me with a cavalier wave of his hand. He tugged at his loosened tie with pudgy fingers.

I kept right on standing.

"What was in the safe, Sam?"

He hunched forward; the top of his head gleamed at me. "I don't know."

"Come on, Sam."

"Silverman called it his edge."

I had heard that before from Evelyn Moss. The pieces were just beginning to fall into place. "You didn't hire me to find Silverman's killer. You wanted Silverman's edge. Find the killer and find the edge and deliver it to you."

"You're smarter than I thought. I don't like that in a P.I.," Sam said. Then he smiled and added, "What's the difference? You go about the case in the same way." He bit down on the moist end of an old unlit cigar he had picked up from an ashtray.

I thought his question over. "Maybe none. Maybe a lot."

"What's the problem?" He was lighting the cigar with a silver lighter he had just taken out of his pants pocket.

"No problem," I said and grinned at him. I took a quick step behind his desk and swung open the picture of the junk that now covered the safe. I looked at the lock.

"I had a locksmith change the combination."

"Except it's empty."

"Only until you deliver what I'm paying you for."

"I know," I said as I came around the front of the desk. We weren't talking about Silverman's murderer anymore.

"So you got anything?" Sam asked.

I dug into my blazer pocket. "These receipts for expenses on the case."

"You cost me more than you're worth," Sam Fan said without looking at the receipts, which included the charge to Body Heat Escorts.

"I've got some leads."

"Like what?"

"Like setting up the prosecution in incriminating or compromising positions."

"Sounds effective. You got proof?"

"I'm close," I said.

"Then what the hell are you doing here talking to me? Go get closer." Sam picked up the receipts and started thumbing through them. He shook his head. "On the way out make sure the door is locked."

I got the message. But before I left his office I had to ask, "How come Silverman didn't let you in on any of this?"

Sam Fan stood up, his hands balled into fists on the desk. "Let's just say we had different areas of legal expertise."

I shut the door behind me. It was eerily silent in the empty office suite; I felt as if I had wandered out of a silver-plated cave. The image of Rick Silverman dead on the rug came back to me and

I realized that the bloodstained carpeting had been replaced.

As I passed Victoria's desk I couldn't help wondering what she was really up to. Still I trusted my instincts that she had not been the one to kill Silverman despite the obvious revenge motive. I also wondered exactly what she knew about Fan's and Silverman's division of labor. This visit had me curious about a lot of things. I closed the outside office door behind me, making sure it was locked. It seemed like a futile gesture. Too many people knew about the other entrance from the parking lot and the street.

As I rode the elevator down I thought about going into the business of blackmail. In this case it didn't bother me. I had a very good idea of exactly what I was looking for. And if I found Rick Silverman's edge I knew exactly what would happen to it. It would end up on the bottom of San Francisco Bay long before it got anywhere near Sam Fan's hands. Although I would feel bad about polluting the bay.

I tried not to imagine the look on Sam's face when I told him.

I waited in my T-Bird on the street across from the parking lot next to Fan's office building. Fifteen minutes later Sam came out and walked over to his Porsche. I started my car up. I let him get on the street before I joined the flow of traffic. I could just as easily have walked. He drove to a restaurant less than three blocks away and left the Porsche by a sign at the entrance that said "Valet Parking." He went into the restaurant while the valet drove his car a few yards over to the Chevron station on the corner and parked it by the rest rooms. Just as Victoria had said, Sam Fan took his Porsche everywhere. I considered waiting for Sam to come out of the restaurant and continuing the tail. I decided I was wasting my time. Besides I couldn't find a parking space. As it turned out, I should have waited.

I drove back to my office and had to park two blocks away. I picked up an evening *Examiner* from old Blind Benny's newsstand and read that we had gone through the hottest summer since the gold rush. I switched to the sports section to read about the 49ers and think about football and autumn. This Saturday was the last exhibition game before the season began.

# 27

My conversation with Sam Fan had not really changed anything. I was going after Silverman's edge and when I had it I had the killer. Simple. Beautiful in its economy. But also theory, and theories don't always work out in their specific applications.

The next morning I called Fan's office, expecting Victoria to answer the telephone. She did. I asked her about the division of labor between Fan and Silverman.

"I don't know much about it." she said softly. "Beyond the obvious."

"Can you look into it?"

"Sam purged the files."

"Not much left?"

"Not much at all."

"Interesting. Anything else you can remember about the day Silverman was shot?"

"No."

"I'll stay in touch." So Sam had purged the files, that was curious, I thought as I hung up.

Leaving Mickey to meet with a prospective client who was coming into the office, Chief Moses and I headed for the courthouse. We had decided on the Chief by playing a game of Texas Hold 'Em between Mickey and the Chief. The winner would go and the Chief had won.

"How come *you* always get to go?" Mickey had complained to me as we started to leave.

"Because my name is on the window, the stationery, and the business cards. I am the eponymous founder of the agency and people expect to see me. That's why."

"Eponymous?"

"Look it up."

A message to Judge Troutvelter that I had something on the Silverman case got me into his chambers during a recess. Chief Moses, dressed in his FSU T-shirt and faded jeans, stayed out in the corridor. I didn't want the judge to think I was trying to intimidate him. Although I had the impression that he didn't intimidate easily.

The judge was dressed in his black robe. I avoided his eyes and looked at the full bookcases rising to the ceiling behind his desk.

"I don't have much time, Mr. St. John."

"I appreciate that. I'd just like to lay out what I have on the Silverman case."

Troutvelter suddenly looked weary. His face was drained of all color. He had aged since our last meeting.

"All right. Lay it out." He pointed to the leather chair and I sat down.

"What turned Silverman into a big winner?"

Troutvelter seemed to look right through me. "Screwups in court."

"Right," I said.

"Don't ask me goddamned rhetorical questions, St. John."

"Sorry, your honor."

"So?"

"The screwups were forced by Silverman. He had something on enough people to turn the screws when he had to."

"In this business everybody has something on somebody," the judge said.

"Even you?"

He just stared at me, letting me draw my own conclusion.

"Who was screwing up?" I asked.

"You mean whom did Silverman control?"

"Yes."

Judge Troutvelter took his time over that one. Finally he said, "Everybody screws up." It sounded like he was handing down a court decision. His eyes were dark holes in his face.

"You know that's not good enough," I said.

"A defendant is presumed innocent until proven guilty. I've lived with that one too long. Look at the newspapers; draw your own conclusions."

There was a knock on the door to the judge's chambers. Troutvelter stood up, took a deep breath, and smoothed his robes with the palms of his hands. I drew my own conclusion that the meeting was over.

As he came out from behind his desk he said to me, "You led me to believe you knew more about the Silverman case than you do. Let me give you some friendly advice. Be careful." Without the desk in front of him he looked frail.

Out in the hall I told the Chief what Troutvelter had said.

"Be careful?" Chief Moses asked.

As we walked towards an exit sign the Chief drew his usual share of stares.

"Don't worry." I said in a loud voice, "I'm just taking him to the gas chamber for execution."

"You feeling self-conscious about me?" he asked.

"I keep telling you that you've got to do something about your clothes. You always look like one of the homeless."

"Sometimes I am one of them, Jeremiah. Sometimes they are my people. Besides I like my Florida State T-shirt. I like the Seminole head on it."

"I know. And sometimes I pass you off as a retired Oakland

Raider. But you need a three-piece suit for certain occasions."

"Bull, you don't wear one."

"I wear a blazer and slacks. Ivy League. Besides I don't look like you."

"The entire Indian nation thanks you for that blessing from the Great Spirit."

"Just one suit?"

"I will give it serious consideration. Can it be a business expense?"

It was another conversation we had at least once a month.

We walked down a flight of marble stairs to the main floor. At the door, Chief Moses stopped and asked again, "Be careful?"

We both wondered what the judge meant.

Back at the office the three of us went over the newspaper stories that Mickey had copied one more time. They had given me Victoria Justice and I hoped that they would provide more. Each of us had a list of possibilities and we made independent notes on each case. We were concentrating on finding basic technical errors in procedure that blew the case and handed it to Silverman on what I called a "Silverman platter." Mickey and the Chief rolled their eyes at that particular attempt at humor. Bad jokes aside we found a lot. Too many to be just a coincidence or a comment on the competence of prosecuting attorneys, arresting officers, and judges.

"Well?" I asked as Mickey put down the last sheet.

She slipped me a folded piece of paper on which she had written a name. Chief Moses did the same. I followed suit. I handed all three to Mickey and she read them off: "Vorflagel. Vorflagel. And Vorflagel. It's unanimous."

"Remember what Arthur Martin said, 'Vorflagel's an asshole.' "

"But we saw him in court," Mickey said. "He was good."

"You picked him too," the Chief reminded Mickey. "Are you changing your mind?"

"When we saw him in court Silverman was dead," I noted. "The heat was off."

"Cause and effect," Chief Moses said.

"You're right. And motive," Mickey added.

The choice seemed clear. "Let's find out about Vorflagel and Silverman's edge."

Mickey rubbed her hands together. "Isn't blackmail fun?"

As we worked together on our plan of action, the red warning light blinked on. Mickey went out to play the receptionist. Whom she brought back was a surprise. And not a pleasant one. I got up.

Impeccably groomed as usual, Detective Chang walked into my office and said, "I want to talk to him. Alone." Chang indicated me with the manicured nail of his right forefinger.

"Have a seat," I said.

Chief Moses left.

"This won't take that long." Chang was not going to sit down.

I sat on the edge of my desk.

"This is your last warning, St. John. The Silverman case is closed. Keep your damn nose out of it."

"Or what?"

"Or I will have your worthless license."

Who was he protecting? There was someone Chang did not want involved in this murder. Which pumped up my adrenaline.

Chang moved to the door and then turned to me: "Not a bad place you have here."

"It's close to Chinatown."

"Every place is close to Chinatown."

I followed Chang out. He barely nodded at Chief Moses and Mickey in the middle office as he departed.

"Don't tell me," Mickey said, "he told you to keep your nose clean."

"What are you going to do?" Chief Moses asked.

"I'm going to be inconspicuous."

"That ought to be easy for you," the Chief concluded. "Now I must go." He was on his way to a date with a USF coed he had met at a John Wayne Film Festival.

I locked the door and shut the blinds.

"What are you doing?" Mickey asked.

"What do you think I'm doing?"

"Fulfilling your fantasy to mix business and pleasure and make love in the office."

"How'd you ever guess?" I asked.

"Women have fantasies too."

"I think that's what I've always said."

We undressed in the shadowy light cast by the lamp in the corner of the room. We made love slowly, savoring each other on the old couch—which I would never be able to look at in the same way again. Finally, control spent, we came together.

After awhile, I said, "Move in with me."

"Why?"

"That's where you belong."

"No."

"Why not?"

"Fear."

"Of what?"

When she didn't answer I repeated my question.

"I'm not sure. I'm not even sure business partners should be lovers."

I thought of my time in the D.A.'s Office.

Suddenly it seemed cold in the room and we shivered in our nakedness. I held her close. I didn't want to lose her.

# 28

The next day was a Friday and I rose early and left before Mickey came in. We had two cases to pursue. One was marital infidelity which the Chief refused to take. I decided to handle it, hoping that a different case might give me a little better perspective on Silverman. The Chief was going to spend the day sticking with a possible embezzler who we suspected would try to disappear soon.

I was tailing a blonde of a certain age who met a dark Hispanic-looking male very much her junior at a corner bar across from a motel off Lombard that promised water beds, X-rated films, free condoms, and other assorted amenities for soul and body. In the bar I drank a Henry's and waited for them to make a move. I didn't have to wait long. They headed off to the motel across the street and with the new miniature Nikon we had bought for the agency I got some good pictures of them going in. Two hours and three

219

beers later I got them coming out. The woman looked like she had just bounced off a trampoline; the man looked like he had spent the time styling his hair. The P.I. business goes on.

It was late afternoon when I got back to the office. I found Mickey trying to console a grumpy Chief. The guy the Chief referred to as the Caucasian male he was tailing had gone through a department store building at Union Square and come out on another street, losing the Chief.

"Buffalo shit," was all the Chief could say in summary. "Some Indian tracker."

"It happens. It's part of the job," I reassured him.

He grunted. "He will be in Brazil."

"So you'll get a nice trip out of it. Right now we have a trap to set." I went back over the details of what we had come up with yesterday before Chang had interrupted us.

The three of us drove over to Sam's office to enlist his help. I would have liked Sam to be the bait but I knew he wouldn't be too interested in the role. We got there as the office was closing for the day. Victoria and the twins were getting ready to leave.

Victoria smiled and said, "He's still in his office." She buzzed him on the intercom. "Go right in."

The three of us marched into the office and took over every available chair. Mickey and Chief Moses immediately became preoccupied with the decor that I had described for them. Sam finally looked at ease in Silverman's old office.

"Are all the troops necessary?" Sam asked.

"We like to give it our all," I explained.

Sam Fan distorted his face into what was to pass for a smile and looked Mickey and the Chief over. They looked back.

"We need your help, Sam," I said.

"Is that what I'm paying you for?"

"Hear me out."

"Okay. So talk." Fan swung his feet up on the desk. His soles and heels were thick and I suspected that he was wearing lifts inside of his boots.

"I want you to get the hell outta here, Sam," I said imitating Sam's voice with Humphrey Bogart gestures.

"What are you doing?" Fan asked as he swung his feet back down. "Getting up an act for Vegas?"

"I'm imitating you, Sam," I said in the same voice.

Sam Fan looked to Mickey and the Chief: "I sound like that?"

"Close enough," Mickey said and the Chief nodded.

"So what's the point?" he asked. His eyes were on Mickey's legs.

"The point is to bait a trap," I explained.

"With me?"

"If you like," Chief Moses said.

"With an imitation of you. That's what you're paying us for."

"Unless you want to stay," the Chief suggested.

"How soon do you want me out?" Fan asked.

"Bye, Sam," I said.

"Don't forget to lock up," he said as he stuffed his briefcase full of papers. Then he and the briefcase disappeared faster than you could say Rick Silverman.

"Why didn't you let Fan call?" Mickey asked.

"We don't have to tell him anything this way."

I worked up my phone routine with my colleagues and they agreed that it wasn't half bad. I was ready.

I got Vorflagel at the D.A.'s Office. In my best Sam Fan voice I told him I had something he would be interested in. Something from Rick Silverman's safe. That got the Deputy D.A.'s attention.

"What?" Vorflagel asked.

"Not on the phone. Come down to my office and we'll talk about it."

"Are you alone?" he asked.

"Yeah."

"Good." He hung up.

"Deputy D.A. Vorflagel wanted to know if I was alone," I said. "He was so interested he believed me when I said yes."

"Do you think he's coming to kill Fan?" Mickey asked.

"What do you think?"

We couldn't have been waiting more than fifteen minutes when the outer door opened. We had left it unlocked so Vorflagel could walk right in. We heard him at the receptionist's desk, trying the interior door. I pressed a button that released the lock. Then there was silence. Vorflagel was moving down the hallway with caution. I sat behind Sam's desk. The Chief stood behind the silver-plated door. Mickey was in an office down the hall.

We had discussed several options and decided to leave the door to Fan's office wide open. There would be less of a possibility of Vorflagel crashing in and firing a weapon if the door was already open and he could see his adversary.

"Fan?" I heard Vorflagel call.

"In here." I didn't bother to disguise my voice.

Vorflagel swung into the open door space, dropped to one knee, and braced his right arm with his left. Pointed at me was the massive barrel of a .357 Magnum.

I raised my hands straight over my head. "Don't shoot," I shouted.

"Who are you? Where's Fan? What's going. . ." Before he could finish the Chief came from behind and trapped him in a bear hug. As he dropped the Magnum a shot went off, tearing into the front of the desk. Shakily, I managed to stand up.

"You're dangerous, Vorflagel."

"Get this goon off of me!"

"MICKEY!" the Chief bellowed.

She appeared in the doorway with a look of relief on her face.

"Get the gun," the Chief ordered. Mickey stooped over and picked it up. She turned the Magnum on the Deputy D.A. It looked huge in her hand.

Chief Moses frisked Vorflagel and released him from his hold. Then he relieved Mickey of the Magnum.

"What happened to Fan?" a very subdued Vorflagel asked.

"He left for his health," the Chief explained.

"What the hell is this all about?"

"About the murder of Rick Silverman."

"I didn't kill him."

"Yet you walked in here with a Magnum ready to blow away Sam Fan. Maybe you're working on closing down the firm."

Vorflagel averted his eyes.

"I know how you performed in court before Silverman's death. You blundered away cut and dried cases because Silverman had something on you. Rick Silverman had you by the balls! And now it was Fan's turn."

The Deputy D.A. stood in silence.

"You taking the fifth?" I asked.

"I just wanted to scare Fan," he said.

I walked in front of the desk and looked at the bullet hole. "That'll do it."

"It went off by accident," he said.

"Did it just go off by accident when you shot Silverman?" Chief Moses asked.

"I didn't kill Silverman!"

The Chief shoved him into a chair.

"I'm a Deputy D.A.," he said weakly. It didn't sound like the threat he intended it to be.

"I know all about the type," I said.

Mickey, playing the good guy, said, "I don't think he killed Silverman."

The Chief laughed.

"She's right."

"Then maybe we can work out a deal," I said.

He looked up at me. "Deal? I don't know what the hell you want. I don't even know who the hell you are."

"I'm Jeremiah St. John, a P.I. trying to find Silverman's murderer."

"Why should I deal with you? The case is closed."

"I can make trouble for you," I warned.

"I'm a Deputy D.A."

"You said that," the Chief said.

"You blew cases because Silverman had you in his back pocket."

"You can't prove it."

"I don't have to prove it. I'm not taking it to court. I'm working with rumor and innuendo and unnamed but reliable sources. They'll ruin a career as easily as a felony conviction."

Vorflagel was squirming in his seat. Perspiration was beading on his forehead and his glasses were slipping forward on his nose. "What do you want?"

"What did Silverman have on you?"

"Then Fan doesn't have it?" Vorflagel asked.

"No."

"And you don't have it?"

"No," I said.

"Then why am I talking to you?"

I pointed to the Chief and the gun. "And because you want to find the real murderer, don't you? And because I know we're talking about Silverman's edge. And sooner or later I'll find it. And when I do it would be a lot better for you to be on my side."

Slowly Vorflagel pulled out a pack of True cigarettes from his inside jacket pocket and asked, "Do you mind?"

"Go ahead," I said. The guy was considerate.

He lit up.

"It came in the mail," Vorflagel said as he exhaled a cloud of smoke.

"What did?" I asked.

"Silverman's fucking edge. Tapes."

"Of what?" I asked.

"There are three of you here. You ought to be able to figure it out." Vorflagel sucked on the cigarette.

"Sex. Drugs. And Rock 'n' Roll!" Mickey blurted out.

"Something for everyone. My wife . . . the D.A. . . ."

"How'd Silverman get this performance?" I asked.

"I met a woman . . ."

"At Monday's?" I asked.

"Yes."

I pulled out my photograph of the Rhoda Bunney painting.

"That's her."

"Where did you go?"

"To her place." He crushed out the half-smoked cigarette in the silver fan-shaped ashtray.

The place Rhoda Bunney was trying to keep me away from.

"The address. Can you remember it?"

"I'll never forget it. Not for the rest of my life." Vorflagel gave us a Russian Hill address. Then he reached for another cigarette from his pack.

"No more," I said.

He looked at me curiously but put the pack away.

"And no one asked for a payoff for the tapes?" I asked.

"No."

"You could just have a copy."

"It was the Master and a copy," Vorflagel said.

"There could be others," the Chief said.

Vorflagel sighed. "There could be but I don't think so. Except for Fan. I was worried Fan had a copy."

"Who do you think sent you the tapes?" I asked.

"A good Samaritan," Vorflagel said.

"Only he got them by knocking off Silverman," Mickey noted.

"I don't know that. But it would be justifiable homicide in my book." Vorflagel looked like that possibility bothered him despite what he said. The man wasn't telling us everything he knew.

"Can I leave?" Vorflagel asked.

"Describe Rhoda's apartment."

He did. In intimate detail.

"Now?" he asked.

I thought it over, looked at my partners, and decided we could let him go.

I nodded my head and Vorflagel stood up.

"Can I have my gun? I need the protection."

"Give the Deputy D.A. his Magnum," I told the Chief.

"Loaded?"

I decided to chance it. "I don't think he's going to murder us here."

Chief Moses reluctantly handed Vorflagel the gun by the handle and he holstered it under his jacket. The bulge from the weapon was noticeable. I wondered why he needed a Magnum. Probably he saw too many movies.

As Chief Moses escorted him out I dug for the bullet lodged in the front of the desk. It popped out into my hand.

When the Chief came back in I held up the bullet for him to inspect.

Mickey said, "We shouldn't have given him back that cannon."

"Maybe he'll shoot himself in the foot with it," I said. I expected him to make some kind of mistake. We had rattled the man.

225

By eight o'clock I was driving to the Russian Hill address Vorflagel had given me when I saw the flashing red, white, and blue bar of a police car in the rearview mirror. I wondered if a taillight had gone out. They signaled me over into a bus stop. Three figures converged on my car. I heard the crunch of splintering plastic. A nightstick had just put out my taillight. I looked up into the face of Detective Chang. Behind him were two huge cops.

"What's the problem, officers?" I tried keeping my tone light.

"Don't give us any lip," Chang ordered.

"Who me?"

Chang reached through the car window and began to apply pressure to my collar bone. I grabbed his hand and tried to free myself.

"He is resisting," Chang announced.

The two cops who looked like they played guard for some semi-pro team instantly had the door open and, almost as quickly, had me out of the driver's seat and spread-eagled against the car. One of them frisked me with his huge paws and came up with my Smith and Wesson.

"Broken taillight, erratic driving, assaulting an officer, resisting arrest . . . Let's search the vehicle," Chang ordered.

"This is bullshit," I protested.

One monster kept me pinned against the T-Bird while the other one searched the car. It didn't take him long to come up with a glassine bag of white powder. Chang took it and held it up in front of my nose.

"I told you to keep your nose clean," he said to me. Then he turned to the searcher. "Where did you find it?"

"Under the front seat," the cop said.

"You bastard, Chang, that's a plant." I said it calmly. There wasn't anything I could do.

"You have the right to remain silent . . ." the other cop began to read to me from a laminated card the back of which was printed in Spanish. I wondered if he had a pack of them with a card for every language spoken in San Francisco. His voice took on the quality of a priest chanting high mass as he performed the ritual.

"Come on, Chang, enough is enough. I get the point. There was no probable cause for searching the vehicle and you know it."

Chang just smiled at me.

"What do you really want?" I asked.

"I warned you. Now it's too late. You're under arrest," Chang said.

"What's the point?" I tried again.

"To put you where you belong."

"You mean to get me out of the way," I said. "To keep the Silverman killing covered up."

"You're a public nuisance. You bother people."

Deputy D.A. Vorflagel had tipped him. And if Vorflagel and Chang were working together, what was going on? I imagined Chang starring in one of Silverman's Made-for-Blackmail tapes. When it came to human behavior anything was possible.

"So Deputy D.A. Vorflagel gave you a call," I said, hoping to get a reaction out of Chang.

He was inscrutable.

# 29

Overhead the cars roared by on the elevated section of Interstate 80 that someone had named the San Francisco Skyway. I wished I were up there trying to get somewhere. Even Oakland would do. Instead I was trapped almost directly beneath the Interstate, moving in handcuffs into the Hall of Justice. Across the street on Bryant every bailbondsman in the city must have had an office. And they were all lit up for Friday night; like Christmas in September.

I was fingerprinted, photographed, and booked. I was in jail. And I wanted to get the hell out. I demanded my right to make a telephone call. I looked through the Yellow Pages once again and came across about a dozen ads for bail bonds. Each indicated a location from a certain point of reference. In descending order I read: 1) "Opposite the Hall of Justice"; 2) "Across from Hall of Justice"; 3) "Across from Jail." I appreciated the basic simplicity of the last. Besides the ad contained the quote: "Don't Die in Jail—Call Frye for Bail" and it promised "5 Minute Service Day or Night." It all reminded me of the Body Heat Escort Service. Only the pictures weren't as cute.

I made my call to Mickey. She and the Chief would take care of it. I guess I sounded scared as well as weary. At any rate, Mickey didn't have any wisecracks, just supportive sympathy and a few curses for Chang.

The bailbondsman they dug up turned out to be a bail bond lady who had to be at least seventy years old. She had cotton candy purple hair and the thinnest wrists, ankles, and neck I had ever seen. The rest of her was completely covered by a long gray dress with long full sleeves. It was hard to believe she had a body under there.

We were sitting in a stark seasick green conference room at a tiny table. I had expected a long row of barred or at least glassed windows, set up the way tellers are lined up in a bank. But there was nothing between us.

"Couldn't this get dangerous?" I asked her.

"If you give me any shit I press that button and a cop comes running." She indicated a button on the wall. It would have taken her three steps at least to reach it; she would never have made it if anyone had tried to stop her. "My name's Queen Faye Frye. My husband owned the business. He was King Frye until a client out on bail mugged him in front of the office."

"Some people have no gratitude."

She looked at me curiously. The purple color of her hair looked particularly odd against the pale green of the wall.

"I've got to get out of here," I said.

"That's what they all say. What's a nice boy like you doing drugs for?"

I didn't bother to tell her it was a frame. That's what they all say.

I spent a sleepless night in jail.

It took until late Saturday afternoon but Mickey and Chief Moses put up the 10 percent for Queen Frye to cover bail, and I was free. When I walked out I felt as if I had been acquitted of mass

murder. Instead, I just had a coke bust to worry about. And Detective Chang. Still, no matter what Chang did I was determined
to continue with the case.

Outside of the Hall of Justice Mickey and the Chief were waiting
for me in the T-Bird.

"You smell like puke," Mickey said. "And you need a shave."

Mickey drove and did a terrible job of shifting on the hills. At
one point she rolled back about ten feet towards a new Jaguar se-
dan before she could get the car in first and going forward.

"Didn't you drive a police car?" I asked her.

"It was flat in Ohio."

After I cleaned up and had something to eat I thought I was
ready to go after Rhoda Bunney again. Instead I fell asleep and
slept through most of Sunday.

It wasn't until Monday that I was ready. I wanted the Chief to go
with me. Mickey didn't protest.

We drove over to the Russian Hill address. It was an old and
elegant apartment house that was being squeezed on both sides by
new and inelegant condominiums. We drove past it several times
like thieves casing the place. Then we drove down the hill. About
two blocks away from the building I got out of the car and told the
Chief to go ahead and park somewhere across from the entrance.

"I wish you didn't have a car built for white midgets." The wheel
was pressed up against his chest.

"Try not to get spotted," I warned him.

"Who's out there?" he asked as he put on a San Diego Padres
baseball hat for a disguise.

"Probably Chang."

"Right." The Chief, looking like an adult in a kiddy car at an
amusement park, made it up the hill.

I decided to walk south and around the block to look for a rear
entrance. I went through a narrow alley between two Victorian
houses that led to a wooden fence. An ugly black dog was barking
fiercely at me from a small side yard. The good thing about barking
dogs is that after a while, like the boy who cried wolf, no one pays
attention to them anymore. Instead, people just curse the racket
they make. I climbed over the fence and landed on a narrow strip

of concrete. The wall of the building was lined with metal garbage cans that were stuffed full. Their tops, unable to close tight, were tilted rakishly. I found a rear door that was unlocked, took the stairs up to the second floor, and found the apartment number Vorflagel had given me.

Even from out in the hallway I could hear the shower running. I took out my Union 76 credit card and slipped the doorknob lock. I did it faster than I had ever done it in practice in my office. The door opened. There was enough hardware for three doors but none of it was in use except the worthless button on the doorknob.

I was assuming that this was Rhoda Bunney's apartment; that Vorflagel had not lied; that the woman I wanted to talk to was in the shower.

The living room suggested that the occupant was at least someone in Rhoda Bunney's line of work. It was decorated like a 19th century bordello with red velvet loveseats, a red carpet, red and black silk pillows, and heavy red and black drapes. All over the wall were prints of Reubenesque nudes in generally solitary play. These were not the work of Diego Hammond. There was an elaborate crystal chandelier hanging over the round black lacquered table that stood in the area carved out as a dining room. The drapes were open slightly, revealing a layer of sheer white material. I walked across the plush rug and looked out on Lombard Street, the Golden Gate, and my Thunderbird. A dark blue Ford passed by slowly. I wondered if someone else was casing the place.

I followed the sound of the shower into the bedroom. In the middle of the room, like a honeymoon suite, there was a heart shaped bed covered with a pink spread and shadowed by a canopy. I looked up under the canopy and saw the mirrors I expected. Next to the bed on a nightstand was a small vial with a little gold spoon dangling by a chain from its neck. It was all just as Vorflagel had described it.

Right across from the bed I found exactly what I was looking for in a cherry wardrobe with mirrored doors. I pulled open the doors and found that on the inside the mirrors were actually one-way glass. Like a huge pair of state trooper reflecting sunglasses. Inside the wardrobe were shelves that held a color/sound Panasonic PK-1160 video system. It was the kind of sophisticated equipment that would focus automatically and record in extremely low light.

I found the button that would activate the camera by the lamp on the nightstand. It was disguised as an electric blanket control. It was an impressive setup. I shut the wardrobe doors, sat down on the edge of the bed, and waited.

I heard her shut off the water. She was humming. There was the sound of a plastic shower curtain folding like an accordion. She shut off the overhead fan in the bathroom. Then a naked Rhoda Bunney emerged drying her red hair with a white bath towel. Her body was as good as it appeared in the Hammond painting.

I expected some reaction when I got up from the edge of the bed and said, "Hello, Rhoda."

She didn't scream; she didn't try to cover up her marvelous breasts or her neatly trimmed triangle of reddish pubic hair—touched with gold highlights. She was accustomed to being naked around men. Then I realized how she was looking at me, like I was a customer whom she had maybe forgotten about.

"Don't you remember me?" I asked.

She remembered. "I see a lot of men. They tend to look alike. Now get the hell out of here."

I took a step over to the wardrobe and pulled the mirrored doors open. "I want to talk about your movie career."

Slowly she wrapped the bath towel into a turban on her head, letting me appreciate the curves and lines of her damp body. Then she said, "Just let me get on a robe."

"You don't have to."

She ignored me, pushing the sliding closet door on the other side of the room open on its track, and took out a black satin robe with a red dragon embroidered on the back. She put it on and gathered it at the waist with a satin belt.

When I saw her hand go for a pocket I was at her side in an instant, my hand tight on her wrist. I pulled her hand out of the pocket, reached in myself, and took out a small caliber one-shot pistol.

"You wouldn't want to shoot me here. The blood would mess up the place something awful. Even with red carpeting. You never get the same shade with blood."

"What do you want?"

"I want the names of the men you and Silverman had up here."

"I don't know what you're talking about."

I looked around the room. "You know exactly what I'm talking about. You've got a nice place here. And a pretty heavy investment in furniture and carpeting. You don't give me what I want and the apartment is trash. The Salvation Army won't take the stuff away when my friend and I are through." Then I lifted her chin. "With your apartment and your beautiful face. It would be such a shame." St. John the Terrible.

I pushed her to the window from which she could see Chief Moses in the car. Just sitting there he looked big.

"The guy in the Padres hat," I said. I put my hand on the drapes. "Should I give him the signal to come up?"

"No. I get the message."

She moved over to her dresser and I came up right behind her. I couldn't be sure how many guns she had planted around the room. Turning her face up towards me, she said, "I'm just getting what you want."

"Like you just put on a robe?"

"How many guns could I have?"

"One more would be enough."

She opened a drawer, removed some lingerie, and then pulled up a false bottom. I had been expecting a safe.

"These are my records. How I kept track." She handed me a flat black book that looked like a solar calculator. Mickey would have appreciated the hi-tech item. And the whole hi-tech setup.

"Looking for repeat business?"

She smiled and said, "You never can tell."

"How does it work?"

"Push the scroll button."

The names ran by the display screen in alpha order. For any name you could call up an address and telephone number. Rhoda had worked her way through the courts. Vorflagel's name was there along with a lot of others I recognized. I had a lot of extra suspects that I hoped I wouldn't need. I put the computerized black book into my coat pocket and started to leave the bedroom.

"Hey, don't take it!"

"Sorry," I said.

Before I knew it she was attacking me, her fingernails like claws going for anything they could get at, including my eyes. I don't like to hit women but I couldn't get her off me. With the back of my hand I hit her across the jaw. She went halfway across the room and started back at me, this time with a pair of scissors she had pulled out of a drawer. She was coming at my throat with them when I caught her arm and twisted it behind her back. I pushed her into the bathroom and jammed a chair against the door. Then I got the hell out of there with the hi-tech black book and my life.

I walked down the front stairs of the apartment building to the T-Bird across the street. I hurried to avoid the blue Ford coming towards me. With my back to the Ford I started to open the car door when the sound of gunfire exploded around me. I dove to the ground as the window of the door I was holding shattered. I tried to get my gun out and turn around to see what the hell was going on. The blue Ford was disappearing around a corner. Inside the car the Chief was struggling to raise himself up from the floor. By the time we got the car started it was too late to try to pursue the Ford.

"Did you get the license?" I asked.

"Did you?"

"No."

"We're even."

The Chief settled into the passenger seat.

I slammed the palms of my hands against the leather-covered steering wheel. Shards of broken glass were everywhere.

There was a clean hole in the door of the glove compartment. I opened it and found a bullet lodged in the old owner's manual. "I knew this manual was good for something," I said. I held the bullet up in the light. It glittered like silver.

Johnny D. complained like hell but in the end he had the ballistic tests done.

"They're identical," he said.

I put the phone down.

"It's time to see our prosecutor," I said to the Chief.

We picked up Howard Vorflagel as he was crossing the street to the Hall of Justice after a late lunch. It was a neat and clean kidnapping. We had Vorflagel and his briefcase crammed into the bucket seat under the Chief.

"I made a big mistake," I said as I drove down Bryant.

"You're damn right," he began as he struggled to get upright.

"I let you keep your gun." I turned the steering wheel sharply, taking the car under the Skyway. On the right side street south of Market no one would care if we murdered Vorflagel in public in broad daylight and he knew it.

"Where are you taking me?"

"Right here," I said.

I pulled around the back of a deserted red brick warehouse. Chief Moses shoved him out of the car; I caught him in mid-flight and pushed him up against the right front fender. In the distance a few small boys watched us from behind the weeds of an overgrown lot.

"Last time you just wanted to warn Fan. What was it this time?"

"I don't know what you're talking about!" His face was bright red and his ears looked like they had filled up with blood. His horn-rimmed glasses hung precariously on his nose. I swung him around against the old brick wall of the warehouse and shook him.

"You don't know what I'm talking about?" I shouted. "You've been leaving too many silver bullets around, Lone Ranger. Ballistics matched up the bullet in Fan's desk with the one you shot at me in the street." I hit his mid-section and he doubled over. "I don't like getting shot at." I propped him up while the Chief watched. He was enjoying himself. I was doing his job for him. "Why'd you do such a dumbass thing?"

"I didn't."

I spun him around and twisted his right arm up to the top of his head. "Talk!"

"I couldn't let you get any closer. I couldn't let it all come out. Not when I had just gotten out from under it."

"Then you killed Silverman," I said more calmly.

"No. I didn't."

"But you know who sent you the tapes!"

"No!"

I gave his arm another turn and he screamed.

"Talk, asshole," the Chief said. "It's not going to get any better for you."

Vorflagel talked. And he decided to pay me the eighty bucks he had in his wallet when I pointed out that I no longer had a car window thanks to him. Then we brushed him off and drove him back to the Hall of Justice. I hoped we hadn't cost him a case on the technicality that the prosecution had failed to appear.

"Nice work on Vorflagel," Chief Moses said. "I am impressed."

"I'm working on my image. Will you mention this to Mickey?"

"That squaw is impressed enough."

"You should have seen me take care of Rhoda Bunney."

Chief Moses just looked at me.

We went back to the office. I made a telephone call to the man Vorflagel had named.

# 30

I sat alone, facing the suspect named by the Deputy D.A. "You killed Silverman," I said softly.

"Why would I do that?"

"You forced Silverman to open the safe. When you had the tapes you killed him."

"Why?"

"And then you sent the tapes to his blackmail victims."

"Why?"

"For the law," I said. "Because you saw the scum of the earth walking out of court free. Because you saw what he was doing to a D.A. like Vorflagel."

"Pretty good reasons."

"And you've had Chang harassing me. Every time I talked to you I set myself up."

"That was ironic," Judge Troutvelter said as he ran a hand over his hard gray hair. He was in his shirtsleeves. His robe hung on a rack in the corner of the office. "You were getting too close. You had to be discouraged."

"So you sent Vorflagel to gun me down in the street."

There was a pained expression on his gaunt face. "I didn't know about that. Vorflagel can be a fool."

"So you did it," I said almost casually.

"I'm not going to make it that easy for you. Silverman turned the tapes over to me during the trial. The day before he was killed."

"Can you prove that?"

"I didn't give him a receipt."

"I'm supposed to believe you?"

"Ask Vorflagel. Why do you think he didn't blow the case?"

"He's a reliable witness? A guy who tried to kill me?"

"I gave him the tapes he was on and he nailed Gomez. It was simple as that."

"He said that you mailed them," I said.

"Not to him. How do you think Vorflagel knew where the tapes came from?"

Vorflagel had lied. I couldn't believe Vorflagel so I couldn't believe the judge. "You're claiming that Silverman just gave you the tapes? He just handed over his edge? Your money cheerfully refunded and all that?"

The judge folded his hands across his chest, looked up at the ceiling, and closed his eyes. He took a deep breath, and said, "I had certain information that could lead to his disbarment. That helped convince him."

"Everybody has something on somebody."

"That's what they say."

"What did you have on Silverman?"

"Silverman was an army lawyer during Vietnam. He got into the drug traffic and ended up court-martialed. He got a year of hard labor and a dishonorable discharge. Somehow he got it all hushed up."

"But not hushed up enough." I should have pursued that damn lead when I got it from Rita.

240

"You're a P.I. You know nothing's ever hushed up enough."

We sat there in the room in silence. White-hot light was pouring through the window. I looked out at a piece of the underside of the Skyway. It wasn't the best view in San Francisco.

"Do you believe me?" Judge Troutvelter asked.

I hesitated. "No," I finally said.

"Then you'll want to call the D.A."

"I don't work for the D.A." I said. Not anymore.

"So?"

I let the question hang in the air for a long time. Then I finally said, "You got rid of a lawyer gone bad. He had turned into garbage."

"It was the cocaine."

"And the money. Let's not forget the money."

"And you? What do you do?"

"I did my job. I located the tapes."

"They've all been destroyed."

"Exactly what I had in mind for them myself." I got up.

"You have a rather unique sense of justice," he said.

"I imagine it's a lot like yours." Then I added, "Would you get Chang off my back? He hung this bust on me and there's this." I gave the judge the parking ticket I got in Sonoma.

"Consider it done." The judge reached into the bottom desk drawer and pulled out a bottle of Wild Turkey. "Let's drink to it." We did.

I walked out of the building feeling good. Maybe because for the first time in my life I had fixed a ticket. Or maybe it was the 101 proof bourbon whiskey. It didn't really matter.

When I got down to the parking lot I found the Chief asleep in the car. Obviously he hadn't been very worried about me.

"How did it go?" he asked when I started the car and woke him up.

"He claimed he didn't do it."

"Did you tell him that is what they all say?" the Chief asked through a yawn.

"Of course."

The three of us went out to dinner at the Tandoori Indian restaurant. It had taken over from a failed pizza parlor and the decor hadn't changed much except for a few hanging curtains and pictures of Indian goddesses with multiple sets of limbs. There was a sitar player where the order counter used to be. We all had the Lamb Pasanda with a deep fried Indian bread called Poori.

It was supposed to be a celebration but the mood didn't seem right. At least not for me. And the Chief made no East Indian-American Indian jokes. On the surface things had been cleaned up as I explained to Mickey and Chief Moses. The judge had taken to vigilante justice, and the tapes, Silverman's edge, had been destroyed. It was only a matter of breaking the news to Sam: he would never have Silverman's edge. And I could tell a few suspects that they were in the clear.

My problem was that I was finding myself almost believing Judge Troutvelter.

Everyone felt like cutting the evening short. We were all drained.

I dropped the Chief off by his pickup truck and drove Mickey to her apartment. Then I drove home. I felt uneasy, apprehensive, and I couldn't put my finger on why. As soon as I walked into the office and switched on the light I knew why. The whole place had been tossed.

"Don't you move!" I heard the command issued in a slow drawl and felt what had to be a loaded gun.

"I'm not moving," I said.

"Where are the tapes, St. John?"

I started to laugh.

"What the fuckin' A's so funny?"

I didn't really know. "You messed up the office," I said.

"How can you tell?" Then he added, "Now I'll mess up your head, boy. Turn around." I really didn't want to see who it was. "Turn around!" he ordered.

I was staring at a gun held in the huge paw of Big Mac McCurdy. I knew I didn't have a chance of taking him.

McCurdy came up and closed the door behind me. He made the mistake of bringing the gun close enough for me to lunge at. I made the mistake of giving it a try even though I knew better and took a powerful left to the stomach that knocked the wind out of me and left me gasping for air.

"Don't try that dumb shit with me." McCurdy pushed me through the middle office into mine. He pulled the gun out of my holster and shoved me down. I landed on the couch while he took my chair at the desk. He checked out my gun and found that it was loaded; then he put away his own. McCurdy looked like he was trying to get comfortable. He took out a cheap cigar, unwrapped it, and lit up with a disposable butane lighter.

I had my arms wrapped around my stomach. I didn't say anything about the cigar. I saw that the window fan had been knocked down. That was how McCurdy had broken in. Chief Moses had been right about the flaw in our security. McCurdy had also broken the ceramic pot and crushed the palm it had contained.

"Where are the tapes?"

"Destroyed."

"Destroyed?"

"They were returned to the victims."

McCurdy looked astonished; his freckles stood out from the skin of his face. "Why'd Silverman do an asshole thing like that?"

The heavy smoke took the shape of a curled up cat. The smell of it was terrible. It was worse than cheap. It reminded me of burning rubbish at the dump.

"The usual," I said. "Someone had something on him."

"Like what?"

"His drug conviction and court-martial in the army."

"Jesus!" McCurdy shouted as he slammed his hammer fist down on my desk. "How'd I miss that?" He stared at me down the barrel of my own gun. "Then I did it for nothin'," he drawled.

That's when I felt panic; I didn't want to understand him. I was telling myself that McCurdy was only another guy trying to put his hands on a few possible valuable tapes. He wasn't the murderer. If he was, then he might have to eliminate me.

"Now you know," McCurdy said.

"Know what?"

"Don't try an' jerk me around."

"How did you know about me?" I asked.

243

"Rhoda Bunney."

That I should have known.

"She was the girl in the sting. Y'all were right about the sting, St. John."

"A lucky guess." Some consolation.

"You don't think Silverman coulda pulled all that together by himself? It was my sting. We were gonna clean up the courts. Put the finger on who was into coke. Who was for sale. The sex and drugs tapes were a little bit of insurance. Then Silverman double-crossed me. Feedin' me a few useless tapes while he used the big ones to pull off his cases. Christ, he gave me a tape of a fuckin' dead man. Died two nights after we had him with Rhoda. Now what the hell good was that? He had been double-crossin' me all along."

I didn't ask him why it took him so long to figure it out; I remembered what the Chief had found out about his record.

Silverman had taken him for a ride and a half. I shifted nervously on the couch and considered making a rush for the door. Fat chance.

"How'd you get Silverman involved?" I asked.

"He was a greedy boy. For money and coke. He had himself a big habit. It was easy to get him in. Just like we'd get the others."

"So you say you killed him?"

He looked at me curiously. "It was self-defense. He said he was going to get the tapes out of the safe. Instead he pulled out a silver pistol and fired at me."

"Because the tapes were already gone!"

He thought about it for a while. "Maybe."

I looked at my gun in his hand. "So then you disarmed him and shot him in the heart with his own gun."

"What?"

"You heard me."

"I fired two shots and got the hell outta there. I wasn't even sure I hit him until I heard the news."

"Then you planted your weapon at Gomez's safe house."

"Yeah."

"And the police used the gun and Gomez to clear the case."

"And now you know too much," McCurdy said between compressed lips.

244

"If you shoot me it won't be self-defense."

"Tough shit, boy." McCurdy raised the gun at me.

"Wait," I shouted. "Listen to me."

"Talk fast."

"You never saw the autopsy results or the ballistics report?"

"Are you kiddin'? I'm a DEA outsider around here. They don't give me shit. It's inter-agency cooperation."

"There were two guns."

"I know that. His and mine. Now quit stallin'."

"No. The two bullets from your gun. One hit the wall safe; the other hit Silverman's arm."

"And?"

I had him leaning forward on his heavy elbows. I had him interested. I only hoped I was making sense. "The bullet that killed him came from his own gun." I looked at my gun in McCurdy's hand again.

McCurdy narrowed his eyes. "Then who all killed him?"

I thought about who would descend on wounded prey.

"A jackal."

"What happens to me?" he asked.

I shrugged. "That part of the case is cleared. The police believe Gomez shot him with the Walther. If we find who put the other bullet into Silverman we may just have the murderer. Nobody would care about Gomez. Or you."

McCurdy didn't want to kill me. He was too relieved that he didn't kill Silverman. He took the cigar from the edge of the desk and puffed a screen of smoke around himself.

"You ever link me to this case, St. John, I'll come after you and I'll get you. No matter how long it takes."

I believed him.

"I want to ask you something. Why didn't you just claim it was self-defense in the line of duty?" I asked.

"You wanna know why? I had lost the tapes. The sting was blown. My record couldn't hold up under another fuck-up and investigation." He paused. "So don't forget what I said."

"Hey, you're just another guy who missed the bag of money."

"Yeah. Just another dumb asshole."

I looked at the cigar but didn't say anything. Instead, I put my hand out for the gun and he handed it over.

"Sorry about the tapes," I said.

"I didn't think I could blow another one," he said as he turned and walked out of my office.

At least I knew who had been protecting Rhoda Bunney.

I slammed the window shut. The palm was dead. I went to get a broom to sweep up the mess Big Mac had made.

# 31

I made two calls that morning. One was to Sam Fan. It was time to tell him about the final disposition of the tapes.

Victoria made the appointment for me.

As I was about to hang up she said, "I remembered something else."

"What?"

"When he left he didn't have his briefcase."

"He always took it?"

"Always."

"Always," I repeated.

I made the second call.

Sam Fan looked remarkably comfortable, in his rolled up shirtsleeves with a loosened tie, behind the desk he had now made his own. Too bad he wouldn't be comfortable for long.

247

"The edge is gone." I told him.

"What do you mean?"

"Silverman had his victims on video; and now the tapes are gone."

"Who got them?"

"The actors."

"Somebody killed Silverman for them and then just turned them over?"

I didn't say anything.

"I don't believe it!"

"Sometimes that's how it goes."

"You didn't get them for me. All you got for me are clichés. You knew what the job was about and you didn't do it." Sam stood up. "You're fired!"

"You owe me for the last three days," I tried.

"Forget it."

I had the urge to pick him up and bang his gleaming head against the wall. Still, I couldn't complain. Enough of Fan's checks had cleared already. I got up and opened the door. Then I took a step back into the room.

"I did the job, Sam. Want to know who killed Silverman?"

"Do you know?"

"I'm the detective."

"Don't play games with me, St. John." He put his heavy bare forearms behind his head. "All right. Who did it?"

"You went out to dinner the night Silverman was murdered. The place you usually go."

"Yeah."

"Like the other night when I was here?"

"Yeah?"

I should have kept my tail on him that night. It would have answered some questions.

"You took your Porsche?" I asked.

"Yeah. I took my car. What the hell is this, St. John?" Sam was standing up.

"Your money's worth." Then I added, "You love that Porsche so much you always take it, whether you're coming back to work or not. Even for a few blocks."

248

"Yeah. I like to show up in the Porsche. It impresses the women. So?"

"You didn't take your briefcase that night. You were coming back to work."

Sam Fan's body went rigid.

"I changed my mind," he said angrily. This was not what he was expecting. "What's this prove anyway?"

I had nothing but theory now. "You could hear . . . Gomez . . . getting away after the shots were fired. You were in your office, just on the other side of the suite. When you went to Silverman's office you found him at his desk bleeding. About to call an ambulance. His silver gun was lying on his desk. You picked it up and you fired it point-blank into his chest."

"Now why would I do that?" he asked. "Where's the motive?"

"He was dumping you. He didn't need your particular expertise. He wasn't interested in plea bargaining for small time felonies. And he kept you away from his big time drug clients. Now he was moving on and taking his clients, his edge and his money with him. It was all in the files you destroyed." I was speculating but it made sense to me. "You would be left holding the bag." Considering the garbage bag full of money that wasn't the best way to put it, but it was the best I could do at an uncomfortable moment. "An empty bag," I added.

"Then why hire you?"

"Because without the edge you were nothing, Sam. And you figured I'd come across it. And you'd end up with it. Only you didn't figure I'd take it all the way. All the way to you."

Fan began moving towards me. The silver revolver appeared in his right hand. I couldn't believe it.

"I wouldn't shoot. Not with Jennifer and Jeanine out there."

"You and me are goin' out for an early lunch. Only you're not comin' back. We're gonna take a little ride up the coast."

"I understand it's cooler up there."

"It won't matter to you."

"I can't believe you kept the murder weapon," I said in amazement.

"It's silver," Fan said.

"Of course."

He reached under my coat and pulled out my .38. He put it in his desk.

"My gun's gonna be right here in my pants pocket, so don't try anything, St. John," he said as he shoved me towards the door.

As Fan moved behind me, Detective Chang appeared in the doorway, his extended arms holding his service revolver.

"Drop it, Fan!" Chang had been my second call that morning. After I spoke to Victoria.

Fan hesitated and then let the gun fall.

"Shit," he said.

"Sam," I said, "look at the bright side. At least it's not murder one." I looked around at the family pictures he had brought into the office. I almost felt sorry for him. Where he was going he would miss them all.

Sam cast the usual aspersions on my origins and I felt less sorry.

"I guess this means no bonus," I said. Then I turned to Chang. "Thanks."

"It was a favor for the judge."

"You do a lot of those."

"I don't like you any better than you like me, St. John."

"Maybe. Don't jump to conclusions."

Chang gave me a silent no comment.

I retrieved my Smith and Wesson revolver from Fan's desk drawer.

"Hey, Chang, don't take it personally. You just cleared a case." Then after a long pause I added, "Again."

# 32

I invited Johnny D. and Rita Silverman over to the office for a party more or less. There were other people I could have invited like Amos Billy but he probably wouldn't have come and if he did he'd reclaim that purple wide-brimmed hat that I had hanging on the coatrack. Evelyn Moss and Rhoda Bunney might have felt out of place. Big Mac McCurdy was probably still explaining how he screwed up his latest sting. Good luck to him.

We were all sitting around the office talking about the weather, the Giants, the closing weeks of the pennant race, the start of the 49er's season on Sunday, eating sausage pizzas and drinking. I had brought in a twelve-pack of Bud, half a case of Henry's in bottles, and two jugs of Mondavi white.

I asked for silence. It was summing up time. I wanted to hear what it sounded like laid out. I was a little worried about Rita but I decided she could take it.

251

"Fan hired me to find Silverman's edge. The video tapes as it turned out."

"He probably figured you weren't very good," Mickey commented.

"Why?" I asked. I should have known better.

"He wanted someone good enough to find out who had been in the office before him but not good enough to figure it all out. He wanted a steady plodder to lead him to the tapes."

"Thanks," I said and continued. "I think Gomez fired the first shots and then got out of there; $700,000 is just a normal business loss in the cocaine traffic."

It was true that Gomez had taken the loss but only because he had a plane to catch and a country to skip and he couldn't wait any longer for the delivery of his refund. He probably would have gotten his revenge at some point, by some means, if Sam hadn't beaten him to it. Sam Fan hadn't left much time for anything to happen. I had wondered why Troutvelter had let Gomez out on bail. It was the possibility that he would eliminate Silverman. The Colombian cowboy on the loose seeking revenge. I had to hand it to the judge; he knew what he was doing all along: playing the hardest game of hard ball. It didn't work out exactly as he planned. But it was close enough.

I felt strange lying to these people but I didn't have anything to gain by implicating McCurdy. And maybe a lot to lose. So I let the case stay closed on the first shooting. Besides there would have been a lot of unhappy cops and prosecutors and an unhappy judge if there were questions raised about the autopsy and ballistics. There was a conspiracy if I had ever seen one. I was giving this D.A.'s Office a break. After my previous experience the irony wasn't lost on me.

"The key was Sam Fan driving his Porsche for just a couple of blocks. Who'd have believed it?" I said. "And he got hung on his briefcase," I concluded.

With my story over I waited for questions. Hell I had become part of the conspiracy myself. I had all sorts of plausible answers prepared for all of them.

No more questions—almost.

Rita wouldn't quit. "Why'd Silverman shoot at Gomez? He had the money for him," she asked. At least she didn't ask why Silverman opened the safe when the money was in a bag on the floor under his desk. To get the gun of course if anyone wanted to know the truth.

"Good question. Maybe it was panic. Maybe Gomez was strung out. High on cocaine. Maybe we'll never know." Next question.

Chief Moses took over. "Fan heard the shots and heard someone running away. He found Silverman wounded in the arm. And he saw the gun. He knew Silverman was cutting him out and it was Silverman who brought in the money. It was Silverman who had the edge. Fan picked up the gun and shot him and then went home, acting like he had never come back to the office after he left."

"So we had two different bullets," Johnny D. said.

"But he didn't have the tapes," Rita added.

"Judge Troutvelter," I said, and repeated the story of the judge and the tapes he took from Silverman. Now we all knew about Silverman and Vietnam and why he never talked about it.

"Why'd Silverman start making the tapes?"

"Part of a sting," I said.

"McCurdy?" Mickey asked.

"That's my guess," I said. A very educated one.

"Another screwup," Chief Moses said and left it at that.

"And Vorflagel and Chang?" Mickey asked.

"They thought they were protecting the judge. I hope they're a happy pair. I should have invited them."

Everybody hooted.

"The judge saved a lot of asses," the Chief said.

"I should have invited him."

We fell into silence until Johnny D. asked, "What sting?"

"You need better relations with the DEA," I said.

"I don't think our brass wants to know what's going on."

"Check into it." I didn't think it would lead him anywhere.

"No thanks. I've put in for that transfer to Homicide."

"Good," I said.

"No. Not for you, Jeremiah. I'm paid up."

"What about interest?" I asked. Then I continued, "You should have brought your wife, Johnny."

"She speaks too much English already. I don't want her to learn more from you."

"Getting back to interest, what happens to the bag of money?" Mickey had the good sense to ask.

Rita Silverman raised her glass of Mondavi white and said, "To me and mine!"

"To the lawyers of America," I said, raising my beer bottle to general curses in the room. "Anyone care to join the PAL?"

"I would." The low female voice came from the doorway. Victoria had made it after all.

With my bottle still raised I said, "And to the woman who remembered a briefcase."

"And a newspaper." She handed me a *Chronicle*. The Sam Fan story was on page two. Almost as good as the front page story on Silverman's murder.

Only it didn't mention my name. Chang got all the credit.

"So much for your new image," Mickey said.

# Epilogue

The following Friday morning Mickey, the Chief and I took that ride up the coast that Sam Fan had promised me. We drove north on Route 1 up to Jenner where the Russian River meets the Pacific. We stopped for an early lunch at a restaurant with a bar that jutted out over the very edge of the ocean. We sat out on the deck enjoying a cool sea breeze. Rita Silverman had given us a substantial bonus and we were all feeling good. She felt she owed it to us for what we had found out about Silverman's death. We weren't about to argue with her. It made up a little for all that money I had left behind.

I tilted my face towards the sky and the sun. My partners were having a heated conversation about what kind of hi-tech equipment we should invest some of the bonus money in. But I didn't pay any attention. It was just another sound like the surf pounding far below us. I was thinking with satisfaction that I had solved my first murder case. It had taken a lot of luck and a lot of help from my friends. And persistence. I had been baptized. Leaving the D.A.'s Office had been the right thing for me to do. I wondered if Sarah was still on Team 1. I put it all out of my mind.

I began to realize that Mickey was talking to me about going back to the city. We paid the bill and I got into the car, which I had parked on the edge of a steep cliff. The Chief and Mickey waited until I backed it onto the road before they got in. They made their usual comments about the size of the T-Bird. I ignored them.

"Why don't you write the Silverman story up for your newspaper? You could use a new press card. And you could mention my name," I suggested to Mickey after we had been riding for fifteen minutes.

Mickey didn't answer. She was squeezed in between us and fast asleep.

At Bodega Bay the car broke down. I let it roll down a hill until it stopped on a patch of gravel shoulder at the edge of the bay. Gulls turned overhead.

"Damn," I said.

Mickey was still asleep.

Chief Moses jumped out of the car, opened the hood, and had the motor running in less than five minutes. He got back into his seat, carrying a six-inch piece of aluminum hose in his hand. "All you had to do was remove this." He held it up then tossed it casually into the Pacific.

I hoped I wouldn't ever need it again.

Mickey had slept through it all.

It was still early afternoon when I let the Chief off in Marin where for some reason related to a new Indian Bingo Parlor he had left his pickup truck. A half-hour later Mickey and I were back at the Victorian. I picked up the stack of mail on the floor under the slot and brought it into my office. Mickey sat down sleepily on the couch. I went upstairs to get a surprise for her. When I came back down she looked like she was trying to make up her mind about something.

"What are you thinking? Wondering if you should move in with me?"

"No. Wondering if I should take up Diego Hammond on his offer. I could be immortalized."

"You are already," I said, holding up the *Playboy* picture I had taken from my locker.

"You bastard! You had that all along. I'm embarrassed."

"You posed."

"Give me that!"

"No." I won the mock battle we fought and she collapsed back on the couch. "I know everything about you. Move in with me."

"Never!"

"I didn't show it to the Chief. He doesn't know anything about it."

"Possessive?"

Maybe I was.

"Move in with me anyway?"

She took a long time to answer. "I'm still thinking about it."

I let her think while I looked through the mail. There was an invitation to Nadine's wedding and an envelope from Evelyn Moss. I didn't open it.

I put my arms around Mickey and said, "Maybe it's your last chance. Think about it."

"I am."

"Promise?"

"Yes."

"Come upstairs with me."

She shook her head.

I went upstairs alone and put back her picture in the locker. I didn't want it to get wrinkled or torn. When Mickey came upstairs with me for good she could have it. I went back down.

Mickey was still there, looking very beautiful. The telephone rang. She switched off the answering machine and answered, "St. John Detective Agency. Michelle speaking." Then she put her hand over the mouthpiece and said, "It's a woman who got your business card when she was looking for a dentist."

The woman with the Chiclet teeth.

"So?" I asked.

"She needs a P.I."

"Tell her to try the Yellow Pages." I was planning to be busy with Mickey.

"Okay," Mickey said into the phone.

She hung up and looked at me.

"Well?" I asked.

"She'll be over in fifteen minutes."

The afternoon was ruined.

"This is a business and we're partners," she reminded me.

"I guess I can wait until tonight," I said grumpily.

"I don't know, Jeremiah. Office romances always lead to trouble."

I coughed. I had never told Mickey and the Chief about Sarah and why I had to leave that D.A.'s Office. I looked earnestly at Mickey and said, "No way."

Mickey shrugged. "That's what they all say."

## DOCTOR WHO: THE CABINET OF LIGHT
## by DANIEL O'MAHONY

Where is the Doctor? Everyone is hunting him. Honoré Lechasseur, a time sensitive 'fixer', is hired by mystery woman Emily Blandish to find him. But what is his connection with London in 1949? Lechasseur is about to discover that following in the Doctor's footsteps can be a difficult task.

*An adventure featuring the Doctor.*
Featuring a foreword by Chaz Brenchley.
Deluxe edition frontispiece by John Higgins.
£10 (+ £1.50 UK p&p) Standard h/b ISBN: 1-903889-18-9
£25 (+ £1.50 UK p&p) Deluxe h/b ISBN: 1-903889-19-7

## DOCTOR WHO: FALLEN GODS
## by KATE ORMAN and JONATHAN BLUM

In ancient Akrotiri, a young girl is learning the mysteries of magic from a tutor, who, quite literally, fell from the skies. With his encouragement she can surf the timestreams and see something of the future. But then the demons come.

*An adventure featuring the eighth Doctor*
Featuring a foreword by Storm Constantine.
Deluxe edition frontispiece by Daryl Joyce.
£10 (+ £1.50 UK p&p) Standard h/b ISBN: 1-903889-20-1
£25 (+ £1.50 UK p&p) Deluxe h/b ISBN: 1-903889-21-9

## DOCTOR WHO: FRAYED by TARA SAMMS

On a blasted world, the Doctor and Susan find themselves in the middle of a war they cannot understand. With Susan missing and the Doctor captured, who will save the people from the enemies both from outside and within?

*An adventure featuring the first Doctor and Susan.*
Featuring a foreword by Stephen Laws.
Deluxe edition frontispiece by Chris Moore.
£10 (+ £1.50 UK p&p) Standard h/b ISBN: 1-903889-22-7
£25 (+ £1.50 UK p&p) Deluxe h/b ISBN: 1-903889-23-5

## DOCTOR WHO: EYE OF THE TYGER by PAUL MCAULEY

On a spaceship trapped in the orbit of a black hole, the Doctor finds himself trying to save a civilisation from extinction.

*An adventure featuring the eighth Doctor.*
Featuring a foreword by Neil Gaiman.
Deluxe edition frontispiece by Jim Burns.
£10 (+ £1.50 UK p&p) Standard h/b ISBN: 1-903889-24-3
£25 (+ £1.50 UK p&p) Deluxe h/b ISBN: 1-903889-25-1

Published November 2003

# About the Author

With a career in the bar and nightclub scene behind him and currently employed in IT within local government, Alistair Langston has previously written lyrics for the stage musical *The Beast in the Tower* in addition to the short musical film *Glamour Overdrive*. He currently lives near Glasgow, Scotland where he has a number of projects in development. *Aspects of a Psychopath* is his first novella.

Visit *Aspects of a Psychopath* online: http://www.aoap.co.uk

## Also available from Telos Publishing

### DOCTOR WHO NOVELLAS

### DOCTOR WHO: TIME AND RELATIVE by KIM NEWMAN

The harsh British winter of 1962/3 brings a big freeze and with it comes a new, far greater menace: terrifying icy creatures are stalking the streets, bringing death and destruction.
*An adventure featuring the first Doctor and Susan.*
Featuring a foreword by Justin Richards.
Deluxe edition frontispiece by Bryan Talbot.
**SOLD OUT** Standard h/b ISBN: 1-903889-02-2
£25 (+ £1.50 UK p&p) Deluxe h/b ISBN: 1-903889-03-0

### DOCTOR WHO: CITADEL OF DREAMS by DAVE STONE

In the city-state of Hokesh, time plays tricks; the present is unreliable, the future impossible to intimate.
*An adventure featuring the seventh Doctor and Ace.*
Featuring a foreword by Andrew Cartmel.
Deluxe edition frontispiece by Lee Sullivan.
£10 (+ £1.50 UK p&p) Standard h/b ISBN: 1-903889-04-9
£25 (+ £1.50 UK p&p) Deluxe h/b ISBN: 1-903889-05-7

### DOCTOR WHO: NIGHTDREAMERS by TOM ARDEN

Perihelion Night on the wooded moon Verd. A time of strange sightings, ghosts, and celebration. But what of the mysterious and terrifying Nightdreamers? And of the Nightdreamer King?
*An adventure featuring the third Doctor and Jo.*
Featuring a foreword by Katy Manning.
Deluxe edition frontispiece by Martin McKenna.
£10 (+ £1.50 UK p&p) Standard h/b ISBN: 1-903889-06-5
£25 (+ £1.50 UK p&p) Deluxe h/b ISBN: 1-903889-07-3

### DOCTOR WHO: GHOST SHIP by KEITH TOPPING

The TARDIS lands in the most haunted place on Earth, the luxury ocean liner the Queen Mary on its way from Southampton to New York in the year 1963. But why do ghosts from the past, the present and, perhaps even the future, seek out the Doctor?
*An adventure featuring the fourth Doctor.*
Featuring a foreword by Hugh Lamb.
Deluxe edition frontispiece by Dariusz Jasiczak.
£5.99 (+ £1.50 UK p&p) p/b ISBN: 1-903889-32-4
**SOLD OUT** Standard h/b ISBN: 1-903889-08-1
£25 (+ £1.50 UK p&p) Deluxe h/b ISBN: 1-903889-09-X

### DOCTOR WHO: FOREIGN DEVILS by ANDREW C

The Doctor, Jamie and Zoe find themselves joining forces investigator named Carnacki to solve a series of strange murd country house.
*An adventure featuring the second Doctor, Jamie and Zoe.*
Featuring a foreword by Mike Ashley.
Deluxe edition frontispiece by Mike Collins.
£5.99 (+ £1.50 UK p&p) p/b ISBN: 1-903889-33-2
**SOLD OUT** Standard h/b ISBN: 1-903889-10-3
£25 (+ £1.50 UK p&p) Deluxe h/b ISBN: 1-903889-11

### DOCTOR WHO: RIP TIDE by LOUISE COOPE

Strange things are afoot in a sleepy Cornish village. Str about the harbour and a mysterious object is retrieved Then the locals start getting sick. The Doctor is perh who can help, but can he discover the truth in time?
*An adventure featuring the eighth Doctor.*
Featuring a foreword by Stephen Gallagher.
Deluxe edition frontispiece by Fred Gambino.
£10 (+ £1.50 UK p&p) Standard h/b ISBN: 1-90388
£25 (+ £1.50 UK p&p) Deluxe h/b ISBN: 1-903889

### DOCTOR WHO: WONDERLAND by MARK

San Francisco 1967. A place of love and peace as th full swing. Summer, however, has lost her boyfrie destroyed by a new type of drug nicknamed Blue friends are three English tourists: Ben and Polly, an But will any of them help Summer, and what is th the Blue Moonbeams?
*An adventure featuring the second Doctor, Ben and Polly*
Featuring a foreword by Graham Joyce.
Deluxe edition frontispiece by Dominic Harman
£10 (+ £1.50 UK p&p) Standard h/b ISBN: 1-9
£25 (+ £1.50 UK p&p) Deluxe h/b ISBN: 1-90

### DOCTOR WHO: SHELL SHOCK by SIM

The Doctor is stranded on an alien beach with madman for company. How can he possibly res the same time as he and the TARDIS?
*An adventure featuring the sixth Doctor and Peri.*
Featuring a foreword by Guy N. Smith.
Deluxe edition frontispiece by Bob Covingto
£10 (+ £1.50 UK p&p) Standard h/b ISBN
£25 (+ £1.50 UK p&p) Deluxe h/b ISBN:
**Pub**

## DOCTOR WHO: COMPANION PIECE
### by MIKE TUCKER and ROBERT PERRY

The Doctor and his companion Cat face insurmountable odds when the Doctor is accused of the crime of time travelling and taken to Rome to face the Papal Inquisition.

*An adventure featuring the seventh Doctor and Cat.*

Featuring a foreword by TBA.

Deluxe edition frontispiece by Allan Bednar.

£10 (+ £1.50 UK p&p) Standard h/b ISBN: 1-903889-26-X

£25 (+ £1.50 UK p&p) Deluxe h/b ISBN: 1-903889-27-8

**Published December 2003**

# TIME HUNTER

A new range of high-quality original paperback novellas featuring the adventures in time of Honoré Lechasseur. Part mystery, part detective story, part dark fantasy, part science fiction ... these books are guaranteed to enthrall fans of good fiction everywhere, and are in the spirit of our acclaimed range of *Doctor Who* Novellas.

## THE WINNING SIDE by LANCE PARKIN

Emily is dead! Killed by an unknown assailant. Honoré and Emily find themselves caught up in a plot reaching from the future to their past, and with their very existence, not to mention the future of the entire world, at stake, can they unravel the mystery before it is too late?

An adventure in time and space.

£8 (+ £1.50 UK p&p) Standard p/b ISBN: 1-903889-35-9

£25 (+ £1.50 UK p&p) Deluxe h/b ISBN: 1-903889-36-7

# HORROR/FANTASY

## URBAN GOTHIC: LACUNA & OTHER TRIPS
### ed. DAVID J. HOWE
Stories by Graham Masterton, Christopher Fowler, Simon Clark, Debbie Bennett, Paul Finch, Steve Lockley & Paul Lewis.
Based on the Channel 5 horror series.
SOLD OUT

## THE MANITOU by GRAHAM MASTERTON
A 25th Anniversary author's preferred edition of this classic horror novel. An ancient Red Indian medicine man is reincarnated in modern day New York intent on reclaiming his land from the white men.
£9.99 (+ £2.50 p&p) Standard p/b ISBN: 1-903889-70-7
£30.00 (+ £2.50 p&p) Deluxe h/b ISBN: 1-903889-71-5

## CAPE WRATH by PAUL FINCH
Death and horror on a deserted Scottish island as an ancient Viking warrior chief returns to life.
£8.00 (+ £1.50 p&p) Standard p/b ISBN: 1-903889-60-X

## KING OF ALL THE DEAD by STEVE LOCKLEY & PAUL LEWIS
The king of all the dead will have what is his.
£8.00 (+ £1.50 p&p) Standard p/b ISBN: 1-903889-61-8

## GUARDIAN ANGEL by STEPHANIE BEDWELL-GRIME
Devilish fun as Guardian Angel Porsche Winter loses a soul to the devil ...
£9.99 (+ £2.50 p&p) Standard p/b ISBN: 1-903889-62-6

# TV/FILM GUIDES

## BEYOND THE GATE: THE UNAUTHORISED AND UNOFFICIAL GUIDE TO STARGATE SG-1 by KEITH TOPPING

Complete episode guide to the middle of Season 6 of the popular TV show.
£9.99 (+ £2.50 p&p) Standard p/b ISBN: 1-903889-50-2

## A DAY IN THE LIFE: THE UNAUTHORISED AND UNOFFICIAL GUIDE TO 24 by KEITH TOPPING

Complete episode guide to the first season of the popular TV show.
£9.99 (+ £2.50 p&p) Standard p/b ISBN: 1-903889-53-7

## THE TELEVISION COMPANION: THE UNAUTHORISED AND UNOFFICIAL GUIDE TO DOCTOR WHO by DAVID J HOWE & STEPHEN JAMES WALKER

Complete episode guide to the popular TV show.
£14.99 (+ £4.00 p&p) Standard p/b ISBN: 1-903889-51-0
£30.00 (+ £4.00 p&p) Deluxe h/b ISBN: 1-903889-52-9

## LIBERATION: THE UNAUTHORISED AND UNOFFICIAL GUIDE TO BLAKE'S 7 by ALAN STEVENS & FIONA MOORE

Complete episode guide to the popular TV show.
£9.99 (+ £2.50 p&p) Standard p/b ISBN: 1-903889-54-5
£30.00 (+ £2.50 p&p) Deluxe h/b ISBN: 1-903889-55-3

# HANK JANSON

Classic pulp crime thrillers from the 1950s.

## TORMENT by HANK JANSON
£9.99 (+ £2.50 p&p) Standard p/b ISBN: 1-903889-80-4

## WOMEN HATE TILL DEATH by HANK JANSON
£9.99 (+ £2.50 p&p) Standard p/b ISBN: 1-903889-81-2

The prices shown are correct at time of going to press. However, the publishers reserve the right to increase prices from those previously advertised without prior notice.

**TELOS PUBLISHING**
**c/o Beech House,**
**Chapel Lane,**
**Moulton,**
**Cheshire,**
**CW9 8PQ,**
**England**
**Email: orders@telos.co.uk**
**Web: www.telos.co.uk**

To order copies of any Telos books, please visit our website where there are full details of all titles and facilities for worldwide credit card online ordering, or send a cheque or postal order (UK only) for the appropriate amount (including postage and packing), together with details of the book(s) you require, plus your name and address to the above address. Overseas readers please send two international reply coupons for details of prices and postage rates.